Faith was almost s...
months pregnant,

Micah knew, and she hardly weighed more than an eiderdown pillow. She needed to eat more. She needed to take better care of herself. She needed to be taken care of.

It wasn't like him to act without a clear plan of action, but on more than one occasion in the past twenty-four hours Faith had provoked him into instinctive reactions that came from the gut. This was one of them. He had no idea why he'd picked her up and carried her into the house after he found her crying outside.

In fact, the only thing he was certain of was how right she felt in his arms, how right it seemed to carry her into his house, how right it was to have her arms around his neck and her sweet breath warm on his cheek....

Dear Reader,

The year is coming to a close, so here at Silhouette Intimate Moments we decided to go out with a bang. Once again, we've got a banner lineup of books for you.

Take this month's American Hero, Micah Parish, in *Cherokee Thunder*. You met him in the first book of author Rachel Lee's Conard County series, *Exile's End*, and now he's back with a story of his own. Without meaning to, he finds himself protecting woman-on-the-run Faith Williams and her unborn child, and suddenly this man who shunned emotion is head over heels in love. He's an American Hero you won't want to miss.

Reader favorite Ann Williams puts her own spin on an innovative plot in *Shades of Wyoming*. I don't want to give anything away, so all I'll say is beware of believing that things are what they seem. In *Castle of Dreams*, author Maura Seger takes a predicament right out of the headlines—the difficulties a returning hostage faces in readjusting to the world—and makes it the catalyst for a compelling romance. Award-winner Dee Holmes checks in with another of her deeply moving tales in *Without Price*, while March Madness find Rebecca Daniels writes a suspenseful tale of a couple thrown together and definitely in danger in *Fog City*. Finally, welcome new author Alicia Scott—a college student—whose *Walking After Midnight* takes gritty reality and turns it into irresistible romance.

And 1993 won't bring any letup in the excitement. Look for more of your favorite authors, as well as a Tenth Anniversary lineup in May that you definitely won't want to miss. As always, I hope you enjoy each and every one of our Silhouette Intimate Moments novels.

Yours,

Leslie Wainger
Senior Editor and Editorial Coordinator

AMERICAN HERO

CHEROKEE
THUNDER

Rachel
Lee

Published by Silhouette Books New York
America's Publisher of Contemporary Romance

SILHOUETTE BOOKS
300 East 42nd St., New York, N.Y. 10017

CHEROKEE THUNDER

Copyright © 1992 by Susan Civil

ISBN: 0-373-07463-8

First Silhouette Books printing December 1992

All the characters in this book have no existence
outside the imagination of the author and have
no relation whatsoever to anyone bearing the same
name or names. They are not even distantly
inspired by any individual known or unknown
to the author, and all incidents are pure invention.

®: Trademark used under license and
registered in the United States Patent and
Trademark Office and in other countries.

Printed in the U.S.A.

Books by Rachel Lee

Silhouette Intimate Moments

An Officer and a Gentleman #370
Serious Risks #394
Defying Gravity #430
*Exile's End #449
*Cherokee Thunder #463

*Conard County series

RACHEL LEE

wrote her first play in the third grade for a school assembly, and by the age of twelve, she was hooked on writing. She's lived all over the United States, on both the East and West Coasts, and now resides in Texas with her husband and two teenage children.

Having held jobs as a waitress, real-estate agent, optician and military wife—"Yes, that's a job!"—she uses these, as well as her natural flair for creativity, to write stories that are undeniably romantic. "After all, life is the biggest romantic adventure of all—and if you're open and aware, the most marvelous things are just waiting to be discovered."

To Leslie Wainger, with great appreciation.
In order to reach its full potential,
every gem needs a gifted jeweler—
and every book needs a talented editor.

Chapter 1

Damn Texan!

Despite the darkness of the wet, misty afternoon, Deputy Sheriff Micah Parish identified the license plates on the car ahead of him. The damn fool was driving too fast for the road conditions. The driver probably had no idea that the thin layer of moisture on the road could turn to a coating of ice at any moment—and probably would. The first winter storm of the season was marching into Conard County, Wyoming, and conditions had been worsening all afternoon. There wasn't any residual warmth in the ground to keep things thawed, and as soon as the air temperature slipped below freezing, that sheen of water on the pavement was going to freeze into a treacherous glaze.

Damn, he hated this time of year. It seemed like the first time road conditions turned wintry, everyone had to learn all over again how to drive, and half of them decided to relearn the hard way. A night like this usually meant he would be lucky if he had time for dinner, but tonight he was off-duty and on the way home. This year, the first storm would be somebody else's problem.

Except for Texas up there. The car wasn't slowing up any, and Micah could now hear the occasional rattle of freezing rain against his windshield. Muttering a curse, he leaned forward and flipped the switch that turned on the rack of flashers on the roof of his Blazer. Red and blue lights revolved, casting eerie swirls of color over the wet, gray countryside.

He only intended to warn the driver of the worsening conditions and advise caution. He figured he could spend five minutes doing that, his conscience would be soothed, and then he could head home for the steak dinner he had been looking forward to all day.

An instant later, he was wondering if he had caused an accident instead. There was a bright flare of brake lights, and then the car ahead of him went out of control, first fishtailing this way and that, then finally going into a full circular spin. If there was any mercy, it was that the car continued to slow down, finally nosing to a stop into a ditch alongside the road.

Micah was by nature a silent man, but as he eased the Blazer to a careful halt on the grassy shoulder, he muttered a string of curses like beads on a rosary. Even in the rain he could see the gush of steam from beneath the other car's hood, and as he approached, he could smell the distinctive odor of antifreeze overheating on the engine block. The cute white Honda was seriously damaged. He just hoped to hell the occupants were wearing safety harnesses.

Damn, he hated auto accidents. Too often it felt like Vietnam all over again: the torn, dismembered bodies, the stink of blood and the cries of anguish. And all too often there were kids.

This time there weren't any kids. This time there was just the driver, a woman who was sitting upright and clutching the steering wheel in a death grip. She appeared uninjured, but it was impossible to be certain. Reaching out, he threw open the Honda's door and demanded, "Lady, are you okay?"

"Yes." She stared straight ahead, unmoving.

Disturbed, Micah bent and peered in at her, wondering if she had banged her head. She seemed dazed. "Let's get you out of there."

"No, really..." Faith Williams turned automatically to look at him, then gasped. If the seat belt hadn't held her in place, she would have scrambled to the far side of the car in panic.

He was a man, he was a cop, and he was big. That alone was more than enough to awaken her terror, but this man looked hard. Cold. Dangerous. His features were sharply etched—all angles and planes, looking as if they had been shaped in stone—and his eyes, as black as night, held absolutely no warmth. She shrank backward.

He saw her panic and fear, and while it was extreme, it wasn't entirely unexpected. He was a big, powerful man, with a harshly chiseled face, a half-breed who looked like a half-breed, a man who looked wild and dangerous. He even recognized that wearing his black hair to his shoulders didn't do much to make him seem more civilized. But civilization was a veneer Micah Parish wore, not part of his nature. He was perfectly content to have women cross the street to avoid him and even more content to have men think twice about giving him a hard time. It made life easier. Simpler. Micah was a great believer in sticking to basics.

He was, Faith thought as she cowered as far away from him as she could get, a perfect male animal. She didn't think she'd ever seen a man who looked so much like a... like a man. Like a predator. Like a hunter. As wildly, violently beautiful as a wolf. As deadly. And about as trustworthy. He was a man, after all, and she knew everything she ever wanted to know about men. Especially men who wore uniforms.

Micah shifted impatiently, recognizing her fright, understanding it, and feeling absolutely in no mood to deal with it. Dinner was waiting, and it was getting damn cold out here. He was, however, a uniformed deputy, and he couldn't leave a woman all alone in the middle of nowhere to freeze to death. Because she *would* freeze to death. Up this road there was nothing for the next eighty miles except his ranch and the deserted Montrose place. Oh, there were a few other ranches way back off the road, but nothing she could get to on foot. And town lay twenty-seven miles behind them. With the weather turning sour, his was apt to be the last vehicle heading this way before late tomorrow morning.

Touch was supposed to be reassuring, so he touched her shoulder. She flinched away as if his hand were a burning brand. Well, hell, he thought, and stepped back, giving her space. "Lady, your car is dead, and you're going to be just as dead if you don't let me take you to shelter. There's a winter storm on its way in. I guarantee you'll be a frozen corpse before midnight." For a taciturn man that was a long speech, so long it surprised even him. And it was wasted.

People had looked at him in all sorts of ways in his life, most of them with good reason, but he couldn't remember a perfect stranger ever looking at him as if he were the devil incarnate. Reaching up, he pushed back his tan Stetson and settled his fists on his khaki-clad hips. Hell and tarnation. He tried again.

"Lady, I'm a cop. A deputy sheriff. My job is to *help* you. I swear that's all I want to do. Just let me help you so I can get the hell home to my dinner and a warm fire, will you?"

As soon as he spoke, Micah wished he could recall the irritated words. The woman flinched visibly and then reached for the clasp of the seat belt with shaking, awkward hands, as if she couldn't comply swiftly enough.

"I'm . . . I'm sorry," she said weakly. "I'm sorry."

Micah released a relieved breath and stepped back a little more, recognizing that the lady evidently had some kind of problem, but that she was trying to keep a grip on it. So okay. He would stand back if she'd just behave rationally.

Unfortunately, he wasn't able to keep as much distance as they both would have liked. She was dressed for Texas, not Wyoming, and her sedate pumps provided absolutely no traction on the ice that was beginning to glaze everything. When she tried to ease out of the car, her foot slipped and she fell back into the seat.

Micah regarded this development with distaste. "I'm going to have to help you," he said reluctantly. She clearly didn't want to be touched, and he just as definitely didn't want to do any more touching. Cops had hard and fast rules about dealing with solitary females, and every one of them involved avoiding any potential appearance of impropriety. He had broken the first rule when he touched her, and now, fool that he was, he was going to break it again—big time.

A stocking cap completely concealed her hair, but she had wide blue eyes and satiny-looking calves a man would kill to stroke. Nice thighs, too, he realized when she slid forward on the seat and her skirt hiked up. Legs that just went on forever. What the hell was the matter with him, anyway?

He knew all about women. They were turned on by his badge, his gun and his uniform. A cop could get laid any time, anywhere. It was appalling how many women were prepared to trade their bodies to avoid a hundred-dollar traffic ticket. Amazing how many times he had approached a vehicle with his summons book in hand only to find some woman baring her body for his view. Yeah, he knew all about women. They were users, connivers, whores. They weren't in it for the long haul, and they were interested only in what they could get.

He also knew himself. He was a sucker for strays and lost animals. He was a one-finger pushover for anybody in serious need of help. Why did he get the uneasy feeling that this woman was in serious need of help? Why did he suddenly have the gut-sinking certainty that he was in the process of committing a major tactical error? He trusted his instincts. Instincts had kept him alive for better than twenty years in defiance of the odds. This time they were telling him to dump this woman PDQ. This time he had to ignore them.

He tried to steady her on the ice by holding her arm, but she kept slipping away, and he figured he was apt to tear her arm right out of its socket if he kept catching her this way. Without further ado, he scooped her up in his arms and carried her to the Blazer, ignoring her weak protests.

"Shut up," he said finally as he struggled to handle her and open the door at the same time. "Just shut up and hold still."

Those gruff commands would have been enough to stir most women up into a full-scale rebellion. He figured she would call him at least one name and take a halfhearted swing at him. She did neither. Instead, she became instantly very still and very silent, and the fear came back to her face. He ignored it. One way or the other, he was *not* going to get tangled up in this woman's problems, even if he had to pretend he was deaf, dumb and blind for the rest of the night.

He set her on the Blazer's passenger seat and let go of her immediately, then stepped back. "You need anything from the car?"

"M-my suitcases. In the trunk."

No, he told himself, he would *not* ask her what she was so scared of, because she might actually tell him. And if she told him, he would probably feel bound to do something to help her. Didn't he always? It didn't take any effort to remember a half dozen times when he'd felt bound to help someone and then had lived to regret it. It was the story of his life, it seemed.

Opening the Honda's trunk with the keys he had rescued from the ignition, Micah considered giving voice to a few choice words. Damn, it looked as if everything she owned were crammed into this tiny trunk. There was even a coffee maker. Suitcases? Which suitcases? All of them? Smothering a sigh, he started carrying them all to the Blazer.

The roads were treacherous now, and freezing rain mixed with snow had begun to fall. Micah climbed into the warm cab of the Blazer and turned over the ignition. "We're going to my place." He heard her swiftly drawn breath, but ignored it. There really wasn't any other option. He'd spent the last ten minutes, while he carted all her gear, trying to think of one. "It's getting too bad out there to drive back to town, and my place is only a couple more miles up the road."

"What about...what about the Montrose ranch? That isn't too much farther, is it?"

"A few miles past mine," he answered, tossing her a curious glance before returning his attention to the road. Surely he would have heard something if the Montrose property had been put up for sale. He was, after all, the likeliest person to want it. He drove slowly, carefully, patiently. On this ice there was no margin for error. "Nobody lives there, though. What do you want with the Montrose place?"

"It's mine now," she said. "Jason Montrose was my father."

In that instant he knew who she was. Faith Montrose. Something wrenched in him, but he forced himself to ignore it. Obviously she didn't remember him, so he could safely pretend not to know her. It had been twenty-five years, after all, and it would be better that way—for both of them.

"Well, you can't go there tonight. I doubt there's enough propane left in the tank to run the heater overnight. You'd freeze. I'll get you there in the morning, and we'll see what needs to be done." He needed his head examined. *We'll* see what needs to be done? Right.

God, she was a babe in the woods, just what he needed for his nearest neighbor. He knew she must be over thirty, and he found himself wondering what kind of life she had led that she didn't know about things like arranging for the power to be turned on, the propane tank to be filled, the pump to be primed. . . . If she had arranged for any of those things to be done, he would have heard about it. No, the Montrose place wasn't ready for occupancy, and wouldn't be for several days at least. Hell. What was he supposed to do with her? Well, when the weather improved he could take her to a motel, he guessed.

At least she wasn't a gabber. She kept perfectly quiet and huddled as close to the door as she could, which caused the shoulder harness to lie right across her throat. He thought of warning her that the seat belt could hurt her throat if they stopped suddenly, but then decided against it. It was none of his business. None of his damn business. As a decent human being, he had to make sure she didn't freeze to death, but he didn't have to do any more than that.

Micah's house was set more than a mile off the county road. At the time he purchased the ranch, there had been a couple of other places in the county he might have bought, but this one had appealed to him because the house was situated among rocky outcrops that gave it a protected feeling. There was only one approach by which a vehicle could arrive, and while that was no longer a necessary consideration in his life, it nonetheless made him more comfortable. The habits of half a lifetime were harder to break than an addiction, and sometimes not worth the trouble. Selecting a defensible location was such a habit. It didn't complicate anything.

Tonight nothing looked appealing, he thought as he jockeyed the Blazer right up to the kitchen door. The outcrops, normally a rainbow of sedimentary colors, were a dismal gray. Even the grass seemed to have become gray under its growing burden of ice, and when he stepped out of the vehicle, ice crystals stung his cheeks. A lousy, miserable, godforsaken night, he thought sourly. He was grateful that he didn't have to be on duty.

He ushered his unwanted guest into the kitchen and paused only long enough to start a pot of coffee. "I've got to check on my animals," he told her. "Make yourself comfortable and have some coffee. When I get back I'll make dinner."

"Deputy?"

Her voice stopped him at the door. Reluctantly, he looked back.

"I didn't get your name," she said, looking like a lost waif in the middle of his large kitchen.

For the first time he realized this woman was tiny. Scarcely an inch or two over five feet. The down jacket she wore nearly swallowed her whole. "Micah," he said after a moment. "I'm Micah Parish."

"I'm Faith Williams," she said politely. "Thank you for rescuing me."

Well, hell, he thought, and crammed his hat tighter on his head. "It's my job," he said shortly, and stepped out into the darkening late afternoon.

Nope. She didn't remember him at all.

It had been many years since Micah had last seen Faith, but he maintained a clear memory of her nonetheless. He'd been a sort of adopted brother to her during her first summer visit to her father. Faith had been six the first time Micah saw her, frightened at being yanked from her Houston home and sent unaccompanied by air to visit a father in Conard County, a father she scarcely remembered. Micah had been eighteen, and to this day he clearly recalled the meeting.

His horse had gone lame in the arroyo that cut between the Wyatt spread and the Montrose ranch where Micah was working for the summer. Micah had been squatting, running his hands expertly up Dutchman's foreleg, when he'd looked up to see a tiny girl with a tear-streaked face and eyes the color of the midsummer sky staring at him. Her hair was long and pale, hanging nearly to her thin little waist, and the hot, dry July breeze blew it across her face like a shimmering veil.

"Are you hurt?" Micah asked instantly, captivated by the eyes, concerned by the tears.

Slowly she shook her head. "No." Her little girl's voice was hardly more than a whisper.

"Are you lost?"

Again she shook her head solemnly.

But Micah knew she was at least four miles from the nearest dwelling, the Montrose house.

Moving slowly so as not to startle her, Micah sat cross-legged on the dirt beside Dutchman.

"Where's your home?" he asked quietly.

"Houston."

He knew then that he was looking at Jason Montrose's daughter. Montrose had made no secret that his girl was coming from Houston to spend the summer with him.

"Where's your daddy?" he asked her.

She shook her head. "I want my mommy." Her lower lip trembled.

Eighteen-year-old boys aren't noted for their sensitivity, but Micah's heart went out to the little girl. "I know," he said.

"Do you have a mommy?"

"She's dead."

Faith's lower lip had trembled even more. "My mommy's in Houston, and I'm going to find her."

Micah wondered what the devil to do now. "It's too far to walk," he told her. "You could walk all summer and still not get to Houston."

"I don't care."

"You'll get cold and hungry, and your mommy and daddy will worry about you. You'll make your mommy cry."

The little face crumpled even more.

"Why don't you let me take you back to your daddy?"

"No!"

Micah sighed and looked down at the dusty clay ground. The little girl stepped closer.

"Are you an Indian?" she asked.

Micah's head shot up, but all he found was honest curiosity. Of course, she was only a child. Moreover, in a spurt of rebellion, he'd let his black hair grow to his shoulders and tied it back with a bandanna around his forehead.

"Half Indian," he answered truthfully. *Half-breed.*

She drew a little closer. "I never saw a real Indian before."

"Well, you have now."

"Can I live with you?"

The question so startled him that he simply stared at her. "What about your daddy?" he asked finally.

"He doesn't care about me. He went away when I was little."

Micah heard the girl's mother in that statement. "Kid, your daddy loves you a whole lot. He told everybody in town how much he loves you and how happy he is you're visiting him. You're gonna make him real sad."

Again the small chin trembled. Micah sighed.

"Tell you what, kid. I'll give you a ride on my horse, and we'll both go back together and talk to your daddy. A real ride on a real Indian horse," he added cajolingly.

It was a long time coming, but finally he got a small nod. Micah lifted her onto his saddle, wrapped her small hands tightly around the pommel, and, with instructions to hang on tight, he walked her and his horse the four miles to the Montrose place.

His welcome by Jason Montrose had been far warmer than a half-breed was accustomed to. And when Micah had knelt in the dust to extract his own promise from Faith that she wouldn't try to run away again, she had insisted that she would stay if he promised to visit her the next day. Looking up at Jason Montrose, expecting the rancher to be annoyed or disapproving, Micah had instead received a nod.

"I second that invitation, Micah," Jason Montrose had said. "You come visit her tomorrow and any other time you feel like it."

Somehow Micah had felt like it quite a bit. He'd been the one to teach Faith how to ride, who'd taught her to swim in the watering hole and how to milk a cow. He was never certain if he was welcomed simply because he made Faith easier for Montrose to handle, but it ceased to matter to him. She was the sister he had never had.

In late August Micah had gone off to the army, and Faith had gone back to Houston. He wrote her a couple of letters from Vietnam and received some crayoned thank you notes in return, but then the horror had gripped him, and he hadn't written anymore.

He'd seen her once again, years later, when he'd passed through Conard County, stopping briefly to visit his buddy Nate Tate. Faith had been fifteen, and he'd been twenty-seven, a very old twenty-seven. Life's currents had carried him into ever more dangerous occupations. He'd come upon Faith at the swimming hole while he'd been out visiting old haunts. The sound of laughter and splashing, such a clean, wonderful sound, had drawn him. She'd been with a group of kids her own age, all having a good time. Micah had hung back, not wanting to disrupt the fun, and decided not to speak to her. He told himself she probably wouldn't remember him, anyway, and would only think he was some kind of creep.

Turning his horse, he'd ridden steadily away, never once glancing back. Life had taught him that there was no way back. That one brief summer with Jason Montrose and his daughter, that one brief time in his life where he had actually felt that he was part of a real family, was a precious anomaly. He cherished it, but he wasn't foolish enough to believe he could ever recapture it.

And now Faith was here, he thought as he pitchforked fresh straw into a stall. Hell.

He straightened abruptly and leaned the pitchfork against the wall. From his hip pocket he tugged out his wallet and flipped it open. There, facing his driver's license, was a snapshot of six-year-old Faith. Hardened, toughened, callused hands had held that photo countless times over the past twenty-five years. She'd been the family he had never really had. She had been the symbol of all he had fought for. His little sister.

Now the symbol was here, and she was not a symbol anymore but very real and fully grown. And he didn't know what in the hell he was going to do about it.

Micah entered the kitchen with a burst of cold air. Snow sprinkled the shoulders of his jacket. "It's gettin' downright unfriendly out there," he remarked and headed straight for the coffee pot. Moments later he leaned back against the counter and raised a steaming mug to his mouth. He had unzipped his sage-colored winter jacket, revealing the crisp khaki uniform shirt beneath and his shiny silver badge. Almost reluctantly, his eyes strayed toward where she sat at the table.

Her hair, he saw, was just as pale as it had been in childhood, an almost colorless blond, so fine it looked as if it had been spun from sugar. It had been long and straight, but now she wore it in a tousled profusion of curls that fell softly past her shoulders. Touchable hair, the kind a man wanted to run his hands through.

Her face was just as delicately etched, but stronger somehow, firmer looking. And pinched. Life had taught her some hard lessons, he thought, as he deliberately dragged his gaze from her softly pink, gently bowed lips.

And then he saw her stomach. His mug froze in midair, and he frankly stared. She was pregnant. Very definitely pregnant. Five months, he'd guess. Maybe even six. The knowledge had a shocking, unexpected effect on him. It twisted and turned in his gut like a flaming knife, a strong feeling of unholy jealousy. Slowly, he lifted his black-as-night eyes to her small, pale face.

"Miz Williams," he said after a moment, "do you want to tell me what the hell is going on here?"

Her hands closed around the mug of coffee she wasn't drinking, and he didn't miss the tight way she held on to it. This lady, he found himself thinking, was a bundle of very raw nerve endings.

Ten seconds or so passed before she answered him. Her eyes never lifted from her mug. "What do you mean?"

He snorted and took a swig of his coffee. "Pregnant women don't go running off into the back of beyond all by themselves."

She bit her lower lip. "Why not?"

"Why not." He repeated the question without the question mark. Cut it out, Micah, he warned himself. If you don't ask questions, you don't get answers you don't want to hear. You don't get involved. You don't collect another stray. And this woman was giving him plenty of opportunities to avoid involvement. She was backing away as determinedly as he ought to be and wasn't.

"Well," he heard himself saying, "most pregnant women get concerned about things like doctors and someone to call on if they need help. So, is your husband arriving in a day or two?" He'd noted the lack of a wedding ring, but that didn't necessarily mean anything. Besides, on second look he thought he could see a thin line of paler skin on her ring finger. Recent divorce, maybe.

Her color receded even more, making her look ashen. What was with her? he wondered yet again. A casual question shouldn't make her look as if she had just been threatened with a firing squad.

"I don't think—I don't think that's any of your business," she answered in a voice that was thin and strained. She looked at him then, a pathetic attempt at defiance.

"Sure it is," he remarked. "I'm going to be your nearest neighbor. The only neighbor close enough to help out in an emergency. That makes it my business, Miz Williams. Are you going to be alone?"

Her blue eyes wavered and fell, as if she had run out of courage. "Yes."

"Well, hell," he said, and sighed. "What else do I need to know?"

Her eyes snapped back to his face, and she was clearly perplexed. "What else?"

"Yeah, what else? Where's junior's daddy? Does he know about this kid? Is he likely to come along and make trouble? Or did he head for the hills and leave you all alone?"

"It's really not your...not your concern," Faith protested weakly. "I'm not going to bother you. I don't want to bother you with anything."

"I know. But you will." Deciding the air had better be cleared, because maybe then she would see sense and pack up and go back to Texas, he pulled out a chair on the far side of the table and straddled it.

"Look," he said. "The Montrose place is thirty-six miles from the nearest town. The nearest neighbor is me, four and a half miles down the road. Beyond that, better than ten or twelve miles away, are the Lairds and the Wyatts. If you run into anything more severe than a twisted ankle, you're going to be calling on a neighbor for help. That's the way it is in these parts. That's the way it has to be for all of us." He looked at her until she nodded her understanding.

"Now, you're going to stay here with me until we get your power on, your propane delivered and your phone installed. There's no way in hell I'm going to let you stay out there alone with no heat, no water and no phone. You can just plain forget it. Anyhow, I don't think you're stupid enough to try it. So, you're my business. You're my business because I'm going to be the person you turn to when there's any trouble. You're my business because it's my job to protect the welfare of the people in this county, so if you move into this county your welfare is going to be my business. Am I getting through?"

She was gnawing her lip, and she gave only the smallest nod. "I won't be any trouble. I promise. I don't want to make trouble for anyone."

There was something about the way she spoke that made him sigh. It also disturbed some deep, dark place inside him. It sounded wrong, somehow, as if she were afraid. As if it were a world-class crime to disturb someone.

He rubbed his chin and considered starting dinner. After all, he'd said more in the last ten minutes than he'd said in the last week. It wasn't like him to offer opinions on the things people chose to do.

And then, as he studied her bowed head, he realized something so strongly and so forcefully that it never entered his head to question the knowledge. "You're running from someone. Who is it?"

She drew a sharp breath, and her head jerked almost as if she had been struck.

"C'mon, Miz Williams. Who are you running from?"

When she raised her face, he wished he hadn't asked. No one should look as old, as hunted and as terrified as this woman did right now. She released a breath so ragged that it sounded as if it had come from a tattered soul.

"My ex-husband," she said.

Chapter 2

There was a whole lot more Micah needed to know, but he didn't ask. Instead, he showed Faith the spare bedroom upstairs and left her with her suitcases, some fresh towels and the advice to change into something a little warmer before dinner. He himself made a quick change into a well-worn pair of jeans and a red flannel shirt.

Downstairs, he took the time to start a fire in the wood stove that stood in the hallway between the living room and dining room, and then he turned his attention to dinner. The steak, meant for just him, would now have to serve two, but he didn't begrudge her.

The fact that she was fleeing her husband, her *ex*-husband, raised all kinds of questions. From the look on her face, he suspected none of the answers would be pretty. A woman running the way this woman was running was hardly trying to avoid a simple attempt to patch things up.

For a moment, as he stood over the stove, Micah saw her in his mind's eye as she had been so many years ago, the child and the blossoming teenager. She had been full of so much promise, and he had always believed her future would be bright and shining. He had needed to believe it. Now this. What had happened to her?

Well, if it was going to concern him in any way, he figured the answers would fall into his lap with time. They always did. When life set out to drag you into the middle of a mess, it didn't hold anything back.

Of course, he could still hope that she would head back to Texas and make her problems somebody else's concern. Gut instinct said she was staying, though. Right here. Just four miles up the road. Bringing all her problems with her.

And he wasn't going to be able to keep clear, because of the little girl she had once been, and because she was pregnant and alone. Between those three things, Micah figured he was tied into this mess but good. He swore, a single, succinct word that punctured the quiet like a thunderclap.

The blood of shamans ran in the veins of Micah Parish. He could still remember one of the rare occasions in his early childhood when his father, a taciturn, unemotional man, had taken Micah on his knee. Amory Parish had made a stab at being a father from time to time, and on one occasion he had spoken of Micah's mother. She had been a Cherokee medicine woman, the elder Parish had told his young son. Micah's grandfather had also been a medicine man, reputedly one of great power and magic. Amory Parish didn't hold with that kind of nonsense, and he was sure the magic had been a matter of imagination, but he wanted the boy to understand that his Indian ancestors hadn't been scum, no matter what anybody told him.

A boy who was already getting bloody noses from taking exception to being called a dirty Indian, a boy who fed his empty, hungry heart with Arthurian legends and read Sir Walter Scott under his blankets with a flashlight—that boy had treasured that small bit of information about his ancestry. It had made him feel special.

It had also explained his feelings. At least, that was what he called them, those moments of intuition when he seemed almost to step outside time and know, just *know* things he shouldn't be able to. He'd never told anyone about those experiences, and he never would. Even to him they sounded crazy.

Right now, though, his intuition was telling him that he was standing on the edge of a precipice, and that nothing would ever be the same again.

The vegetables and instant mashed potatoes were on the table, and he was taking the steak out of the broiler when Faith returned to the kitchen. She hovered uncertainly in the doorway, as if she feared she were trespassing.

"Pull up a chair," Micah said. "Chow's ready."

"Can I—can I help?"

"Nope. It's all done." He didn't want to look at her, but somehow he couldn't stop himself. He saw the shadow in her blue eyes, a shadow of fear so old she wore it comfortably, unaware that it wasn't natural. He saw, too, an amazing vulnerability. Whatever life had hurled at this woman, she hadn't learned how to protect herself. She hadn't grown calluses or developed a shell. Hell! Somebody ought to tell her that a little emotional armor was a useful thing.

He set the table just like a man, Faith thought as she took her place. Flatware had been dumped beside the plates. A roll of paper towels stood in the center of the table in lieu of napkins. The potatoes had been served in the saucepan, and the broccoli had already been placed on the plates. In spite of herself, she felt the corners of her mouth lift in amusement. She wondered when a woman had last sat at Micah Parish's table.

Micah caught sight of that smile, the faint, tentative shimmer of humor, and he was suddenly aware that Faith was a woman. A warm, sweet-smelling, soft-looking, enticing tidbit of femininity. And despite the swollen curve of her abdomen, plainly evident beneath the soft folds of an oversize blue sweatshirt, she was a sexy tidbit of femininity, too.

Aw, hell. Not that, too!

He turned swiftly away and went to the refrigerator for milk. He would have his nightly beer, but she was going to drink milk. He didn't even bother to ask her. He couldn't have said exactly why, but something in her vulnerability told him this baby was important to her and that she would take every precaution to ensure its well-being.

"Thank you," she said when he placed the tall glass of milk before her. She was touched by his thoughtfulness, and a glimmer of warmth crept into her voice. She looked up, trying to smile. Blue eyes met black, and Texas sank into the dark velvet of a Wyoming night. So deep, she thought. So dark. So mesmerizing. Those eyes were dark pools, beckoning, bottomless. Beyond them, she felt, was something bright and shining, something so bright that it needed to be hidden in those deep, dark pools.

Micah blinked and looked away, uneasily feeling he had looked into the eyes of destiny. Refusing to let the superstitious, fanciful part of his nature get the better of him, he pulled back his chair and sat, giving his attention to his meal.

"That's far too much steak for me," Faith protested when he tried to serve her. "I couldn't possibly—"

"You're eating for two," he interrupted.

"Well, yes," she said uncertainly, "but one of us only weighs a couple of pounds."

Micah's eyes snapped up to hers, and what he saw there had him smiling against his better judgment. It wasn't much of a smile, just a twitch at one corner of his mouth, but Faith saw it, and the great, cold knot of fear in her eased a little more.

He spoke. "But one of you is growing fast."

"Both of us are growing fast," she said ruefully. "But not fast enough to eat all that steak."

The other corner of his mouth reluctantly rose to join the first. As a smile it was small and faint, but it had the most amazing effect on his face, Faith realized with a sense of wonder. Micah Parish no longer looked hard, forbidding or cruel. He passed her the plate holding the steak.

"Cut off whatever you want," he said roughly.

Her hands trembled a little, aware of his eyes on her, and she sliced off about three ounces of the beef. She doubted she was going to be able to swallow even that much if this man kept staring at her this way.

He didn't think that was nearly enough, but he kept quiet about it. He'd already argued too much about something that was none of his business anyhow.

He did, however, cherish a high reverence for life. It seemed a funny thing in a man who had made his living by the sword for so long, or perhaps it was the natural outcome of seeing life valued so cheaply for so long. He held a particular reverence for new life, for the innocent unborn, for the women who carried life in their bellies.

He found himself thinking, as he ate his dinner, that Faith Williams would have been a hell of a lot easier to deal with if she wasn't expecting a baby. A pregnant woman needed someone to look out for her, to look after her, and he had the definite feeling she didn't have a soul in the world.

The first thing he needed to do, he decided reluctantly, was find out something about her husband—what kind of threat he was, and how she was involved. If the man was really a danger to her, he might have some kind of police record, and if he could just get the man's name and the city where he and Faith had been living, he could check it out. But before he invaded her privacy that way, he was going to make one more stab at getting her to tell him herself. Remembering the way she had reacted earlier to his questioning, he didn't think it was going to be easy. After dinner, he told himself.

She wanted to help with the dishes of course. She'd clearly had a very proper upbringing. He wondered, as he passed her a freshly rinsed plate to dry, what she would think of his upbringing. If you could honestly call it an upbringing at all.

His dad had been an Army enlisted man. His mother, a full-blooded Cherokee, had left her husband and eldest child just before Micah's second birthday, taking her newborn second son with her. Micah's father had claimed the division was a fair one, a son to each parent. Micah just plain didn't think about it much at all. He had never seen his mother again and had heard that she'd died within a year.

After that, Micah's upbringing had been catch-as-catch-can, and devil take the hindmost. His father had bounced from one Army post to another, dragging Micah with him and finding a succession of women to look after the boy. None of them had particularly cared for the silent child, and along about the time Micah turned ten, his father stopped trying to pass the women off as housekeepers. Micah had always known better, anyway. His attitude toward women had practically been born in the cradle with him.

He was wiping down the stove when he realized that he had passed the last hour or more in the company of a woman who hadn't talked him to death. In fact, she hadn't seemed to be disturbed by his silence, either. That must be some kind of first.

Turning, he sought her out with his eyes and found her at the kitchen window, looking out at the blowing, whirling snow that was illuminated by the porch light. She had her arms protectively wrapped around her stomach, a pregnant woman's perennial pose.

She seemed to sense his attention and turned her head quickly his way. She made an attempt to smile. "I've never seen a blizzard before," she confessed.

"Never?" He stepped toward her, turning his gaze to the window. Here was his opening. "Whereabouts in Texas are you from?"

"San Antonio."

"I thought you folks got some snow from time to time down there."

"Oh, we do, but nothing like this. Once every few years we'll get a powder, maybe even a couple of inches. But nothing like this." She pointed to the blowing, drifting snow. "How much do you think will fall?"

"The weather report's calling for ten to twelve inches."

She utterly astonished him then by hugging herself and smiling like a delighted child. "Fantastic!"

"Fantastic?" he repeated gruffly, then caught himself. Hell, there was no point ruining her fun by telling her just what kind of extra work a blizzard created for a rancher, or how much fun it was going to be trying to plow out his mile-long driveway. Naw, just let her enjoy it.

But she had heard the implied disagreement in his tone, and right before his astonished eyes, she flinched away from him and shrank into herself. What the hell? And why was she covering her womb as if she expected a blow there? Right there.

"Miz Williams..."

She shrank back even farther, watching him warily as she backed up. "I'm sorry," she said almost blankly. "I'll get out of your way."

"Miz Williams..." She was still backing up, and he saw the danger she was unaware of. Right behind her was a chair, and if she stumbled over it... "Faith, don't move. You're going to—"

The bark in his tone scared her even more, and she took another quick backward step. That did it. Heedless of her fright, Micah leapt forward and grabbed her, catching her just as the back of her leg collided with the chair.

"Damn fool woman," he swore. "If you'd fallen over that chair—"

But she didn't hear what he was saying. She heard his tone, and total panic seized her. Like a wildcat, she fought his hold on her, trying to escape. He felt her panic but didn't dare let her go for fear she would hurt herself trying to scramble away from him. Unable to do anything else, he tightened his hold and took her blows as she flailed wildly at him.

"Miz Williams... Faith... it's okay. I won't hurt you. I swear I won't hurt you...." He murmured as soothingly as he could, using the same tone he used on his frightened or hurt livestock. Again and again she pounded his shoulders and chest with her fists, shoving at him, trying to break his hold. She might be giving him a small bruise or two, but she didn't know a damn thing about protecting herself. Sighing, he braced himself against her hammering and kept murmuring a soothing stream of nonsense, hoping to penetrate her terror with his tone.

Finally he managed to pin her arms to her sides and hold her snugly against him. She wiggled, but she was rapidly tiring.

"You'll hurt the baby," he said. "Shh... It's okay. Shh."

It was exhaustion that quieted her finally, not anything he said or did. She sagged against him, all the fight worn out of her, and her face fell against his hard chest.

"Shh," he whispered. "It's okay. You're safe here, Faith. You're safe."

It was a good thing she didn't look up at his face just then, however, because she would have become terrified all over again. At that moment Micah Parish had a pretty good idea what Faith Williams was fleeing from, and at that moment he was in a mood for murder.

With weary astonishment, Faith felt Micah's grasp on her change. His arms ceased to imprison her, and his hands began to stroke soothingly from her shoulder to her hip, as if he were stroking a kitten. She would never have imagined him to be gentle, but he was gentle right then, touching her with a kindness that made her throat tighten.

He felt the wetness of tears soaking his shirt, and he expelled a breath, letting go of the anger. It wouldn't do a damn bit of good to be angry. Not right now, at any rate. And hell, he didn't want to get all tied up in knots with this woman—or any woman—anyway.

But he sighed again, sensing that the knots were already being tied. Damn, he was a sucker for strays.

Bending, he scooped her up and carried her toward the stairs as if he were carrying a bride over the threshold.

"Easy," he said, when he heard her sharp intake of breath. "Easy. I'm just going to take you to your room. You're tuckered out and need to rest. You have to take care of that baby, Miz Williams."

Upstairs, he shouldered his way into her room and put her down gently on the bed. She stared up at him in the light from the hall, her expression one of wondering disbelief as he pulled the quilts over her.

"You rest a while, Miz Williams. You just rest. If you want to come down again later, you come. I usually like to make some cocoa around bedtime if that interests you."

He paused a moment, then touched her cheek awkwardly. "Was your husband's name Williams, too?"

"Yes." Her voice was nothing but a cracked whisper. "Yes. Frank Williams." She closed her eyes, hoping he would leave it at that.

He didn't, though. "He wouldn't have had any trouble with the law, would he?" A man like that often did, especially if his wife had any spunk at all. And this woman had spunk, all right.

Faith turned her face away. "He's wanted right now," she said wearily. "He escaped from custody three days ago."

Escaped from custody? He was very definitely going to check this out. "Well, don't you worry about him none. If Frank Williams sets foot in Conard County, he'll be dealing with me. Now just you sleep."

He closed the door quietly behind him as he left her.

Back in the kitchen, he pulled the phone off the hook and placed a call to the Conard County Sheriff's Department.

"Fred, it's Micah. Listen, if you're not real busy, I was wondering if you could do me a favor? Yeah, I'd like you to get a hold of the San Antonio police and see if you can get me a rap sheet on a Frank Williams. Might be Francis Williams. I understand he recently escaped from custody, and

I have reason to believe he might be headed this way. Thanks, Fred.''

After he hung up, he stood looking out at the drifting, blowing snow in the yard off the kitchen, trying to concentrate on the things he needed to do for his animals. He didn't have a whole lot of livestock, a few horses, a few head of cattle, just enough animals to make the place feel like a ranch. Working for the Sheriff's Department, he really didn't have the time to ranch, and he really didn't have the know-how, either, though he supposed he could hire help.

There wasn't any point in it, though, he thought for the umpteenth time. Since youth, he'd wanted to live on a ranch, to have his own spread, to be able to get on a horse and ride until he got tired without leaving his own land. He could do that right now. He'd fulfilled his dream. Building anything bigger, anything more complex, was something a man did when he wanted to leave something to the future. Micah didn't want to do that. Oh, if he had a son or a daughter he probably would, but you couldn't get a kid without a woman, and he'd be damned if he would take any woman into his life. No way.

He knew better. He'd nearly fallen into that trap once, and Micah wasn't a man who ever made a mistake a second time.

Faith cried a little, but tears came easily to her since she'd become pregnant, and they dried just as quickly. She slept for a little while, feeling the day's fatigue deep in her bones.

When she woke, it was nearly ten p.m., and the wind was howling like a banshee around the corners of the house, making the windows rattle and the frame structure creak and groan with each renewed blast. A draft curled across the room and touched her nose with chilly fingers. From downstairs she heard a bang, signifying that Micah Parish was still up and about.

It was lonely in this strange room, and the sounds of the storm were eerie, forlorn. She tried for a while to go back to sleep, but eventually she gave up. At last she sat up and switched on the small lamp on the bedside table. The pink shade cast a warm glow, and Faith wondered if Micah had purchased this house furnished, or if at some time a woman, perhaps a sister, had slept in this room. With all its pink frills, it was certainly not a room Micah would have created, nor was it the kind of room a grown woman would have decorated for herself.

The wind rattled the windows again and howled a desolate note. Sighing, Faith climbed out from under the quilts, deciding that even the company of a man was better than this creepy solitude. At least, the company of a man like Micah.

For a moment, when her feet touched the floor, she paused, remembering. She had acted like a crazy woman, she admitted. He must think she needed to be locked up. Despite that, he'd been incredibly gentle with her. Incredibly caring. The only other man she had ever known to show such kindness to her was the Texas Ranger who had saved her. Garrett Hancock. But Garrett had had a reason for understanding. His sister, he had told her, had once been married to a man like Frank Williams. How was it Micah understood? How was it he was so caring and gentle?

Or was he? *Better than thirty percent of the women in this country are victims of spousal abuse.* Her counselor had told her that shocking statistic. So many! And that meant an awful lot of men were like Frank. An awful lot. And that was why she shouldn't trust Micah Parish, no matter how kind he might seem. He could very well be another of them. Perhaps that was why he lived alone. Perhaps he'd driven a previous wife away.

She shivered as the wind moaned yet again and the draft snaked across the room to wrap her in an icy embrace.

Whatever Micah Parish was or wasn't, she didn't need to worry about it. She had dated Frank for months before they had married, and it wasn't until they'd been married nearly a year that he had hit her for the first time. An abuser sel-

dom showed his colors to strangers. So, for the time being,
and as long as she developed no kind of relationship with
the man, she was safe.

And all of that was rationalization anyway, she admitted. Micah had somehow managed to make her feel safe
when he had held her and endured her blows without retal-
iating. Something in his voice, in his eyes, in the way he
touched her...those things made her feel safe.

Or perhaps it was just coming back to Conard County
that made her feel safe. After her initial resistance to visiting her father, she had come to treasure her summers here
as a hiatus from an increasingly sour mother and a stepfather who preached damnation over the slightest infraction
and used his belt as a punctuation mark.

And there had been that Indian boy...Mike, she thought.
He was like a soft, warm memory, a feeling more than a visual image. Closing her eyes, she could almost, just barely,
recall the incredible security she had felt in her sixth summer, knowing that her father or Mike was watching over her
every moment. She had never fallen, slipped or tripped
without one of them catching her up in strong, sheltering
arms and drying her tears.

But then she had gone home to Texas to find her mother
remarried, and Mike had gone to Vietnam and after a couple of letters he had never written again. He must have died,
she thought, and felt the dry whisper of an ancient loss. But
it was the search for what he had given her that had brought
her back to Conard County.

Feeling calmer and more in control, she stood up and
tugged her sweatshirt down over her swollen belly. The baby
kicked, a soft poke that instantly brought a smile to her lips.
She loved being pregnant. She loved the child growing
within her. She could hardly wait to hold her son or daughter.

Downstairs, she found Micah in the kitchen, stirring a pot
with the promised hot chocolate. He glanced up when she

stepped into the room and gave her a nod that said nothing one way or the other.

"It sounds terrible outside," she said shyly, truly seeing him for the first time. He was a man, yes, and a cop besides, but he had carried her upstairs as carefully as a baby and tucked her in with a gentleness that she had never before experienced, not once in her entire life.

Micah turned and looked at her fully. He wondered if she had the vaguest idea how sexy she looked at this very minute, with her hair all tousled from her nap and her cheeks still flushed from sleep. Probably. Women always knew when they looked sexy. It was their stock in trade.

But there was something in her soft blue eyes, a kind of wistfulness that reached him despite his barriers. He was a little astonished to hear himself clear his throat and speak.

"After we have our cocoa, I'll find some boots and warm clothes for you. Anybody who's never been out in a blizzard really shouldn't miss a chance to see what it's like."

Her face lighted. There was really no other way to describe the change in her expression in response to his suggestion. In that instant she seemed to forget whatever was worrying her, terrifying her, driving her.

"Really? We can go out in this? It's not dangerous?"

He felt his mouth trying to frame a smile. He never smiled, but here he was smiling for at least the second time in one day. "Only if we were out in it too long, Miz Williams. We'll only be out a few minutes, just long enough for you to get a taste of what a blizzard is like."

The smile she gave him was warm, genuine. She suspected that he didn't especially want to go out in this, that to him it was nothing but a major inconvenience, yet here he was proposing to take her out just so she could see what it was like. But somehow she felt he wouldn't appreciate an emotional display of gratitude, so she offered him the only other thing she could. "I'd be honored if you would call me Faith, Deputy Parish."

He looked away, giving his attention to the pot he was stirring. Faith waited, wondering if he meant to ignore her, and why he should hesitate over what to call her.

Eventually Micah cleared his throat and spoke gruffly, feeling even as he did that this was another mistake in a day full of mistakes. "You can call me Micah," he told her.

That was not an offer Micah Parish made often, Faith realized. There was something about the rusty way he said it that revealed it was a rare concession.

"Thank you," she said politely.

He made a sound in his throat, sort of a grunt of acknowledgment. "Pull up a chair," he said roughly. "Cocoa's about ready." He glanced at her again and then snapped his gaze back to the saucepan.

"Earlier," he said, and cleared his throat, "earlier, I grabbed you because you were about to fall. I didn't mean to terrify you." That had been troubling him since he'd carried her upstairs, that she still might not understand why he had grabbed her that way. He knew how easily such things could be misunderstood. "The chair was right behind you, and you were backing up. There just wasn't time to be polite about it."

Seated at the table, her hands folded protectively over her stomach, Faith tried to find a way to let him know she understood, and to apologize for her own behavior. The problem was, she didn't see how she could apologize without explaining about Frank, and she didn't want to do that. Talking about it meant thinking about it, and she wasn't prepared to do that, either. Talking and thinking didn't help. Forgetting was the only way she could deal with it.

He was such a large man, she thought as she watched him set the mugs full of steaming cocoa on the table. He tore a paper towel from the roll and folded it awkwardly before he passed it to her. The gesture was touching, somehow, as if he were trying to polish up his world a little to make it more palatable to her.

He should only know, she thought wearily, where she had been. He would hardly worry about whether folding a paper towel would make it a more acceptable napkin.

He sat across from her, and she watched his huge hands cup and lift his mug. Big, capable hands, she thought. She would willingly bet that there was very little this man didn't know how to do with those hands.

And she had to apologize. Now. Before too much time passed.

"I'm sorry," she said abruptly, committed now to saying it.

He looked up sharply, as if he had forgotten she was there. He hadn't. He had, however, grown accustomed to her silence. She was a peaceful presence. "Sorry?"

"Yes. I've been so stupid today. Running my car off the road and putting you to all this trouble... And then the way I acted when—before, when—I can't believe I—I'm just so sorry!"

Well, hell, Micah thought. Maybe he didn't want to see it, and maybe he didn't want to tangle with it, but this woman's face reflected fear, uncertainty and utter misery. Some things a man just couldn't ignore, however much he might want to.

Reaching out, he captured one of her hands in a gentle grip. The gesture was meant to be soothing, but once again he was reminded that for her it was not. She flinched as he reached out, and at his touch she grew perfectly still, perfectly quiet. Kind of like a mouse caught by the eye of a snake. It was a survival kind of stillness, the stillness of the hunted.

Well, hell, he thought again, and let go of her. He damn well better get this woman established at the Montrose place before he got to actually caring what happened to her. He didn't want to think about the kinds of things that could make a woman so scared that she would run this fast and hard with her belly full of baby.

He muttered an oath that caused her to flinch again. Seeing her reaction, he got mad. Not at her, exactly. Maybe at himself a little. Whatever, he was mad.

"Look," he said harshly, "I've never in my life hit a man or a woman who didn't hit me first, and plenty of times I didn't hit back even then. I've got nothing to prove to anyone, least of all that I'm a bigger, tougher, meaner hombre. It's none of my business who made you so skittish, and I'm not asking. Just understand, you have nothing at all to fear from *me*."

She could almost believe him. She was surprised to realize that she *wanted* to believe him. Intellectually, she understood that not all men were abusive, but emotionally she knew only one thing—that she had once trusted, and her trust had been completely betrayed.

Micah accepted her silence for what it was, and was satisfied. He was, after all, not going to have any more to do with this lady than he absolutely couldn't avoid.

He drained his mug and scraped his chair back from the table. "I'll go see if I can find something for you to wear on your feet in the snow." At the kitchen door he hesitated and looked back. "Faith? Did you bring any winter gear except your coat?"

She shook her head, not looking at him. "I thought I had plenty of time. I didn't expect to come up here so soon."

Or so suddenly, he finished silently. Helter-skelter, harum-scarum, that was how she'd fled from Texas and her ex-husband. Fast. Suddenly. Without warning.

Well, hell.

"Does your ex know about the Montrose place?"

She blanched a little. "I don't think so."

But she was not one hundred percent sure. Great. Saying nothing more, he headed for the back hall closet, where an assortment of winter clothing had collected over the years from previous owners and occupants. He'd considered throwing everything away when he bought the place four years ago, but he couldn't bring himself to be so wasteful.

Much of his adult life, as a member of the Army Special Operations branch, he'd lived and worked in underdeveloped countries. The clothes in that closet were by no means worn out, and every time he thought of dumping them, he remembered plenty of people who would have treasured such leavings. As a result, the closet was still full of unused clothes that he had no use for. Periodically he swore he'd give them to the next church rummage sale, and every time he forgot about the stuff until it was too late.

It didn't take him too long to find a lady's pair of blue boots, some bright red mittens, a long, knitted scarf and the stocking cap she'd been wearing when he met her.

"Where did you get these?" Faith asked in amazement as she looked at Micah's offerings. "Do you have a sister or daughter stashed somewhere?"

"Not that I know of. The last owners evidently did, though."

"I wonder why they left this stuff. And my—the bedroom you're letting me use, is obviously a little girl's."

He'd wondered about that himself, a time or two, but he'd never wondered hard enough or long enough to think of asking anyone about it. "I don't know. I heard the last owners had some kind of trouble, but I never poked into it."

Faith looked up at him. "You're not a very curious person."

"Oh, I get curious enough at times," he admitted grudgingly. "But the older I get, the less time I seem to have to waste. I pick and choose what I spend my efforts on these days." Also, he liked to keep life simple, but that was hard to explain to folks. Most people ran around making their lives more complex with every breath they took.

"Come on," he said gruffly. "Pull on the boots. We'll get you your first taste of a real Wyoming blizzard." And maybe it would be enough to send her flying back to gentler climates. A man could always hope for a miracle, not that he ever got one.

Thirty seconds after they stepped out into the kitchen yard, he knew he wasn't going to get his miracle this time, either. Or maybe he *had* gotten a miracle of sorts, because he was damned if he could remember the last time he'd seen anyone light up with sheer joy the way Faith did as she discovered winter. Whatever she had been through, she hadn't lost her capacity to enjoy life, and that understanding made him just a wee bit uncomfortable, because he realized that he had lost his. He couldn't remember the last time he'd been plain glad to be alive. Maybe he had never felt that way.

And surely he had never, at least since earliest childhood, turned his face up the way she did right now to the falling snow. Certainly he had never stuck out his tongue to catch a whirling flake, and he was damn sure he'd never laughed with such glee. She was going to make a good mother, this woman, he thought as he watched her laugh and romp. She hadn't entirely lost the child within her.

Turning, Faith caught sight of Micah watching her as if she were some sort of puzzle to solve. A tan cowboy hat shadowed his eyes from the porch light, but she could almost swear the corners of his mouth had lifted a little. Just a little. As if he wanted to play, too, but had convinced himself he was too old and staid. Too mature and adult.

Before she had time to talk herself out of it, she scooped up a handful of snow and began to pack it. "Is this how you make a snowball?" she asked Micah.

"That's the way," he answered, coming a step closer. "You never made a snowball, even when it snowed in San Antone?"

The wind gusted around the corner of the house, snatching up a cloud of icy snow and flinging it right in Faith's eyes. She jumped backward instinctively and gave a small shriek as the ice crystals blinded her. Immediately, she was steadied by a strong hand on her elbow.

"Are you okay?" Micah asked.

"Just startled." She ought to be afraid, she thought as Micah caught her chin and tilted her face up. She ought to be, but somehow she wasn't. She blinked at the snow on her eyelashes and felt the flakes melting coldly on her cheeks. A soft gasp escaped her, though, when his fingertips fluttered softly against her skin, gently—oh, lord, how gently!—wiping away the dampness.

"There," he said roughly, and stepped back, releasing her immediately. "Are you cold? Do you want to go in?"

"Not yet." She hesitated. "Do you—do you mind?"

"Naw." The blizzard, which until a few minutes ago had been merely an unavoidable inconvenience of another Wyoming winter, had become a wonderland for him. He wasn't sure why, and he refused to analyze it. All he knew was that he was enjoying Faith's enjoyment, and it had been a long time since he had enjoyed much of anything at all.

She was still holding her little snowball, a somewhat rounded, not very ballish ball. She glanced down at it, and then over at him, and in the instant before she hurled the snowball, he saw what was coming in the mischief that lighted her eyes.

"No," he said, and ducked to one side just as she threw. Without a moment's hesitation he scooped up snow in his bare hands and began to pack a considerably more professional piece of cold ammunition. "You asked for it," he said gruffly.

So she had, Faith thought, and reached for more snow. This time she packed it with more confidence, and as a result achieved a much more credible ball. Certain that just one hit from a snowball packed by Micah would damp her enthusiasm, she hurried to get a couple of throws in before he could strike her with a bull's-eye. By the time he finished packing his one very large, very round, very smooth snowball, Faith had hurled three of her own at him and was working on a fourth. She hadn't managed to hit him yet—he was extraordinarily fast on his feet—but she didn't think she really wanted to. What if he got annoyed?

Micah had no intention of hitting her, either, or of even coming close. He was afraid she might slip on the snow and hurt herself. Instead, he kept dodging her rounds and working on his own snowball until it began to seem that he was creating the ultimate weapon.

Faith grew breathless from her exertions and laughter. She couldn't seem to stop laughing. It was exciting and fun to be out here in the dark with the snow blowing and whirling around like fairy dust in the cold wind. For this brief, precious time, she felt young and free and unafraid.

She hit Micah finally, with a big, soft ball that splattered against the middle of his chest. His eyes remained shadowed beneath the brim of his hat, but there was something definitely wicked in the way the corners of his mouth suddenly lifted.

"Now," he said, "it's your turn."

He started toward her, holding his huge snowball out in front of him like a threat.

"You're not going to rub my face in that," Faith said, backing up.

"No. Wouldn't dream of it."

"Why don't you just throw it, then?" She backed up another step, aware of the tension creeping into her. The fun was gone, she realized abruptly. The sight of this huge man bearing down on her was no longer part of a game. It was beginning to feel horrifyingly real, a nightmare revisited. "Micah?"

He was an astute man, highly sensitized to conversational and physical nuances after years in Special Operations and law enforcement. He heard the very faint quaver of doubt enter her tone, felt her sudden tension like a pocket of high voltage electricity in the cold air. At once he halted and dropped the snowball.

"It's all right," he said gruffly. "I was just teasing you." Teasing, for Pete's sake. Micah Parish didn't tease anyone, ever. What the hell was he doing? "Let's go in before you get a chill."

Her fear evaporated the instant he stopped advancing on her, and she felt like a fool. A cruel fool. Words escaped her before she could stop them. "Micah, it's not you."

He looked away a moment before he answered. "I know, Faith. I know. Come on. I'll make some more cocoa."

"What do you know?" she asked, too surprised to move.

"That your husband abused you," he said curtly. "Is that why they put him away?"

Faith shook her head slowly as things inside her began to tremble from unnamed fears and feelings. "Not—not entirely."

"Well, it doesn't matter a whole bucket-load of manure in a barnyard, I reckon." Moving slowly, he reached for her arm. "Come on. Whether you like it or not, you've already been out here too long, and a chill won't do you a damn bit of good."

She let him guide her up the steps and into the enclosed porch, where they could shed their boots before entering the kitchen. He was a caretaker, she thought as he knelt before her and pulled the boots off her feet. Before she even had a chance to set her sock-clad foot down in one of the damp spots, he had slipped her sneaker on and tied it.

"Now the other one," he said.

She shifted her balance and steadied herself with a hand on his shoulder. He didn't even know her from Adam, yet he was taking care of her as attentively as if she were his . . . his wife. The way a wife *should* be cared for, though not the way she had been treated herself, of course.

She could feel the play of his muscles beneath her palm, and she looked down, only to see the curve of her swollen tummy and the top of Micah's head.

In that instant, as if somebody had suddenly cast her backward in time, she was six years old again, and a boy with long black hair was kneeling before her to tie the lace of her shoe.

She caught her breath, but just then Micah looked up at her, an older face. A remote face. A cold, impassive, unapproachable face. This couldn't possibly be Mike from her first summer visit here.

Could it?

"Come on," he said gruffly as he rose to his feet. "You look frozen. Let's get something hot into you."

No, she thought, her heart hammering as she allowed him to tug her gently into the kitchen. That boy was lost to her forever. Even if Micah Parish had once been that boy, he was obviously gone. One look at his face was enough to tell anyone that he had learned life's lessons the hard way.

But she looked at him as he made more cocoa and wondered.

And suddenly she was sure. The boy who had taught her to ride and swim and build forts out of hay bales was standing across the room from her, looking as if life had treated him even worse than it had treated her.

And because he hadn't said anything about knowing her, she kept the knowledge to herself. Maybe he had forgotten her. Maybe he didn't want to admit he knew her. Maybe, if he remembered her at all, he recalled her as the boss's pesky daughter who had tagged after him all the time.

So she kept quiet, drank her cocoa and headed for bed.

And wished until she ached that she could be six years old again.

Chapter 3

Micah stayed up long after Faith excused herself and went to bed. The next two days were his regular days off, so he felt no particular pressure to retire. He would still have to get up at the same time in the morning to tend the animals, but then he could go back to bed if he felt like it.

The blizzard continued to blow and howl around the corners of the house, and periodically the windows rattled from the force of a gust. There would be some fantastic drifts across the road come morning, he thought as he poured himself another hot drink. The plows probably wouldn't reach the end of his driveway before early afternoon.

And that was just fine with him. Apart from his unexpected guest, he wouldn't mind being snowbound a while. A little time cut off from the world was just what he needed after a week like this past one. At least the blizzard would keep Jeff Cumberland's mind off his mutilated cows.

Cattle mutilations occurred from time to time in the area, and after a lot of initial uproar—well before Micah's time as a deputy—people had stopped worrying about UFOs and cultists. Most ranchers still weren't entirely convinced that this was some strange behavior on the part of coyotes, but there was little useful evidence that it was anything else. It was one of those troubling things that people finally learned to live with because they had no other choice.

Micah, who'd seen his first mutilation four years ago during his second day on the job, still found them disturbing. The state lab said the seemingly surgical precision of the wounds was an effect of shrinking flesh around the wounds, and Micah figured they were probably right, but he'd never seen anything quite like it. And he still had trouble believing that a predator would kill a cow and then eat nothing but the tongue and testes or udders.

Two days ago Jeff Cumberland had called the Conard County Sheriff's Office, madder than all get-out. Not one but three of his cattle had been found mutilated in widely separated areas of his ranch. Micah was a highly skilled, experienced tracker, so the Sheriff, Nathan Tate, had asked him to take a look. Micah had looked, had spent the last two days looking, in fact, and had found not one damn thing.

Sitting in his living room now, listening to quiet country-western music on his stereo, he cradled his mug of cocoa on his chest and thought over what he'd seen, and what he hadn't seen.

The weather had been cold and dry for the last month, so the ground had been hard as rock. Micah hadn't expected to find anything as useful as a paw print to identify the predator, but there should have been a sign of some kind. Circling away from the dead animals in an ever widening search, he should have found spoor at least. Something, somewhere, should have betrayed the fact that some hunter had made his meal on that damn cow. There hadn't been a thing. Not a thing. Not around any of the animals. Micah was sure of that. There wasn't even a shadow of a doubt in his mind.

All indicators said those animals had been killed somewhere else and dumped at various places around Jeff's ranch. Micah had heard that claim before, and he had always been inclined to brush it aside, thinking that most people could easily miss the slight signs an experienced tracker would recognize. This time, he was ready to make the claim himself, because he knew his own skill, and he knew he hadn't missed anything. There had been nothing to miss.

And that didn't add up.

Now this blizzard would take care of the whole thing. They wouldn't be able to look for anything else, and the state lab was bound to send down the same results when it finished with the carcasses. Jeff had asked Micah if he was just wasting time and money sending the carcasses in for examination, but Micah hadn't been able to answer. Something just didn't feel right. It was itching at the back of his neck like unfinished business, nagging at the corners of his mind.

He'd taken a lot of photos of the scene. Most of them were at the lab being developed, but he had some instant photos out in the glove box of his Blazer, and for a minute or two he toyed with the idea of going out to get them. Then the wind howled again, and he smiled ruefully into his cup. Nope, it could wait. He'd spent too many years at the mercy of the elements, and tonight he just wanted to enjoy his freedom to stay in from the cold.

By 9:30 the next morning, Micah had plowed the full length of his driveway with the heavy blade attached to the front of his Blazer. Every year in Conard County, the plows were attached to the front of the Sheriff's vehicles on October fifteenth. In this isolated area, lives could depend on a deputy being able to get through on the worst roads. Last year Nate had raised funds and bought a helicopter for emergencies, but people still needed to be able to plow.

Snow was still whipping and whirling around and the sky had a leaden look to it, when he reached the county road only to discover that, as he'd expected, the county plows hadn't been through yet. He had hoped they had though, he thought as he turned the Blazer and headed back toward the house, largely because he wanted Faith Williams safely ensconced in a motel.

It wasn't that she was a troublesome houseguest. Far from it. He hadn't even seen her this morning, though he had thought he heard her stirring when he came downstairs. No, the trouble was himself. Something about Faith Williams was making him aware of a certain . . . emptiness in his own life. The existence of holes. Gaps.

He muttered an obscenity and down-shifted as he pulled into the yard near the kitchen door. Turning, he dropped the plow to the ground and cleared the yard between the house and stable.

It was just sex, he told himself. He hadn't gotten laid lately. Not in a long time, as a matter of fact. Not since two years ago when he went to Chicago on vacation to pay a little visit to Billy Bald Eagle. Billy, an old Army buddy, had introduced him to a school teacher who had a thing for Indians. God, how he hated that! Didn't always keep him from taking advantage of it, though. But since he didn't believe in soiling his own nest, he considered the ladies of Conard County to be off-limits, and a man was bound to get a little hungry at times.

He was hungry right now. No use denying it. Sexual irritation was running in his blood, making his nerves acutely sensitive, drawing his attention to things he would ordinarily never notice, like the tight fit of his jeans. Or the way Faith Williams smelled. God, that woman's scent was sheer, distilled *female*. Clean, sweet temptation.

So, no matter how quiet and unobtrusive the lady was, she had to go. Soon. The sooner the better.

Muttering another curse, he parked the Blazer by the door and climbed out. He wanted some coffee, and he couldn't put off going inside a moment longer. There was just so much tending the animals needed, just so much plowing he could do. Damn, he was acting like a foolish kid, hiding out here like this.

The kitchen was filled with the aroma of freshly brewed coffee when he stepped in. Looking around, he saw that his guest had not only made a fresh pot, but she had also cleaned up the kitchen, giving it a sparkle he seldom bothered with. And from the other side of the house he heard his vacuum cleaner growling. Hell's bells! Forgetting his desire for a mug of coffee, he headed for the living room, determined to stop the foolish woman before she hurt herself.

This morning she wore black slacks and a cotton-candy pink maternity top that stopped him dead in the doorway. There was something so softly feminine about that top that he felt like a stranger in his own world. She turned to smile at him, and Micah came face-to-face with all the things he had sacrificed and all the things he had fought his entire life to preserve. She was satin and silk, soft femininity and gentle perfumes, milky skin and blue eyes. He'd seen women like her many times, but always from the far side of a glass barrier he couldn't cross. They weren't meant for him, these gentle creatures, but they embodied all the things he had dedicated his life to protecting. He had lived on the dark underside so that women could be silky and soft and gentle for other men, so they wouldn't have to scramble in the dirt and live in privation and oppression.

It sounded stupid as hell, and he would have gone to the stake before he would ever have admitted it out loud, but somewhere deep inside he had always cherished a kind of icon of womanhood that was in diametric opposition to all the women he had ever known. Inside him, he believed in a woman who wasn't grasping, selfish and cheap. A giving, loving, generous woman. A woman who would bring softness to a life that was all hard edges and jagged peaks.

"Micah?" Faith's smile faded as he stood there and stared at her with an expression that was almost a scowl. Her heart skipped and began to race as she wondered what she had done to anger him.

His scowl deepened. "Leave that vacuum alone, woman. You'll hurt yourself."

"A little vacuuming won't—"

"Damn it, you're pregnant. You shouldn't be doing this kind of work!"

She hadn't been mistreated long enough to become totally crushed. She could still feel defiant, and right now she did. It sparked in her eyes, though she didn't know it, and tightened the soft, lush line of her mouth. Inside her, words struggled to be free, words telling him that she was capable of doing a stupid little job such as vacuuming, that being pregnant didn't turn her into a weakling or an invalid, but she bit the words back. She *had* been mistreated long enough to fear angering a man.

He saw the defiance rise in her, saw her back stiffen and her chin come up, saw the snap of it in her eyes, and he felt the craziest, most contradictory urge to grin. He stifled it. "Go on," he said gruffly. "Spit it out, little lady."

She didn't like the way he called her "little lady." It was derogatory, and she suspected he meant it to be. Again words filled her throat and caught there, unspoken.

He waited a moment, then turned away in utter indifference. If she wouldn't speak up for herself, it wasn't his problem. And he wasn't going to let it become his problem.

Faith watched the big man turn away, and his indifference prodded her more sharply than anything he had said. For too long, nothing she had felt had mattered. Her feelings had been discounted and ignored. She had been made to feel insignificant if the right shirt wasn't ironed or whether dinner wasn't ready exactly on time.

In the past couple of months she had made some headway, with help. The changes were small, but lately, for the first time in her life, she had begun to believe that what she felt *was* important, as important as what anybody else thought or felt. And if her feelings were important, then nobody, *nobody,* had a right to trample on them.

Hardly aware of what she was doing, she charged after Micah into the kitchen and caught up with him just as he was pouring a mug of coffee.

"Just one moment, Deputy Parish," she said. Her voice quavered, and shock at her own temerity tried to silence her. She clasped her hands and felt her heart climb into her throat. Had she lost her mind?

Micah heard her uncertainty, her fright. He turned slowly and leaned back against the counter with his legs casually crossed at the ankles, trying to look as unthreatening as possible for a man of his size and untamed appearance.

"Yes, ma'am?" he asked, keeping his voice quiet.

"I..." Oh, God, she was having a panic attack. There suddenly wasn't enough air in the room, and her heart raced so rapidly that there seemed to be no space between beats. Nonetheless, she forced the words out. "I...don't like the way...you t-talked to me!"

Her words were little more than a ragged gasp, giving him a clear notion of just how much it cost her to speak them. He felt a glimmer of admiration. "Well, I reckon I can understand that," he agreed mildly.

Faith, who had been expecting lightning bolts to strike her dead for her effrontery, felt her mouth fall open. "Y-you can?" she asked in a whisper.

Micah folded his arms across his broad chest, giving her another measure of security. "Sure can," he said. "Would you like some herbal tea? I keep it for a neighbor lady. She's pregnant, too."

Faith edged into the kitchen, stunned by his calm reaction to a situation that for her had held all the potential deadliness of a nuclear bomb. "Which neighbor lady is that?"

"Mandy Laird. She and her husband will be your nearest neighbors on the other side."

"Oh. When is she due?"

"Late May. Tea?"

"Uh, yes. Please." She edged closer, still amazed that nothing bad had happened to her. "Uh, Micah?"

"Yeah?"

"You aren't . . . you aren't mad at me?"

He turned from filling the tea kettle. "Now why in the hell would I be mad at you?"

"For..." For what? For telling him she didn't like the way he talked to her? That sounded incredibly foolish. She took her courage into her hands once more. "I don't like being called little lady. You're talking down to me as if I were a child, and I am not a child."

He set the kettle on the stove and turned on the gas burner. "Reckon that's a matter of perspective," he said in his slow, deep voice. "I'm forty-three years old, little lady. I've seen things that make grown men weep and sweat with terror. I figure that makes me about as old as Methuselah. However old you are, you're still a far sight younger than me."

There was no way she could retort to that, except possibly to claim that four years of marriage to Frank Williams had made her about as old as Methuselah herself.

She watched him move around the kitchen with athletic grace, taking the box of herbal tea from the cupboard, opening the packet that held the tea bag with hands so big it seemed impossible they could perform such a delicate task. The kettle whistled, and he poured hot water into the cup.

As she accepted the cup from him, Faith looked up into obsidian eyes set in a harsh face. In that instant a trickle of awareness passed through her, a little niggling thing that touched her core with warmth and made her knees feel suddenly weak.

"Easy." He steadied the cup as a tremor passed through her. "Faith? What's wrong?"

Wrong? Only that she was standing closer to a man than she could believe, and doing it of her own free will. Only that some part of her was thinking of that man touching her, *wanting* that man to touch her. God, she knew better! Didn't she? Oh God!

The cup fell from her hand and shattered, splashing hot tea everywhere. Faith's slacks protected her as she turned and ran from the kitchen.

Micah took a quick step after her, then caught himself. Well, hell. She had her problems, which he damn well knew, and he wasn't going to get any more involved than he already was. No way. Uh-uh. No sir.

Yet he took another step after her anyway. Damn, he was a sucker for the wounded of the world. He sure as hell ought to know better by now.

The phone rang, giving him a blessed out. Now he couldn't go after Faith and he didn't have to feel guilty about his reluctance.

"Morning, Micah," said the gravelly voice of Sheriff Nathan Tate. "I just received a rap sheet from San Antonio. You want to tell me why you're so all-fired interested in a guy named Francis Williams? And why he's so important that this rap sheet was hand carried up here by a Texas Ranger?"

Micah's knock on her bedroom door startled Faith. She sat up immediately, unconsciously pulling the pillow over her stomach like protective armor. She wasn't ready to face Micah yet, but it seemed he was going to give her no choice. He probably wanted to demand an explanation for her weird behavior, and he was certainly entitled to one. Or maybe he wanted to yell at her about the broken cup and the mess. Frank would have yelled about it. Frank probably would have hit her two or three times and then stood over her while she cleaned it up. He might even have kicked her while she was on her knees. He'd done that a couple of times. She was always very careful not to break anything when he was around.

"Faith, I need to talk to you," he called through the door.

"I'm sorry about the cup," she said uneasily.

The cup? In the hallway, Micah stared at her door in perplexity. His thoughts had moved far away from the shattered remains of the cup that still rested in the middle of his kitchen floor. "Don't worry about the cup," he said roughly. "The damn cup doesn't matter. Faith, I need to talk to you. Can I come in a minute?"

The fact that he was asking finally penetrated her uneasiness. Frank wouldn't have asked. He would have come through that door all the madder because she had closed it. "Come in," she said. Nervously, she scooted farther back on the bed and hugged the pillow more tightly.

Micah saw it all, of course, but he had too much on his mind to think about it now. "I just had a call from my boss. Do you know a Texas Ranger named Garrett Hancock?"

Her breath escaped in a whoosh. "Yes. Oh yes! He saved . . . He helped me. Is he hurt? Is something wrong?"

"He's not hurt," Micah hastened to reassure her. "He wants to see you, though. He's here in Wyoming."

"Here? Why?" Her eyes were wide with surprise. And then understanding shook her. "Frank. He's the one who arrested Frank. Oh, my God, he followed Frank up here. . . ."

"No. No." Automatically, he crossed to the bed, intending to reassure her, but when he saw her flinch backward he stopped, remembering that this woman had no reason to trust any man. "He's here because I sent for your husband's rap sheet last night. I wanted to know what you were up against. Anyhow, I guess Hancock thought I might have run across Frank or had dealings of some kind with him."

Her heart had been beating fit to burst, and now it didn't want to slow down. It *couldn't* slow down, not with Micah standing over her, making her wonder what it would be like not to be afraid. Oh God, she was so tired of being afraid!

Moving slowly, very slowly, Micah sat on the edge of the bed and faced her. She watched him with huge eyes and flaring nostrils, with exactly the same kind of wild fear he had seen in a horse's eyes when faced with a rattler. She would bolt if he gave her half a chance.

So he didn't give her a chance. He wasn't sure why he was doing this, but he knew someone had to try to help this woman over her terror, and there didn't seem to be any other volunteers in sight. Knowing this was another deadly mistake in the chain of mistakes he'd been making since he set eyes on her, he reached out and took her trembling shoulders. Then, ignoring her whimpered protest, ignoring her terror, he hauled her up against his chest and wrapped her in his arms. "It's okay," he said softly. "Just rest against me. It's okay."

She didn't fight him this time, but whether that was good or bad he couldn't say. It might be terror keeping her there, as evidenced by the ripping shudders that tore through her body, or it might be the early beginnings of trust. He didn't know, and at this point he really didn't think it mattered. It was going to take more than one hug to make this woman trust him or any other man, just like it would take more than one good woman to change his mind about the whole gender.

He understood the chain reaction of panic, understood that she would need time to calm down again. Unconscious of what he was doing, he began to rock her gently, unaware of making soothing sounds in the back of his throat. In far-off lands, under conditions that defied description, he had calmed others this way, hardly even aware of doing it. He had held terrified children, dying men and injured women, and he'd done it because it needed doing. The gift of human touch and human warmth was the most priceless gift in life, and too damn rare, from what he'd seen. As long as a man had strength in his arms, it was his responsibility to give that gift wherever it was needed. Micah believed that. He believed it at a level so deep it wasn't even conscious. He just acted on it.

Faith's panic receded, quieted by the incredible gentleness of this savage-looking man. With her ear pressed to his heart and his arms snug around her, she felt safe. The feeling stunned her, and for the longest time she could only lie against his chest and try to absorb the miracle of feeling safe for the first time in years.

"Have you seen a doctor about this panic?" Micah asked eventually, when he realized she was calm and nearly limp against him.

"My family doctor wanted to give me tranquilizers."

"You're pregnant."

"Exactly. I wouldn't take them, anyway. I don't want to be doped up." She could hardly believe she was having a conversation like this with a man. A man who was a cop. Her heart gave a single, uncomfortable lurch and then settled down again. There was no threat in hands and arms so gentle. Not at this moment, at any rate. Surely she could be allowed, for just this little space of time, to seize this feeling and store it up against the future?

Micah cleared his throat. "Sometimes...sometimes when somebody's been through something really bad, professional help can be useful."

She nodded, unconsciously rubbing her cheek against his chest. Micah was conscious of it, though. He was suddenly acutely aware of exactly how many days and nights he had been celibate. His body responded in a healthy fashion to this woman's femaleness, and he clenched his teeth in self-denial. She wasn't his type, he reminded himself. She wasn't looking for a casual, uncomplicated relationship. Hell, she wasn't in the market for *any* kind of relationship.

"I was seeing a psychologist," Faith said after a moment, and moved a little closer, nearly forgetting everything in a growing desire to be just a little nearer to the warmth, the heat, the strength and solidity, of this man who held her with a gentleness she would have sworn no man was capable of.

"Was it helping?"

"A little." She sighed, finding the thud of his heart beneath her to be a wonderful, somehow reassuring, sound.

Her hand, with a will all its own, crept around his waist, hugging him back. Just a little. He probably didn't even notice.

But he did, and his throat tightened. He pushed down the feeling. "I don't know if we have anyone nearby who can keep on helping you, Faith."

"It doesn't matter. What it all comes down to in the end is time. I mean, yes, it helped to have someone tell me that it wasn't my fault that Frank beat me. I needed someone to say I had nothing to be ashamed of, that I hadn't done anything wrong. It was nice to hear, Micah, but believing it is something else."

"I know." Yeah, he knew. "What made you come running up here? Why do you think Frank's going to hurt you again?" It seemed to him that if the man had escaped from custody, coming after his wife would be the last thing on his mind. The guy would have to be a real fool to show up the one place where the authorities would be expecting him—wherever Faith was.

"Three—" Her voice cracked, and she started again, growing tense against him. She didn't want to think about this, wanted to dive under the pillow and pretend that none of this had ever happened, but she had an equally strong need to explain to this gentle, savage-looking man just why she was acting in such crazy, inexplicable ways. "Three months ago, while he was out on bail, he came to my apartment. He was mad because I had filed for divorce and he got even angrier when he realized I was pregnant. Why he was mad, I don't know. He was the one who forced himself on me. I shouldn't have told him, but I didn't want him to hurt the baby. I thought it would help keep him out. I tried so hard to keep him out." Her voice had thickened, and her breath started coming in huge sobbing gulps. "When he got in, I tried to get away, but I couldn't. He was so strong...." This time a real sob escaped her, and Micah's arms tightened.

"It's okay, Faith," he said roughly. "It's okay. You're safe here."

She drew another sobbing breath and buried her face against Micah's shoulder. "Garrett Hancock saved me," she said in a choked voice. "Frank was going to kill me. When Frank got out on bail, Garrett was watching him, hoping he might get some more evidence or something. I think...I think maybe Garrett thought I knew more about Frank's doings than I'd said. I don't know. I just know he was there...." Her voice shattered, and she began to weep in earnest.

She regained control swiftly, though. Micah figured she'd had a lot of practice at hiding her feelings.

"Anyway," she said when she again lay quietly against him, "they rescinded Frank's bail because of what he did to me. He's been in the county jail awaiting trial, and as long as he was locked up, I felt... Then he got out. And I wasn't going to wait around to see if he came after me again. I just wasn't going to!"

"No, of course not." Somehow his fingers had worked their way into her long, silky hair, and he massaged the back of her head gently. "Don't you have any family to help you get through this, Faith? Or friends?"

"The friends are all Frank's," she said bitterly. "As for family, they're all dead except my stepsister, and she's in a convent. What's *she* going to do?"

Nothing, he guessed. And there was no way, now, that he would be able to dump her at the Lazy Rest Motel. No way. Hell. He wouldn't sleep for wondering if Frank would manage to find her in such an obvious place.

The baby chose that moment to kick, but instead of simply meeting the soft side of Faith's womb, the little foot met the hard wall of Micah's stomach.

"Well, I'll be..." he breathed quietly.

Faith glanced up and caught her breath. His obsidian gaze was fastened to the swell of her abdomen, and there was no mistaking the reverence and awe on his face. For months now she had longed to share this miracle with someone, to share the wonder and excitement of the life growing within her.

"Does it hurt?" Micah asked gruffly.

"No. It's just a little poke." Here was her opportunity to share, and she didn't even think to hesitate. Seizing his hand, she pressed it to her womb, and they both held their breath as they waited. A minute passed, then another, and just as Faith was about to give up, she felt it, the feeling of movement, and then the soft little push from the inside. Right against the palm of Micah's huge hand.

"Well, hell." It was his favorite expression, and it was totally inadequate to the moment. He lifted his eyes to Faith's, and then a small, genuine smile cracked the granite of his features. "Well, hell," he said again, and felt another poke.

Something about the way he was looking at her made her feel as if she had done something totally awesome, though she hadn't done anything spectacular at all. And something about the way he smiled at her made her smile back.

Then, suddenly, as if the unfamiliar feeling of smiles on their faces had jarred them both back to reality, Micah became irritated at himself, and Faith became edgy at being so close to him. An instant later she had slipped away from him and he was already moving toward the door.

"The road should be plowed in a couple of hours," Micah said over his shoulder. "After lunch, we'll go into town to talk to your Texas Ranger."

Boots, Micah thought as he turned the Blazer onto the freshly plowed county road. The woman needed boots. She was wearing the blue boots again, but he was sure they didn't fit properly. She needed boots and mittens and a warmer hat, and snow pants.... She needed a million things, but he would see to the most essential ones before he brought her home tonight. He leaned over and tweaked the heater up a little higher for her benefit, wondering if he had

lost his ever-loving mind. It was one thing to rescue someone from imminent danger. It was another to adopt them.

Sitting beside him, Faith tried not to keep looking at him,
but he might as well have been a lodestone. Time and time
again her gaze was drawn to him, and each time she looked
at him she felt a strange, tugging response in her womb.

He was, beyond any doubt, the epitome of masculinity.
Even his shoulder-length black hair, with its few betraying
threads of gray, did nothing to diminish his powerful male
impact. Beneath the brim of his Stetson he wore mirrored,
aviator-style sunglasses that seemed to complement the
harshly chiseled planes of his face. He looked as forbidding as the snow-drifted, barren countryside outside the car.

She wondered what had made him so hard. That hardness was a veneer, she thought, because she had seen something of the man beneath, a man who opened his house and
his arms to a frightened stray, and who offered his protection for no better reason than that it was needed.

Biting her lower lip, she looked away and wished she had
the courage to question him a little bit. What had happened to him in the twenty-five years since she had last seen
him? Why had the quiet, gentle youth she remembered
turned into such a hard, guarded man?

He turned his head toward her and caught her staring at
him. She felt color rise hotly into her cheeks as she stared at
her own distorted reflection in the mirrored lenses.

"You look like a curious kitten," he said in a deep, rum-
bly voice. "What are you wondering about?"

Suddenly she was wondering about a whole pack of
things, and none of them had to do with the facts of his
past. The question had held a sensual undertone, and as inexperienced as she was, Faith nevertheless picked up on it.
Surely she had misunderstood? This man couldn't possibly
find her sexually attractive! Not when she was misshapen
with almost six months of pregnancy!

He had returned his attention to the road almost as soon
as he spoke, leaving her to wonder why the thought that this

man might find her attractive didn't terrify her. And leaving her to conclude that he couldn't possibly find her attractive, anyway, so her terror, or lack of it, was irrelevant.

She stole another glance his way and again felt the impact of their differences. He was all male, and she was a woman who understood better than many the threat of a man's greater size and strength. This man surely outweighed her by a good hundred pounds, and he towered over her by more than a foot. He was considerably older than she, vastly more experienced. And he was solid. She felt that about him, just as she felt he was utterly self-contained. He needed nothing and no one, yet anyone who needed him would not be disappointed. He was a rock to lean on.

Dear Lord, how she wanted to lean! For so long she had been alone with her demons and her terrors, without anyone to turn to for even a shred of comfort or support. The strength of her need gave her breath a ragged sound as she quickly turned her head and looked out the window. It wouldn't be fair to Micah to lean on him, of course. And it wouldn't be good for her, either. She had a child to think of, a child who was going to need a strong mother who had found direction in her life.

She needed to get her act together during the next several months, and letting someone else handle her problems wasn't the way to achieve that. It was time for Faith Montrose Williams to finish growing up.

There was bitterness in the thought, because she had been raised to be a wife, to make a home for a man who would deal with all the realities while she created a haven for him. Nobody had bothered to suggest to her that she might have to be self-supporting, or that a child might depend on her meager, uneducated abilities. Nobody had ever warned her that being a wife might be a nightmare, that the man who was supposed to care for her might routinely beat her bloody and then try to kill her. Nobody had ever warned her that a man might be so jealous of his own carelessly planted seed growing in her belly that he would kick her in the womb.

God, she felt so betrayed! She could still hear her own mother's voice telling her not to let anyone know she was smart, because boys didn't like brainy girls. She could still hear the naggings that she had to be sexy, but not bright, that she had to make a man feel important, even at the cost of her own intelligence and pride. She had to be a reflection of a man's whims. Her own needs and wishes were to take second place. A good wife was one who kept her man happy, whatever it took. Yes, she could hear it all, and in retrospect she could see how she had been betrayed. She had never been asked what she liked or wanted, had only been told over and over again what appealed to men. It didn't take a genius to see the implication that was never stated: that *she* didn't matter.

And when her husband was unhappy and hit her, it was *her* fault, of course. If she had kept him happy, he wouldn't have hit her. If she hadn't served chicken, he wouldn't have hit her. If she hadn't fallen asleep before he got home, he wouldn't have hit her. If she hadn't spoken pleasantly to that nice clerk at the store, he wouldn't have hit her. If she had known how to be a woman, how to be a wife, he wouldn't have hit her. It was all her fault, because if she had mastered a woman's role, which was to please a man, her man wouldn't have been so unhappy with her. Each blow, each curse, had labeled her a failure as a woman. And each blow, each curse, each criticism, had made her feel more guilty, more ashamed, more deserving of the violence he showered on her.

"But it wasn't my fault!"

"Faith?"

She had been so caught up in her thoughts, in her anger and grief, that she only now realized she was crying again, and that she must have spoken at least some of her thoughts out loud, because Micah had pulled to a stop.

"Faith?"

She refused to look at him as humiliation began a slow burn in the pit of her stomach, right next to the rage that never faded, the icy, cold knot of anger that never eased. "Sorry," she said thickly. "I cry a lot since I got pregnant."

"You need to cry," he said roughly. "Here." He handed her a wad of tissues and then shifted into gear again. Least said, soonest mended. It was time to quit getting in deeper.

Thankful he didn't question her, Faith wiped her eyes and sniffled her tears away. God, she was so tired of it all—tired of being afraid, of feeling sad, tired of being tired of everything.

By the time Micah pulled up in front of the Sheriff's office, she once again had a grip on her feelings.

The office was right on the main street of Conard City, in the shadow of the courthouse. Most of the town looked to be of recent vintage, but the courthouse had been constructed by someone with a yen for Victorian style Gothic architecture, and the result produced a rather pleasant feeling of age and charm. The Sheriff's office was in a corner storefront overlooking the courthouse lawn and most of the town's businesses. On this cold, snowy afternoon, there were few people about, giving the town an almost deserted air.

Inside, Micah guided Faith through the front office with a nod for Charlie Huskins, who had just returned to duty after being wounded two months earlier during a kidnapping attempt. It was the most excitement Conard County had seen in years, but Micah had the uneasy feeling they were about to have a lot more excitement.

"How're you feeling, Charlie?" Micah asked.

"Great. Just great." Charlie's smile was broad and warm. He figured he owed Micah his life, because Micah was the one who had found him and carried him out of the rugged terrain where he had been shot. "Nate and the Ranger are waiting for you in Nate's office."

Micah nodded and touched the small of Faith's back gently. "Through there," he said, nodding toward Nate's door.

Faith tensed, every instinct telling her to turn around and walk out. It was cowardly, she knew, but it seemed as if Frank were going to haunt her forever, as if she would never be able to escape from all the fallout. If it was a bad dream, she wished it would all just go away. But of course it wouldn't.

Because his life had so often depended on it, Micah had become an astute judge of men. He approved of Garrett Hancock the instant he clapped eyes on him, and after a moment Hancock evidently came to a similar conclusion about Micah.

Sheriff Nathan Tate was an old army buddy of Micah's. They had served together in Vietnam long ago and kept in touch over the years. Four years ago, when Micah had retired from the army, he had stopped in Conard City to say hello to Nate and accepted a position as a deputy. He had never regretted his decision.

Except possibly right now, Micah thought grimly as they all settled into chairs around Nate's desk. Things here were getting out of hand. What had started out as a neighborly hand to a stranded motorist looked like it was about to get messy and complicated.

"Are you doing all right, Faith?" Garrett Hancock wanted to know. He looked, Micah thought, like a successful Texas oilman in his neatly tailored gray suit and lizard skin cowboy boots. When he moved, the badge pinned to his shirt became visible. "You weren't hurt when your car went off the road?"

"No, I'm fine, Garrett." And relieved that Micah had evidently explained her present circumstances. "Deputy Parish has been very kind."

Garrett nodded to Micah, as if he considered Micah's help to Faith to be a personal favor. "You took off like lightning, Faith. Nobody knew where you'd got to, and I was more than a little worried.''

"I didn't want to hang around when I heard Frank had escaped." All her attention focused on the Ranger. "Is he coming this way, Garrett? Is that why you came all the way up here?"

Garrett smiled crookedly and shook his head. "I came flying up here because late last night the San Antonio police got a request for Frank's rap sheet from the Conard County Sheriff's Office and I thought Frank might be here. Now that I know *you're* here, I consider it a definite possibility that he might show up in the area." He looked at Nate and Micah.

"So let's have the story," Nate said. "I take a personal interest in the doings in my county."

"Francis Avery Williams," Garrett said, "is a former San Antonio police officer. He's charged with a whole range of felonies, some of them federal. It appears he's been the kingpin of a large drug smuggling operation, that he was operating several houses of prostitution, and that he had his fingers in a fencing operation. He's also wanted for the attempted murder of his wife, and I would personally like to wrap my hands around his throat." He smiled without humor.

"He's been responsible for shepherding drug shipments up from the border, and we've begun to suspect that he has some major organized crime connections, though we still haven't put together all the pieces on that. It appears that Williams isn't a cop who went bad but a criminal who became a cop to get on the inside track. Nor was he the only cop involved in the drug trafficking. We expect to make another ten or fifteen arrests very shortly."

"No small-time operator, then," Nate remarked.

"Far from it. All the alarms went off when we got your fax last night, because we've long suspected he had at least one out-of-state connection, but we haven't been able to put

our finger on where." He turned to Faith. "Does Frank
know about your father's ranch?"

Faith's hands were knotted so tightly into fists that her
short nails dug into her palms. "I don't know," she said
tautly. "I didn't think so, but I'm not completely sure." It
was the nightmare again, she thought despairingly. Questions about Frank coming at her from every angle, no one
ever able to believe how very little she knew about the man
she had lived with for four years. An endless, awful nightmare, until she wished she could just throw back her head
and howl.

And suddenly, unexpectedly, into her unending nightmare, came a gentle, reassuring, strong touch. Micah, inwardly cursing his own weakness, reached out and closed his
large hand on her small, soft shoulder. That touch was like
a beacon in the night, telling her that even if she couldn't
escape the nightmare, she wasn't alone in it.

"Is there a possibility he could have known?" Garrett
asked.

Faith tried to think, but somehow her mind kept veering
to the large hand on her shoulder, toward the man who had
touched her womb with such reverence only a couple of
hours ago. And why, she wondered raggedly, did they keep
questioning her as if she had done something wrong? She
wasn't the criminal, but Micah was the only one who seemed
to understand that.

Something inside her snapped like a string stretched too
tightly. "I don't know," she managed to whisper, and then,
in a single, swift movement, heedless of what Garrett or
Nathan Tate might think of her, she swung around in her
chair and buried her face tightly against Micah's powerful
shoulder.

Well, hell, he thought. But the surge of protectiveness that
rose in him was fierce, and his arms closed around her,
supporting her, sustaining her.

Slowly he lifted his head and looked straight at Garrett. "That's enough, Hancock. She's not the criminal here. I'm not letting you or anyone else badger her."

Well, hell, Micah thought, looking into Nate's face and seeing a reflection of his own surprise. That sure tore it. He was a one-finger pushover for anybody in trouble. Yep, he sure was.

Chapter 4

It was bad enough to announce to the Ranger and his own boss that his objectivity was shot to hell. But not as bad as putting his arms around this woman and letting *her* know that she could count on him to place himself between her and any threat.

That counted as sheer stupidity on his part. He'd been around the block enough times to know that there were women who wouldn't hesitate to use that kind of knowledge to take advantage of a man and tie him up in so many knots that he'd never get the kinks out. What did he know about Faith Williams except that as a six-year-old she'd stolen his heart? Twenty-five years had passed since then, and she could be any kind of person now. God, at his age he shouldn't be a sucker for icy blond hair and sad blue eyes.

The sheriff opened the door of his office and called out to Charlie Huskins. "Charlie, you take Mrs. Williams into that empty office across the way and see that she gets a hot cup of that herbal tea I keep around here for Mandy Laird."

Faith sat up reluctantly, hating to leave the security of Micah's embrace, but aware that she was being pointedly dismissed. She hesitated, looking deep into Micah's dark eyes and registering his complex tangle of feelings. "I'm sorry, Deputy," she said unsteadily.

Rising, she lifted her chin and looked straight at Nate, realizing that, from Micah's point of view, he was the important person in the room. The sheriff must be wondering what had gotten into Micah to defend a woman who was supposedly a stranger. From the outside Micah's actions would certainly appear unprofessional, and Faith felt a need to defend him against that presumption. "Deputy Parish and I were acquainted many years ago, Sheriff. In fact, he was like a brother to me the first summer I spent up here with my father. He naturally feels protective."

So she remembered him after all, Micah realized with unexpected pleasure. He didn't want her defending him, but on the other hand, it said something about her that she wanted to. Maybe Faith still had some of that little girl in her, after all. Not that it was going to make any difference. His mystical, superstitious side kept trying to tell him that these events were destined, that there wasn't a damn thing to do but plunge ahead and hang on for the ride. It was difficult for a man with the blood of shamans strong in his veins to believe he had found Faith by accident on the road yesterday.

When the door closed behind Faith, Nate sank into his chair and regarded Micah across the scarred desktop. "You know better than that, you crusty old Injun."

One corner of Micah's mouth took a short, upward hike. Nate had been teasing him that way since their days in the jewel green jungles of Southeast Asia. "Reckon so," he agreed.

"She wouldn't be the towheaded tyke in your wallet, would she?"

Micah gave a short, silent nod of confirmation. The hell of living in Conard County with friends like Nate Tate and

Ransom Laird, who went all the way back to the Stone Age with him, was that they knew things like that about him. They knew what he carried in his wallet; they knew what made him sweat and what made him scream.

"Well, that explains it," Nate allowed. He'd known about the picture, but this was the first time he'd ever connected it with Jason Montrose's daughter who, as a summer visitor nearly twenty years his junior, had seldom crossed his path. "I just about forgot you worked out there that summer. So, what do you think about this, old son?"

Micah spared the Ranger a glance. Garrett Hancock, surprisingly, didn't seem disturbed by these developments. "I think," Micah said after a moment, "that she's been mistreated something fierce. That she's scared to death, that she came here to try to find some kind of safety and security for herself and her child. You Rangers have a different idea?"

Garrett's lips tightened for a moment. "We just can't afford to take chances, Parish. The woman was married to Frank Williams for four years. It's entirely possible that she may have had some idea of his activities. She may know things she doesn't realize she knows. We can't afford to overlook that possibility."

"Badgering her isn't going to get anything out of her," Micah said flatly. "She panics the minute a man gets on her case over anything. Hell, she panicked last night when I said something sarcastic. That man must've been all over her all the time."

"He was rough on her," Garrett agreed. "You might be interested to know that on two occasions she called the police for help. The first time, when they arrived and found out that Williams was a cop, they walked away. An hour later a neighbor brought her to the hospital with a broken arm, two black eyes and a lacerated scalp. She claimed to have fallen down the stairs."

Micah swore savagely, and even Nate looked a little stunned.

"The next time, the cops didn't even bother to answer the call," Garrett said. "Faith wound up in the hospital that night, too. She never called the police again. Not even the night he tried to kill her by stabbing her. By the time I broke down the door, he'd inflicted a couple of pretty deep wounds."

Garrett sighed and eyed Micah grimly. "Personally, Parish, I don't think she knows a thing about what Williams was up to. Unfortunately, mine isn't the only opinion that matters. And I'm worried that Williams will come after her. After what I saw that night three months ago, I don't think the man will quit. He wants her dead."

"Why?" So much for his notion that Williams would have the sense to stay away from the one place he would be looked for.

"Why?" Garrett shrugged. "The psychologist who interviewed Williams said it's simply so nobody else can have her."

So nobody else can have her. Micah ran that assessment around and around in his head as he drove himself and Faith back to his ranch. Before leaving Conard City, he had taken her to Freitag's Mercantile and gotten her properly garbed for the weather. Then he'd stopped by Bayard's Garage and told them where her Honda could be found. Dirk Bayard promised to dig it out and call with an estimate in the next day or so.

When Faith quietly protested that Micah had better things to do with his time and she would take care of things herself, he simply looked at her with his black-as-night eyes and didn't say a word. Faith subsided immediately.

There had been a few more stops, first at the rural electric co-op office, where she paid the required deposit and arranged for her power to be connected. Then came the telephone office, where the procedure was repeated, and the propane company, who promised to check out her gas appliances when they filled the tank.

And everywhere they went, people treated Faith like family. Warm smiles met her, people promised to look after her needs immediately, and she was made to feel as if she had always lived here.

Inevitably, she turned sideways on the seat and watched Micah as he drove. He had said nothing one way or the other about her claim that they were old friends from her childhood, and she wondered if he remembered, or if he thought she was making it up.

"You're looking curious again," he growled when they were a few miles out of town. "Go ahead and ask. I don't promise to answer."

The mirrored sunglasses swung around toward her, and Faith caught her breath, thinking what a male archetype he was: huge, dark, his black hair flowing warriorlike to his shoulders. He wore snug denim that sculpted powerful thighs and embraced his masculinity with a boldness that made Faith's mouth turn suddenly dry. His shearling jacket hung open, revealing that even when he sat his stomach was so hard that not an inch of flesh bulged over his belt.

Faith licked dry lips, and Micah turned his attention back to the road. "Well?" he asked. He was afraid that if she licked her lips again he was going to forget all his good sense and lick them for her.

"Do you . . ." she licked her lips again. "Do you remember that summer you taught me to ride?"

He didn't even hesitate. "Yeah, I remember. I remember finding you out in that arroyo at the boundary and wondering if a fairy had suddenly popped up from the dust. You sure were the tiniest little thing. Still are, I reckon." He sent a brief glance her way. "I thought you didn't remember me."

"I didn't, at first. It was when you helped me with my shoes last night that I suddenly remembered a time when you tied my tennis shoe for me. It's funny," she admitted, looking away for fear she would betray her wealth of emotion, "I remember calling you Mike, but other than that, I remember you only as a feeling."

Micah didn't reply immediately, and Faith listened to the engine's grumble with a heart that tapped time in an uncomfortable rhythm. Had she embarrassed him somehow with that admission? Perhaps. As a rule, any discussion of feelings had men hunting for a six-pack and a ride to the nearest fishing hole.

Just as she concluded that Micah meant to say nothing more to her, he spoke, his deep voice like the rumble of distant thunder. "A feeling? You mean you don't remember that you used to think I was the 'bestest Indian' in the whole world?"

An embarrassed little laugh escaped her even as she felt a quiver of pleasure that he was unexpectedly teasing her. To look at him, a woman would never imagine Micah Parish as a tease. "I really said that to you? How did you ever stand me?"

"It wasn't too hard. You were such a little mite, and so serious all the time." He had spent a ridiculous amount of time trying to think up ways to make her laugh, too, but he left that unsaid. The boy he had been then was so far removed from the man he was now that it was like looking back on a stranger.

He did admit one thing, though, because it reminded him of something he could never afford to forget. "You were the first person who ever called me an Indian as if it were something to be proud of."

Faith turned immediately on the seat and looked at him, a frown creasing her brow. Micah showed her only his profile, a strong, stony profile. "I guess you've faced a lot of prejudice."

He gave a small negative shake of his head. "Not since I reached full size and joined the army."

No, Faith thought. Few people would want to tangle with someone Micah's size, especially someone who looked as if he could handle himself with deadly ease in any kind of situation. For the first time in months—maybe years—she felt interested in someone else and wondered how to ask for more information. "Were you . . . did you stay in the army very long?" That seemed a safe enough question.

"Twenty-one years."

"That's a long time."

"Sure seemed like it sometimes." He braked and turned slowly onto the county road leading to his ranch. The sun had begun to melt the snow from the plowed pavement in a few spots, but in others the slush was treacherous. It gave him an excuse to stay quiet for a minute or two. All this talking was unusual for him, yet he kept feeling compelled to do it. Something about Faith wound his vocal cords up like a toy motorboat.

"Did you ever marry?"

The question caught Micah sideways, because he was expecting her to continue with questions about the army. Before he had a chance to choose his words with his usual care, he answered her. "Came pretty close once." Well, hell, he thought, tightening his grip on the steering wheel. Now she was going to want to know what happened. Women always did, and he had no one but himself to blame for what was coming. Damn it, what was wrong with him today?

"What happened?"

There was, buried deep within him, an old festering anger. In childhood he had learned that to be a half-breed was to be the lowest of all the races of humanity. Neither Anglo nor Indian, wanted by no one, belonging nowhere. The young child had hurt, but hurt toughens and hardens. In the place of pain he had cultivated anger, and in the place of caring he had grown calluses.

His saving grace had been his ideals, unwittingly planted in his soul by the books he had read to fill his empty days. Mythical and historical tales had filled his mind with great deeds and high ideals. Nurtured in the stony soil of anger, he had developed a strong sense of the importance of honor, loyalty and duty. He had discovered compassion for those who were weaker, and reverence for life.

But the anger remained, festering, and sometimes the poison spilled out. Now, on the snowy country road, with signs of yet another storm building in the west, he slammed on the brakes and brought them to a rough halt.

Turning, he stared at Faith from behind the mirrored lenses. "What is it with women?" he asked her, his voice a quiet whip crack in the truck cab. "I never met a woman who didn't want to poke her nose into places it didn't belong."

Faith instinctively shrank back against the door, seeking to place more distance between them. Micah's hands remained on the steering wheel, gripping it tightly, giving her no cause to think he might strike, but she was afraid anyway. Conditioning like hers was not easily overcome. "I'm sorry," she said faintly. "It's none of my business."

"No. It isn't." But he didn't release the brake. Instead he turned his head, staring straight ahead. "I was just back from my first tour in Vietnam," he said after a moment, telling her and wondering why he was doing it, but doing it anyway. "She was the prettiest thing I'd seen since—in a long time. She wore my engagement ring for a week. Just long enough to make her father good and mad. I didn't measure up to a Mercedes and her allowance."

Shrugging, he started driving again.

"You mean she dumped you because her father threatened to cut her off?" Faith couldn't imagine it.

"Yep." He wanted this subject closed *now*. He was afraid the poison would spill out if he tried to tell anyone all the other things he had learned from Dawn Dedrick. Things like it was okay to take a savage into your bed and show him off like a pet jungle cat, but a half-breed sure as hell wasn't good enough to marry.

In retrospect, Micah often wondered why that had come as such a shock to him. It wasn't as if he hadn't long since realized that half-breed was about the dirtiest word in the language.

"Micah?" Faith spoke tentatively. "I'm sorry I made you mad."

He sighed. Two more days, he reminded himself. He just had to hang on for two more days, then she would be at her own place and he could get back to normal.

He wasn't too worried about Frank Williams. Since the man had never been to the Montrose ranch, according to Faith, he wasn't going to be able to find it without asking for directions. In a place as underpopulated as Conard County, it was the easiest thing in the world to alert people to be on the lookout for someone asking for the Montrose place. Here, the frontier mentality prevailed. People as isolated as they were knew how much they depended on their neighbors, and they considered it their duty to look after one another. It was one of the reasons Micah stayed here. Some of the citizens of Conard County would never accept him, but enough of them treated him decently to make the place feel like home.

And the land. He loved the land. He felt a mystical connection with it and cherished the way it weathered the seasons, always changing yet continually unchanged. Sometimes he wondered if the connection he felt sprang from all the years he had spent being bounced around from army post to army post. The land was so enduring, while he himself had always felt so transient. Perhaps he felt a part of the land because he felt a part of so little else.

Turning into his driveway, he felt a sense of belonging that helped satisfy needs he had never really analyzed. When you lived your life on a knife-edge, as he had for so many years while in the Special Forces, you didn't have a whole lot of opportunity to philosophize, or very much inclination to do so.

People assumed—and Micah was content to let them— that the Special Forces spent all their time training for eventualities that had rarely occurred since Vietnam. In truth, Micah had been an active operative, had parachuted into deserts and jungles and frigid tundras, and had collected military intelligence from within the borders of many unfriendly nations. In the dead of night he had jumped from cargo planes with orders to gather certain kinds of intelligence and no way home except through his own skills and daring.

And when he walked out from behind supposedly impenetrable borders, when he set foot once again on free soil, he had neither the time nor the inclination to ponder life's mysteries. Instead, he would drink a couple of beers and get laid, not necessarily in that order, and then begin planning the next mission. And in between missions, there was always the training, the endless training, that kept a man honed to his uttermost limits. Self-indulgence had no room among the Special Forces.

This ranch was, in fact, the only real indulgence of his life. Here he had the space he had always craved, the absolute physical solitude to match his emotional isolation. He was a solitary, self-contained man.

So what the hell was he doing with this woman?

"Conard County, Conard City, Conard Creek," Faith remarked as they neared the house. "I always meant to ask Dad if there are any Conards left in Conard County."

In spite of himself, Micah chuckled quietly. "There's one. Emmaline Conard, generally known as Miss Emma, runs the Conard County Library."

Faith felt her own mouth curving into an unexpected smile. "She's ninety and never married, right?"

"Nope. She's about your age, and never likely to marry."

"Why not?"

Micah braked near the kitchen door and switched off the ignition. The sudden quiet seemed almost loud. "Well, it was back before my time, but I've heard rumors about a traveling man who neglected to mention he was married. What I know for sure is that any man who's ever been bold enough to show any personal interest beyond a question about the Dewey decimal system has been run off in no uncertain terms. Nobody bothers to ask anymore.''

"That's sad."

Micah paused, his door open and one booted foot on the ground. "Is it? I would have expected you to feel she's better off avoiding men."

Faith averted her face, feeling inexplicably, ridiculously, near tears again. "Not all men are like Frank," she whispered huskily.

He almost didn't hear her. It was a whisper so soft and so eloquent of unshed tears that he felt suddenly transported back in time to the child who had missed her mother and the half-breed Indian boy who had tried so hard to make the pain easier for her.

He'd had no right then to dry her tears, and he had even less right to do so now, but that didn't stop him.

With a muttered oath, he climbed out of the Blazer and came around to Faith's side. He yanked the door open, and before she could move a muscle, he scooped her off the seat and carried her into the house. Almost six months pregnant and she hardly weighed more than an eiderdown pillow. She needed to eat more. She needed to take better care of herself.

She needed to be taken care of.

It wasn't like him to act without a clear plan of action, but on more than one occasion in the past twenty-four hours, Faith had provoked him into instinctive reactions that came from the gut. This was one of them. He had no idea why he had picked her up, no idea what he intended to do with her as he carried her into the house.

In fact, he realized with a sudden pang of uncharacteristic trepidation, the only thing he was certain of was how right she felt in his arms, how right it seemed to carry her into his house, how right it was to have her arms around his neck and her sweet breath warm on his cheek.

"Micah..."

''Hush.'' He spoke softly, almost gently, as he kicked the kitchen door closed behind them and headed for the stairs. Distance. He had to keep his distance, but he was failing abysmally at that, and had been ever since the instant he set eyes on her. He'd never been able to keep any distance from her, not even when she'd been only six years old and knee-high to a mushroom.

Solitude. He needed it, craved it, hungered for it. He was his own best friend, and the only person in the world he truly trusted, other than Nate Tate and Ransom Laird. He was complete unto himself and seldom regretted it.

And he was shaman. Over the years, over the miles, that fact had come to take on a wealth of meaning through experience. He saw what others failed to, felt the threads of reality as a tangible thing. In his blood he sensed the currents of life in ways beyond the ordinary. A sixth sense set him apart, guided him and goaded him.

His army comrades had said that Micah Parish could track a ghost across water. They had claimed he had eyes in the back of his head. They had said he could hear sounds in the silence before they were made. They had not nicknamed him Chief or Geronimo, or even Breed, as they often did with other Native Americans. No. They had called him *Brujo*. Sorcerer.

But being a shaman wasn't helping him right now. It wasn't making a bit of difference to the fact that something inside him was cracking wide open and letting need pour through. The solitary man suddenly didn't want to be solitary. The self-sufficient man was suddenly insufficient.

It was time to get his distance back.

Strangely unafraid, Faith clung to Micah's powerful shoulders as he carried her up the stairs. His expression was grim, controlled, his eyes like a dark fire.

For years now Faith had resented her own diminutive size, believing that people would have been far less likely to shove her around if she hadn't been so small. Micah made her feel that smallness acutely, but in a different, provocative way.

He made her feel fragile but protected, small but cherished. He made her feel that his great size was not a threat but a shield.

He shouldered his way into her room and gently laid her on the bed. Then, standing over her, he drew a deep breath and closed his eyes. After a moment, he spoke.

"You take a nap. It's been a long day. I need to go out for a while."

Her voice stopped him at the door. "Will you be gone long?"

The question held undertones he didn't want to deal with. "A while," was all he said. "I'll be out a while."

He didn't go far. He didn't even take the Blazer. Instead, he stomped out into the cold yard, and around the rear side of the barn, then climbed a narrow trail in the rock face that stood guarding his buildings. It was a long, taxing climb, worse in the snowy, slippery conditions. No novice could have made it, but Micah took it steadily, with only a slight deepening of his breathing. In places he needed to go nearly hand over hand, but he never paused. Frigid meltwater soaked his knees, but he scarcely felt the chill of it.

At the top, nearly knee-deep in last night's snowfall, he stopped to look down at his house and barn.

It looked just the way he had dreamed it for years. In the growing twilight, with the snow all around, it looked exactly like the place he had envisioned for so many years in so many alien lands. Even the white smoke curling up from the chimney was a part of the dream. In his gut, in his shaman's soul, he understood that nothing happened, absolutely nothing, unless first it was dreamed.

Throwing back his head, he drew a deep lungful of the cold, clean air. A fresh storm was marching in from the west, as yet a low line of clouds scarcely higher than the mountains in the distance. It would soon be dark, and he debated for a moment whether to return immediately along the treacherous path he had just climbed or to take the longer, safer way around. Tilting his head a little, he judged the encroaching night. It would have to be the longer way.

Turning, he headed away from the setting sun and the approaching storm. With each step, his control settled more firmly into place, and the silence and solitude returned to his soul. This was how he was meant to be, he thought, as night gathered softly around him. Alone in the cold, surrounded by the vast barrenness of the Wyoming winter. One with the wilderness.

Dreamless.

Half an hour later, Micah had just reached his driveway again and was striding toward the pinpoints of light that came from the house. He was cold, his jeans were soaked from the knees down, but the discomfort scarcely penetrated his awareness. Hard, mindless exercise was a focus that lifted consciousness out of its ordinary rut to an altered state. Discomfort and pain ceased to have any meaning, and all the garbage was cleared from his mind.

He felt the vehicle before he heard it. The vibration came up from the frozen ground, muffled a little by the soles of his boots, but alerting him nonetheless. He paused, and shortly he was able to make out the distant rumble of the approaching vehicle.

What now? he wondered, just as the flare of headlights swung toward him into his driveway. Standing back to the side of the drive, one foot braced in the mound of snow he had earlier plowed out of the way, he waited for the visitor's arrival.

A minute later a familiar black Suburban pulled up beside him. The window rolled down, and Gage Dalton leaned out. As usual, he sported a couple of days' growth of dark stubble on his cheeks, a marked contrast to the premature silver of his hair.

"Howdy, Micah."

"Gage." Micah nodded. "What brings you out this way?"

"Jeff Cumberland's got two more mutilated cattle."

"Well, hell," Micah sighed. It never rained but it poured. "How fresh are they?"

"Fresh enough. Since last night's snowfall."

"I suppose the ground's all trampled up now."

"Nope. That's why I came to get you. Nate's ordered up some floodlights, and they're hoping you'll take a look before it gets all messed up. Near as I can tell, these two weren't far apart, and both were spotted this afternoon by Cumberland's foreman. His horse's tracks are the only ones in sight."

Without another word Micah walked around to the passenger side and climbed in. "I need to go up to the house and change first. I'm soaked to the skin."

"Right."

Gage shifted into gear and accelerated smoothly. In the dim light from the dashboard, a jagged scar was visible on his cheek. The gossips of Conard County speculated endlessly about it and other rumored scars, but then, Gage Dalton was the kind of man who, scarred or not, would have been the subject of avid gossip. Mystery cloaked him. The story of those scars was a tale Gage had never told anyone in the county, but Micah suspected they had something to do with the background that had made Nate hire Gage as a part-time investigator.

"I hear Jason Montrose's daughter is staying with you," Gage remarked.

"Just until her power's on. What are folks saying?"

"Just that her ex might be looking for her with trouble in mind."

"She's had a bad time of it," Micah said.

"So I hear. By now I reckon most everyone is keeping an eye out for strangers. After what happened to Mandy and Ransom Laird, you hardly have to convince people that trouble can come to Conard County. Everyone I talked to today seems eager enough to help out. If Frank Williams sets foot in the county, we'll hear about it."

Micah pretty much figured they would, too. He just hoped they'd hear in enough time.

"I sure don't think anybody's going to get directions to the Montrose ranch from anyone in this county," Gage remarked as he pulled to a stop beside Micah's Blazer.

"Come on in for some coffee while I change," Micah suggested. Gage needed no more urging. It had been a long, cold day.

Faith was in the kitchen when they entered, in the middle of frying the pork chops she had found thawing in Micah's refrigerator. At first she had hesitated about making herself so at home in his kitchen, and then she had decided that whenever he came back in from the cold he was going to want a meal.

That was *something* she could do, she thought with a twinge of bitterness. She could prepare a good, nutritious meal. She could keep a spotless house, get ink stains out of uniform shirts and iron a perfect set of military creases. Some résumé.

Micah paused just inside the door, taking in the incredibly domestic scene in his kitchen. Complete, he realized with a sense of shock, down to the frilly pink apron Faith wore over the swelling mound of her belly. In that instant, an instant during which time seemed to abruptly halt, he realized that he had dreamed this, too—in unguarded moments. Hell!

"Faith, this is Gage Dalton. He and I need to go out to the Bar C ranch on business as soon as I change."

"Ma'am." Gage tugged off his black Stetson, revealing silvery hair, startling in a man who appeared to be only in his mid to late thirties. His eyes were a stormy gray-green, like the sky before a squall. Faith dragged her gaze away from his disfigured cheek, thinking he must have been as handsome as sin before he got hurt.

"I offered Gage some coffee...." Micah's voice trailed off. He felt awkward in his own kitchen, he realized. Awkward telling her that he'd offered Gage coffee, as if he should have cleared it with her first. Man, he was losing his mind!

"I just made a fresh pot," Faith hastened to say. "Should I pour you some, too, Micah?"

"Yeah. I'll be back in a minute." He left without a backward glance, glad to escape the sensation that reality had just shifted course in some way, and that nothing was at all the way he'd thought.

Faith set two mugs on the table and filled them, signaling Gage to take a seat. "Are you a deputy, too?" she asked him. He wasn't wearing a uniform, but he'd apparently come on official business.

"Not exactly. I work on a part-time basis for the sheriff as an investigator, but I don't do any of the daily law enforcement stuff."

"Has there been trouble out at the Bar C?" She cast her mind back to the summers she had spent here as a child, trying to recall the Bar C. "That's the Cumberland ranch, isn't it?"

"Just a couple of cattle mutilations," Gage answered. "We're hoping Micah can pick up some kind of sign as to what did it. Sure would be nice to put the mystery to rest."

"I've read about those," Faith said, turning the chops. "Don't some people think aliens do it?"

"There was a whole uproar about it maybe fifteen years back. Some folks claimed it was devil worshippers, others thought aliens must be taking samples of some kind. The state lab insists that it's just normal predator activity."

"What do you think?"

Gage gave her a slow smile. "Well, ma'am, it might be aliens, but I sure think they'd want samples of something besides cattle."

Faith laughed. "That's a good point. But if it's wolves or coyotes or whatever, why do they take only a few parts?"

Gage shrugged. "If it was easy to explain, people wouldn't be talking about aliens."

Micah heard the laughter as he came back down the stairs dressed in a freshly pressed uniform. The sound was so out of place in this silent, empty house that he paused to listen to it—and to battle an unreasoning surge of jealousy that it was Gage who had first drawn that sound from her. Ridiculous, he told himself, squatting by the wood stove to ensure that the fire would keep Faith warm until he returned. Childish.

Convinced that he had sternly squashed the ignoble portion of his nature, and that the fire would keep the house warm for hours yet, he returned to the kitchen.

Faith turned toward him immediately with a welcoming smile that tightened when she saw his uniform and the gun belt hanging low on his hips. It wasn't exactly the same utility belt that her husband had worn, with all its little pouches, but it was close enough to stir the memories.

Somehow she had forgotten her instinctive tension around the police, but now it returned in an uncomfortable rush. But this is Micah, she told herself. *Micah*. Micah who had soothed her tears and put bandages on her small cuts when she had been a child. Micah who had treated her so gently since he helped her from her car yesterday. Micah who had shared her awe at the baby's movements. There was absolutely no reason to be afraid of him.

But she was tense anyhow, and her eyes followed him almost warily as he crossed the room and reached for the mug of coffee she had poured for him. Such a big man, she thought, towering over her by much more than a foot. Such a strong, powerful man.

He glanced over at her. "Are those chops burning?" The question was mild, non-accusatory, but Faith jumped.

"Oh!" She turned swiftly and found the chops had almost passed the point of being edible. "Oh!" Quickly, she forked them out of the pan onto a plate with trembling hands. "I'm sorry! Oh, I'm so sorry."

For a long moment there wasn't a sound behind her in the kitchen; then Micah said, "I'll follow you in my car in just a minute or two, Gage."

"Sure." A chair scraped, and booted feet clomped across the floor. Seconds later the door closed behind Gage.

Faith clung to the counter, her back to Micah, trembling so hard it was visible. He was going to hit her. That was why he told Gage to go ahead. Frank always hit her when she screwed up like this. He wouldn't care that the meat would only be just a little dry, that it wasn't ruined at all. He would hit her. Instinctively, she tucked her chin down to her chest and drew her shoulders up. Tensed in expectation, she awaited the inevitable blows.

"Faith." Micah's tone was soft, gentle, a coaxing murmur. He stepped toward her.

"I'm sorry," she whispered. "I don't know how it happened. Really... I shouldn't... I... I'm sorry! I'm such a screwup!"

Huge hands, hands that could have snapped a man's arm in two as if it were a dry matchstick, huge, powerful, dark-skinned hands, closed with ineffable gentleness on her small, trembling shoulders.

"It's all right, Faith," he murmured. "It's all right. Really. No one's going to hurt you. No one's mad at you. You're not a screwup. Hush... just hush..."

Ignoring the resistance in every muscle of her body, he gently but firmly turned her around and then wrapped her snugly in his powerful arms. With her head buried against his breastbone and his arms holding her close, she no longer feared that he was going to hit her. After a moment, a long, seemingly interminable moment, she sagged against him.

"That's better," he murmured, stroking her riotous blond curls. "That's better. I promise you, Faith, I will never, ever hit you. Never. And as long as I'm anywhere in sight, no one else will ever hit you, either. I swear it."

A shudder passed through her, and then she leaned even closer against him, telling him silently that, for the moment at least, she believed him.

"I wish I could stay," he said, keeping his voice pitched soothingly, "but Nate needs me out at the Bar C. I'll probably be gone for a few hours, but I sure would like one of those chops when I come back."

"I . . . I ruined them. . . ."

"No. No. They're not ruined. Nothing's ruined." Except him. His objectivity and his distance were shot to hell. His fingers were combing through hair that had the texture of silk and lightly brushing against a neck that felt like warm satin. Womanly aromas filled his nose along with the homey ones of cooked food, and Micah Parish was wondering why he couldn't have some of those things he had spent his whole life fighting to protect.

The foot of an unborn child kicked him gently, a soft reminder that time was an endless flow and it was a man's purpose to pass his seed to the future. A man was driven to it, and right now he wanted like hell to mate. The urge was rising in him, fed by soft femininity, by full breasts pressing against him, and even by the swelling womb of a woman who was fulfilling her God-given purpose by bearing life.

Life was that simple, really, but people turned it into a complex maze of pitfalls. It was the pitfalls that made Micah step back and turn for the door.

"I'll be back in a couple of hours," he said over his shoulder. "If you need anything, call the Lairds. The number is by the phone."

Shaking, shaken, Faith watched him go.

Chapter 5

The remote corner of Jeff Cumberland's Bar C Ranch looked like a scene lifted from a movie. Dark storm clouds, limned in silver by a crescent moon, were beginning to scud across the star-strewn sky. Floodlights on tall tripods had been set up at both mutilation sites, a jarring eruption of modernity into the timeless winter landscape.

Micah understood the politics of being sheriff—as an elected official, Nate had to keep the voters reasonably happy—but he wished to hell that this time Nate had spared the overkill. Sure, Jeff was upset. That was natural. Cattle weren't exactly cheap commodities, and Jeff's herd was more valuable than most, since he ran a prize-winning breeding program, but it wouldn't help Jeff or anybody else if all the evidence was destroyed in an attempt to look as if the sheriff were doing his job.

"I know, I know," Nate said to Micah as the latter slogged up to him. The vehicles had been kept at a good distance, and there was a deputy to warn all comers to keep to the already trampled ground. "Fred and I were the only ones to approach the carcasses, and we never got closer than fifteen feet." He handed Micah a hand-held floodlight. "You won't find diddly."

Nate was a good tracker, too. Maybe a little rusty, but good, so Micah figured there was no point in looking for anything obvious. If the mutilators had slipped, it would be in some barely detectable way.

"This is an awful lot of mutilations in a small area," Gage said as Micah and Nate joined him at the edge of the circle of light.

"Yeah." Nate's agreement was sour. A couple of these a year could be ignored. Five in three days was the kind of thing that could raise a lynch mob in quiet Conard County—if the folks found a target.

Squatting, Micah sifted fresh snow through his fingers. It wasn't dry enough to have blown away all signs of whoever might have been here, or to have blown off the dead animal. That meant the steer that lay in the middle of the circle of light had been dropped there since the snowfall. Or just as it was ending. Otherwise, the carcass would have been drifted over by snow.

There were no tracks in the fresh snow, and Micah was already reaching some hair-raising conclusions by the time he squatted beside the carcass. The tongue was gone; he saw that immediately. The eyes had been left alone, though, and they were a delicacy most predators didn't pass up. The genitals were also gone, another typical sign, and the excision was typically neat, looking as if the cuts must have been made with a knife. The day had been dry and cold, but cold enough to shrink the wounded flesh so much?

Micah had never been squeamish, but he really didn't care for this part of his job, he thought as he moved the steer's limbs and examined the wounds. Ah, this one had been disemboweled, too. That was new. He sat back on his haunches thoughtfully and studied the animal.

A while later he moved around to the other side and studied the animal from that angle, too. Not much blood at all, but that was usual for these kills. Nothing new. Except that if the animal had died here, its body heat would have melted the snow around and beneath it.

He signalled Nate and Fred to come over and help him lift the carcass a little. He didn't particularly want to move a ton of dead beef, but he needed to see just how far the animal had melted itself into the snow. If it had died here, there should be a layer of ice beneath it.

There wasn't.

"Well, hell," he said to no one in particular. "Where's Jeff?"

"Right here," Cumberland answered from behind one of the floodlamps. "You want me to come over?"

"Yeah. There's no sign to disturb. I want you to see this, though. You, too, Gage," he added to the investigator.

Both men joined him, Nate and Fred beside the dead steer.

"If this animal died here," Micah said flatly, "its body heat would have melted the snow, and then, as it cooled, the meltwater would have refrozen. I figure a ton of beef should have melted its way right through the snow to the ground. It didn't. See that? The snow is compressed from the weight, but it didn't thaw and refreeze."

Jeff Cumberland swore. He didn't need a diagram.

"Let's go look at the other one," Micah said, straightening. "I reckon we'll find the same thing, though."

Once again he checked very carefully for any kind of sign in the snow, and once again he reached the same conclusion.

"These cattle were dropped here," he said flatly. "Right now, I'd bet somebody brought them out here on a helicopter, already mutilated, and shoved them out."

The five men looked at one another, none of them voicing the obvious question: Why?

"I think," Nate said roughly, "that we'd all better keep our mouths shut about this for the time being. For now we'll say it's a typical mutilation." He looked at Cumberland. "Jeff?"

"Yeah. Fine." The rancher looked angry, but more, he looked disturbed. The most obvious conclusion, one that went as unspoken as the obvious question, was that someone was out to give Cumberland a hard time. None of the men gathered around the carcass had any idea why that should be. Cumberland was both well liked and well respected.

Nate turned to Micah. "Thanks for coming out here. Sorry I interrupted your break. Take Friday off, too, if you want. Mrs. Williams might need some help getting settled."

"She might. Thanks." With a nod, Micah turned to walk away. Gage moved alongside him. Neither of them said anything until they reached their vehicles, when Micah turned to the other man.

"You have some connections at the state lab, don't you?"

Gage nodded. "You need me to call in a favor?"

"I'd sure appreciate it if they'd put the Bar C cattle on the top of their priority list. These aren't the usual mutilations. Any of 'em, not just the one that was disemboweled."

"I'll call them in the morning," Gage promised.

"Thanks." Micah swung up into the driver's seat and shoved his key into the ignition. Now to go home and find out if Faith had recovered from her earlier fright.

Damn! Imagine a man hitting a woman like that. The memory of how she had hunched up and waited for the blows made him ache, and it made him mad. Nobody—man, woman or child—should ever have to feel like that.

The back porch light was on to guide him, and the dim light over the sink was on, too, but Faith had evidently gone to bed. He was relieved. Things were churning in him, things that weren't pretty or very nice. Needs, savage from long denial, kept trying to rear their heads, and he just didn't feel like wrestling with even the least provocation right now.

His dinner sat on the counter next to the microwave. It was wrapped in plastic, ready to be heated. The thoughtfulness touched him. Not once in forty-three years had anyone left a meal out for him.

While he heated the meal, he removed his gun belt, then unbuttoned his shirt and pulled out the tails, making himself reasonably comfortable. He knew he'd made a mistake when he heard Faith's soft "Oh!" behind him.

"I didn't hear you come in," she said. "I must have been dozing."

He hesitated a moment, then shrugged inwardly and turned to face her. A man's partially bared chest hardly constituted indecent exposure, and surely she had seen chests before.

But never one like his, Faith thought, staring in spite of herself. Never one so smooth, so muscled, so free of hair, with such a warm, coppery tone. Never one that tapered down to a belly so flat that every ridge of muscle showed. She suddenly didn't find it at all incredible that she should want to reach out and touch him. It somehow seemed like the most normal thing in the world to yearn to press her palms to that warm, smooth skin.

Micah saw her breasts rise with a sudden, deep breath, saw her pupils dilate, but he couldn't tell whether it was fear or arousal that caused her reaction. Probably fear, he thought, and reached instantly to button his shirt. He turned to face the microwave.

"Thanks for leaving dinner out for me," he said.

"You're welcome." Frank had never once said thank you for anything, least of all something as small as leaving out a plate of food for him. She edged closer, recognizing yet again that this man was not like Frank. Not like Frank at all. The idea of a man so utterly different from her ex-husband drew her like a warm fire on a cold night. Fantasies cherished in childhood surged to the forefront of her mind, reminding her that once she had believed in a good and gentle man, a man whose touches would be welcome, whose caresses would be pleasurable. Her life so far had made a mockery of those dreams, but perhaps Micah...

"I thought you were asleep," he said gruffly. "I figured you'd gone to bed."

"I...I waited up," she said, gathering her courage in both hands and taking a step toward him. She had promised herself that she was going to stop acting like a mouse, and while she might periodically backslide, as she had earlier, she was still resolved to show some courage. "I wanted to apologize."

He turned and stared at her, his black-as-midnight eyes steady but unrevealing. "What for?"

"For acting like such a ditz. I'm sure I embarrassed you, and Gage must have thought he'd walked into a madhouse."

Micah muttered a word Faith was not accustomed to hearing. Shocked, she blinked and felt a blush rise to her face. "I'm not very good at that, either," she said in a breathless rush.

He stared at her hard, doubting his ears, and what he saw made a chuckle rise in him. It didn't quite escape—his laughter rarely did—but it curved the corners of his mouth upward into an unmistakable smile. Faith, he realized, was bravely trying to make a joke. It was there in the tentative sparkle in her eyes, the hopeful set of her mouth. She was trying to step aside from her anxiety and act normally. She was trying to bridge the gap her fear kept opening between them. The smile he gave her now brought an answering smile to her lips and lightened the shadows in her blue eyes.

There was so much courage and trust inherent in that small attempt to reach out to him that emotion momentarily tightened his throat. "Come here, woman," he said roughly, and opened his arms to her.

She hesitated, as he had known she would, but not long enough for him to regret his impulsive invitation, not long enough for him to rescind it. And suddenly she was there in his embrace, willingly and freely this time, offering him a trust so great that it pierced his solitary soul.

Yielding a long, deep sigh, as if everything in him had awaited this very moment, he closed his eyes and bowed his head until his face was buried in the soft, silky curls atop her head.

"I've been worrying about you all evening," he said reluctantly, his voice hardly more than a rough murmur. "I hated to leave you alone when you were so upset."

"I'm used to being alone, and I'm used to being upset, Micah." What she wasn't used to was being utterly comfortable and content in a man's embrace.

The microwave pinged, and Micah released her, thinking that he'd damn well better be careful about taking Faith into his arms, because he could easily grow accustomed to the comfortable way she fit there. Accustomed? Hell, he could get addicted!

She had set his place at the table earlier, so she couldn't do even that much to help as he sat down to his dinner. With a casual movement of his hand, he invited her to join him at the table, so she poured herself a glass of milk and sat across from him.

"Were you able to find out what happened to the cows?" she asked.

Micah gave a small, negative shake of his head. "Just a mess of things that don't add up." He didn't want to discuss it right now. He had told Nate and Jeff all he knew, and they were the only ones who really needed to know. Until he heard something from the state lab, he had nothing to add that wouldn't be pure speculation, and he wasn't the speculating type. He had been trained as a fighter, as a killer, as a commando, and as an intelligence gatherer. He dealt in facts, in the way things really were, and he tried never to pass beyond theory into speculation.

But inside, where no one else could see, ancient instincts were telling him that things were not as they seemed. What met the eye was sometimes an illusion. Troubled, he stabbed his fork into a chop and then, suddenly, looked up and caught Faith staring at him.

"Do I amuse you?" he asked. She watched him a lot, he thought. Closely. Frequently. It might be from fear or uncertainty, it might be something else altogether. Whatever, he chose his words to anger her, hoping that if he pushed her past caution she might bring some of her fears out where he could deal with them.

Instead of getting angry or withdrawing, she shocked him. "You fascinate me," she admitted, coloring brightly.

His black eyes imprisoned her. "How so?"

"You seem . . . so sure of yourself. So strong. So independent. I was wondering what it must feel like not to be afraid of every little thing."

He finished his second pork chop and started on his third before he replied. By then Faith had concluded that she had sounded foolish to him. After all, he feared nothing and probably couldn't imagine why she was such a quivering coward about everything. And then he spoke, his voice like deep, dark velvet.

"Fear is a survival instinct," he said slowly. "Everyone feels it. That's why most people don't stick their hands into the flame on the stove."

He made it sound so simple, so natural, yet she knew that the fears she felt were not natural.

"The circumstances that threaten us determine our fears," he continued just as slowly, his voice flowing like a lazy summer river. "When our circumstances change, gradually our fears change, too." He turned his head and met her gaze squarely. "Yours are changing already, Faith."

They were, she realized. Just a little. "What are you afraid of?" She had no business asking, but she needed to hear this strong, self-contained man admit to just one thing that frightened him, even if it was of no consequence. It would make him seem more human, more approachable. Closer to her.

It was his turn to astonish her, to shock her, and he did it as if compelled, revealing something he had never told anyone else in the world. "I'm afraid of being buried alive."

Speechless, she stared at him, her blue eyes huge. Micah looked down at his plate and sighed. That had sure as hell torn it, he thought grimly. Now would come the questions, and he had no one but himself to blame. She would ask, and he would have to decide whether to answer or to be flat-out rude. He wasn't afraid to be rude, but he didn't want to treat Faith that way. She deserved something better than that.

So he didn't wait for her to speak. Shoving his plate to one side, he rose. "Let's go sit in the living room," he said harshly. If he had to bare his soul even this little bit, he was going to do it comfortably, with a cup of hot coffee in his hands in an environment as far as he could get from the nightmare that still haunted him.

He sat on one corner of the couch and felt momentarily surprised when Faith sat at the other end instead of taking the safer position on the easy chair. Her chin was lifted in a way that told him it had been a conscious decision, another act of defiance in the face of her conditioned terrors.

The lamplight was a warm, golden glow. Wind rattled at the window panes and gave him an excuse to postpone the explanation.

"Another storm is hitting tonight," he told Faith. "I radioed the office a little while ago, and they told me about it. We don't usually get this much snow around here."

"Really? Why not?" Somehow she had thought of this place as being deeply buried in snow most of the time.

"We're in the rain shadow of the mountains. Most of the snow and rain falls up there, which is why we have so few trees around here. Last night we got half the normal snowfall for an entire winter."

"What about tonight?"

"Just a couple of inches, but the way the wind is blowing, it'll probably drift up real good." It always drifted deeply around his house and barn, which, along with the rocky terrain that provided protection, created a wind-break where snow caught. It created a lot of extra work, but Micah had never been afraid of hard work.

And the question was still hanging between them. He could see it in her eyes, could almost hear it on her lips. Well, he could have kept it light. He could have said he was terrified of snakes, or getting old. No one had forced him to say something so obviously real. No one had dragged him over the line from sociable chitchat to stark honesty. Now, however, feeling compelled to finish it, he didn't know how to begin.

Faith settled it. Astonishing him with her perception, she spoke softly into a silence that had grown far too long. "What happened, Micah?"

He wasn't a man who ever flinched from the tough things in life. When he set out to do something, he did it. He had decided to tell her, and he didn't attempt to make light of it or minimize it. He didn't shrug it away. He handed the truth to her without varnish, evasions or omissions.

"Back during the Vietnam conflict, I was wounded and taken prisoner by the VC. The Vietcong. We called them Victor Charlie, or just Charlie." He watched her, waiting for withdrawal or denial, but she only nodded acceptance and understanding.

"They held me for about seventy-six hours," he said, revealing that he had counted every single one of those hours. Every one of those minutes. "In a hole in the ground. It was so narrow I couldn't sit. I had to stand. Most of the time they kept the top of the hole covered so that no light at all got in. There was just me, the dark and the bugs." He heard Faith's soft murmur but ignored it. "Anyhow, from time to time, when they got to feeling really nasty, they shoveled dirt in on me."

"Oh, my God..." It was a whisper. He looked at her, saw the horror. Now he did shrug.

"It kind of stayed with me," he said.

"How... how did you escape?"

"A good buddy of mine, Ransom Laird. You'll meet him before long, since he's your neighbor. He came back after the firefight to find my body and take care of it. He's that kind of guy. When he didn't find me, he realized I was still alive, so he came looking for me. By the time he got me out of that hole I was so weak from infection and dehydration that he had to carry me over his shoulders. To this day, I don't know how he managed it."

She broke free then. She broke out of the prison of terror that had been hammered into her by blows and words. She overcame a hurdle so high that only minutes before it had appeared insurmountable. Caring carried her over it effortlessly.

Without a thought, without room for fright, driven by a need to comfort, she moved down the couch and threw her arms around Micah. Pressing her face into the curve between his warm neck and his shoulder, she leaned into him, chest to chest. She didn't say anything. Silently she clung to him, holding him fiercely, telling him with her arms what she could not find words for.

Amazement held him still for a moment, but then he closed his powerful arms around her and felt her sigh as he hugged her close. It felt as good to her as it did to him, he realized as he sensed the whisper of her sigh against his neck. She wanted him to hold her. God!

His thoughts strayed, and he let them. The nightmare of being buried alive barely touched him anymore, only haunting him on rare occasions. It seemed far away right now. Other things seemed far more important, like this woman's warmth and femininity, her enticing fragrance, her gentle weight on his chest. He needed her to touch him, needed it ferociously, both as a man and as Micah Parish.

It was easy for him to care, but hard for him to need. He had discovered a long time ago that as long as he needed nothing, he could not be hurt. His strength and his solitude resulted directly from that understanding. He could love, but he refused to need to be loved.

But right now, with this soft, warm woman curled up against him, he felt those needs, and for this moment, he didn't batter them down. He ran his hands along her back, feeling the graceful, smooth line of her, the delicacy of the skin and muscle over her ribs. So small, dainty and fragile. There was something about that fragility and her inherent vulnerability that drew him, mesmerized him, made him hungry.

She needed his protection. She needed his strength and his care. And for Micah, the need to be needed was the biggest need of all.

His shaman's blood rose powerfully in him then, battering back thought, reason and caution. For just this sweet, short time, he chose to simply be. To feel. To drift in the current that claimed him.

Lifting Faith, he turned her and settled her onto his lap so that her shoulders were cradled in his arm. With his other hand he captured her small chin and turned her face up to his. For long moments he studied her, hunting for any sign of fear or reluctance. What he saw, all he saw, was a shimmering, scarcely born hope.

Releasing a breath he hadn't been aware of holding, he bent his head and lightly, softly, caressed her lips with his own. To his absolute wonder and amazement, he felt her respond shyly. Hesitantly. As if not quite certain of what he wanted or whether she could provide it.

Micah was a man of wide experience. Sweet and slow, hot and savage, these were matters of mood for him. His only stricture on sexual intimacy was that it be mutually consenting. Mutually pleasurable.

In Faith's tentative response to his kiss he felt a hopeful ambivalence. He thought of pulling back, but then her hand slipped upward from his shoulder and her fingers slid into his hair. Gently, almost unconsciously, she pressed him closer.

A ragged sigh escaped him, and he moved his lips just a little harder against hers, demanding nothing, simply ask-

ing for whatever she chose to give him. Until he was sure she
knew she had nothing at all to fear from him, he would press
her for nothing. Every move would be of her choosing.

But she was not yet drawing any lines. Her other hand
found his cheek, her soft, warm palm coming to rest gently
against the jaw muscles that moved slowly as he kissed her.
Micah wasn't accustomed to gentle touches. Even when
making slow, sweet love, women tended not to be gentle
with him. No one thought he would break; no one thought
he wanted it or needed it.

He had not known until this very moment just how much
he craved it. How much he needed someone to care about
him in a way that made her treat him gently.

Shaken to his roots, he took his mouth from Faith's and
pressed her face to his shoulder. No more, he thought. No
more. This woman had a power in her, a power to touch him
in places he had never, ever let anyone touch him. She had
the power to strip his solitude from him. She was dangerous.

"Micah?"

Reaching up, she touched his face again with the same
gentleness, a touch that implored him to look at her. Helpless against such a plea, he looked down. Her eyes were
wide. They were also hurt and embarrassed. Hell, he hadn't
meant to hurt her!

"Faith, I . . ." I what? he wondered. What could he possibly say?

"You don't have to explain," she said quickly, her color
rising. "I know I'm not very good at sex, and being so
pregnant I'm not even—"

He covered her mouth with his fingers, silencing her
quickly. "You don't know what you're talking about."

He felt her lips part beneath his fingers, felt her draw a
breath to speak, and realized that this woman was losing her
fear of him. Here she was, lying across his lap, her hip
pressing against him intimately enough that she surely must
realize he was aroused, and yet she was preparing to argue

with him. That understanding made him want to laugh. Instead, he smiled.

"Hush," he said. "You're playing with fire."

No, she hadn't realized how aroused he was. That became apparent to him when she went suddenly very still and her gaze strayed downward. And then a delightful pink tide rose into her cheeks. *Now* she knew he was aroused.

"Oh," she said. A small, quiet sound.

He waited for her to grow frightened, anticipated a wild attempt to get off his lap. Instead she simply lay there. After a second or two she stole a glance upward from the corner of her eye.

"A woman is beautiful in all her seasons, Faith." He thought it a simple truth, but she saw it differently. His hand still cupped her chin, his forearm resting innocently between her breasts. She caught that hand and moved it to her stomach. Moments later he felt her child move.

"I've been feeling fat and ugly and very much alone, Micah Parish," she said softly. "You've made me feel beautiful and safe." A small smile curved her lips, and a little sparkle came to her eyes. "But I'm still fat. I'd like to relieve you of my crushing weight and spare you any more discomfort, but I'm afraid I'm stuck. I can't do sit-ups anymore."

She might feel fat, but as far as he was concerned, she didn't weigh anything at all. He lifted her easily and set her on the couch beside him. It would have been wiser to preserve a distance, but when she displayed no desire to move away, he gave in to his own desire to wrap his arm around her shoulders and hold her against his side. Seemingly content, she rested her cheek against his shoulder.

Presently he spoke, addressing a very different subject. "Are you sure you want to move out to that ranch all by yourself?"

"Yes." She tilted her head, trying to see his expression, but saw only the underside of a very strong chin.

"I wish you'd think about it some more," he rumbled. "If anything happens, it'll take time for help to reach you. There won't be another soul for miles—unless you arrange for some kind of live-in companion."

"Don't worry about it, Micah. Believe me, I'll be safer out there all by myself than I have been at any time in the last four years."

"You haven't been pregnant before."

"What difference does that make? At this point there's absolutely no reason to believe I won't finish my normal term without any complications. Believe it or not, I was in a lot more danger driving Loop 410 in San Antonio."

A faint smile lifted the corners of his mouth. She was right about that, but he wasn't suggesting she go back to San Antonio. It was clear after his talk with Garrett Hancock earlier today that moving back there would be a big mistake. Garrett was concerned not only about Frank himself, but about Frank's cohorts. Some of them might think Faith could testify against them.

"Why are you so determined?" he asked finally.

"It's something I have to do, Micah." She leaned forward and looked directly at him. "I've been dependent and helpless for too long. If I'm ever going to be a good mother, I need to be able to stand on my own two feet. I need to be able to take care of *myself* first."

He couldn't argue logically against that. He could only point out alternatives. "You don't have to be utterly alone to learn independence, Moonbeam."

The nickname he had given her that long-ago summer slipped out before he even knew he'd remembered it, and the sound of it brought a surprisingly delighted smile to Faith's face. "I'd forgotten you called me that," she said clapping her hands. "I'd forgotten! I loved it, Micah."

He reached out and caught a handful of her soft, silky curls. "It still looks like moonbeams," he said gruffly. "I've been all over the world, but I've never seen hair quite this color anywhere else.'' And only then did he realize he had even been looking.

Moonbeam. Well, hell.

Faith had gone up to bed, and Micah sat alone in his living room with the company of another mug of coffee and Lee Greenwood singing he was proud to be an American. Then Lee started singing about taking his baby on a morning ride, and Micah changed tapes.

Moonbeam. The long-forgotten nickname should have awakened countless memories of Faith as a child, should have made it possible for Micah to reestablish his emotional distance. Instead, in that flash of time when he had spoken it, it had taken on an entirely new quality. A sensual quality. This woman was moonbeams and lace, satin and silk, soft murmurs and gentle heat. She was a promise of all the soft, warm, womanly things that he had never had in his life.

She had none of the brassiness or confidence of today's working woman. And he guessed she was going to have to develop some if she was to stand on her own two feet in today's world, even in Conard County. Damn shame.

Micah was no male chauvinist. He didn't feel women were less capable or less intelligent than men. He simply felt they were different, with every right to that difference. Their bodies were designed to nurture life, and men's bodies were designed to protect life, and he just plain didn't understand why so many people had a problem with that. There were many modern arenas where men and women were equally competent, and he was perfectly willing to acknowledge that. Why those arenas become a battleground where men and women tried to deny their respective differences or to lord it over one another was something he plain didn't understand, and didn't want to.

What he did understand was that in his personal life he was old-fashioned. He wanted a woman who wasn't afraid to be a woman. A woman who didn't feel threatened by his masculinity. A woman who could accept his size and strength and his role as protector. A woman who wouldn't need to diminish him in order to strengthen herself. A woman who wouldn't feel diminished by him.

A woman who would realize that he needed gentleness, too.

He muttered an oath and headed for the kitchen to refill his mug. He hadn't let himself think about these things for a long time. Ages ago, when he had been a young man, he'd pondered things like this during long, solitary nights in hostile lands. Then he had realized that solitude was his fortress, that he could be whole unto himself.

He *was* whole unto himself. And he wasn't going to let a few restless yearnings change that. No way.

Micah Parish didn't need anyone or anything. Not even the gentle touch of a moonbeam.

Chapter 6

The next morning, Micah was called in to work. Jed Barlowe, the county drunk, had gotten a little disorderly. He had, in fact, taken over the bell tower at Good Shepherd Church and was firing potshots at passersby.

"You'll be careful?"

Faith's words caused Micah to pause as he fastened his body armor over a T-shirt. Once again he had thought her safely in bed, and once again he had been wrong. She moved with amazing silence on her very light feet. He turned to find her in the open door of his bedroom.

"Careful of what?" he asked casually.

"I'm not a fool, Micah Parish," she said sharply. "I was married to a policeman long enough to realize y'all don't wear those damn vests unless somebody is shooting."

"We're supposed to wear them whenever we're on duty, Faith."

"I know that. I also know none of you do, except maybe rookies. What's going on?"

With a sigh, he fastened the last tape and reached for his uniform shirt. Well, hell, he thought, and here he'd been thinking it might be nice to have a woman around. This one in particular. But now she was staring at him in that way a man recognized in his gut, that I'm-not-going-to-give-an-inch-so-you'd-better-just-tell-me look. The one that said she was prepared to be a royal pain in the butt.

"Jed Barlowe's up in a church belfry," he said finally. "He's drunk, and he's got his peashooter, and we just need to keep people off the streets until he passes out or runs out of liquor, whichever comes first. No big deal."

She edged farther into the room, watching as he buttoned the neatly pressed shirt. The vest beneath added just enough bulk to make the shirt snug around his middle.

"You're not going to try any fancy SWAT moves, are you?"

Micah looked at her. "Honey, Conard County doesn't have a SWAT team."

"It has you."

She was genuinely concerned. He wasn't accustomed to seeing that look on anyone's face, in anyone's eyes. And being unaccustomed, he had no defenses against it. "Don't worry. I didn't survive twenty-one years in the Special Forces just so a drunk could shoot me. I'll be home for dinner. Will you be okay?"

"I'll be fine." She wasn't going to let him change the subject that easily. "It's your day off. Why couldn't they handle this without you?"

He reached for the button of his pants and hesitated, looking at Faith. Seeing she had absolutely no intention of budging, and that she didn't seem at all concerned that he was about to unbutton his pants so he could tuck his shirt in, he went right ahead and did it. She never batted an eye.

"They need all the help they can get," he said, answering her question. "Nate can't call everybody off patrol and leave the whole county unprotected because Jed Barlowe got a wild hair."

He faced the mirror over his dresser and turned up the collar of his shirt. Faith continued to watch as he drew on a dark green tie and knotted it. Then he picked up his badge, a shiny silver star, and leaned forward to see better as he pinned it on.

"Here, let me," Faith said. Along with ironing military creases, she was a whiz at pinning on badges and collar insignia. The layer of armor prevented the contact from becoming in any way intimate, but her hands trembled nonetheless. With each passing hour, her desire to touch this man grew. How could she possibly explain the wild urge she had to touch his strength, to see if she could make him tremble, too?

He saw her hands tremble and misunderstood. He thought of the courage it must take for her to come this close and offer to help him with a task she must have performed often for the man who had mistreated her. Looking down, he could see only her soft curls and her shaking hands, and he needed to see more.

"Faith, look at me."

Slowly, she tilted her head up and looked straight at him. He looked so magnificent, she thought. So untamed. "Take care, Micah," she whispered. "Take care."

Then, before she could betray any more, she turned and walked from the room.

"Nobody knows what the hell got into him," Nate told Micah when the latter arrived at Good Shepherd Church, a medium-sized white clapboard structure near the center of town. "Reverend Fromberg was out here shoveling snow for half an hour at least before Jed started shouting obscenities from the belfry. He didn't see Jed get past him into the church this morning, so he must have been in there last night when Fromberg locked up. Probably passed out," Nate added with disgust.

Micah nodded, but his attention was centered on the church and possible means of access. They were all standing well back, behind barricades and a row of sheriff's vehicles. All the occupants had been removed from the surrounding houses and businesses and were awaiting the outcome in the high school gymnasium.

Maude Bleaker, whose diner was directly across the street from the church, and whose usual breakfast business had been interrupted because of this incident, shouldered her way up to Nate, ignoring the deputy who tried to hold her back.

"Nathan Tate," she said angrily, "you've got to stop this now! That man's been nothing but trouble in this county since he had his first taste of his daddy's home brew. I don't think a soul would shed a tear if that man were shot right now."

"Maude, Maude," said the gently chiding voice of Reverend Fromberg, "that's a harsh, unforgiving attitude."

"I know it, Reverend, but that man is beyond forgiveness. He's been vulgar and troublesome all his life, and now he's threatening the good folks of this town." She turned her anger back at the sheriff. "We've all been hearing what a great marksman this Cherokee deputy of yours is! Let him prove it!"

"That'll be enough, Maude," said Nate. He knew Micah's hide was thick, but his own wasn't. Nothing got Nate's dander up faster than the feeling that one of his friends was being attacked. He turned away from Maude and looked at Micah, whose face was chiseled granite behind his mirrored glasses. "What do you think?"

"If somebody can keep him distracted for thirty seconds, I can reach the building. After that, it'll be a snap. Hell, Nate, the man's drunk out of his mind."

"If it's that easy, I'll have one of the other deputies do it. You're on break." Nate didn't for a minute believe it would be easy, which was why he'd sent for Micah in the first place. It just stuck in his craw to hear Micah speak as if it were a piece of cake.

Micah swung his head around and looked down at Nate. "It's that easy for someone with my training. I'm the only one who's trained. I'll do it."

While Jed Barlowe shot another couple of wild rounds at the sheriff's vehicles and missed by a country mile, Micah went into the diner, ignoring Maude as if she were invisible, and pulled on winter camouflage over his clothes.

"What weapon do you want?" Nate asked him.

"Just my side arm and knife. He's so drunk I can probably take him down without using any weapon if you can just keep him occupied with what's going on outside."

Nate half smiled. "Maybe I'll have Maude holler at him through the megaphone. That ought to rile him good." Across the room, Maude gave a snort.

"Yeah." Bending, Micah checked the knife he always kept holstered in his boot. "Okay, I'm ready. I'll circle around through the alley and come up behind the church. I'll radio just as soon as I'm in position, and then you start the diversion. I'll have to maintain silence after that so he doesn't hear me. Give me at least thirty seconds to cross the open ground, just to be safe."

"You'll get it," Nate promised.

Maude Bleaker, watching this exchange, had grown mercifully silent. As Micah brushed past her toward the diner's rear door, she reached out and stopped him. Slowly he turned his head and looked down at her. He disliked being distracted at a time like this, but his expression revealed nothing.

Maude spoke. "I didn't mean anything by what I said out there, Deputy. I was just mad."

He regarded her stonily for a moment, then gave a brief nod. "Forget it, Miz Bleaker. I have." He'd long ago become deaf to such inferences.

"The name's Maude, Micah Parish," she hollered after him. "Don't be forgetting *that.*"

An invisible smile tugged at the corner of his mouth as he stepped out into the snowy alley. Maude Bleaker was a long-standing believer in lawmen who shot first and worried about it later. She had also said something nasty to everyone in the county at one time or another. All things considered, he had come off lightly.

He paused, drawing a couple of deep breaths, shifting his mental focus to an almost tunnel-like awareness of the task at hand. Last night's snowfall had drifted deep in the alley. Someone had started plowing it out and then stopped, probably because of the excitement Jed Barlowe was stirring up.

At places the snow reached nearly to his hips, but Micah slogged through it as if it weren't there. Ten minutes later he stood in the alley by the corner of Houlihan's Hardware and reached for the microphone attached to the collar of his camouflage. "I'm in place," he told Nate quietly.

He could see the steeple clearly from here, and just as clearly he could see Jed Barlowe. Jed was leaning against the rail that ringed the cupola where the bell hung just beneath the spire. His attention was fixed on the crowd of cars and deputies in front of the diner, and Micah could see only the back of his head as he leaned out and shouted something.

Now! Micah thought, and darted across the open ground toward the back side of the church. Distantly he heard the report of a .357 Magnum, and registered that Jed was shooting again. He was damn glad the man hadn't brought anything more heavy-duty on his little spree. He would be a hell of a lot more dangerous with a high-powered rifle of the kind a lot of locals kept for hunting predators.

Take care, Micah. The memory of Faith's parting words joined the swarm of impressions he was drinking in with every sense. The snow beneath his boots made a dry crunch that muffled his running steps. The cold air knifed his lungs and made his earlobes ache. Every sense was fine-tuned to hypersensitivity.

He was one with the wind as he ran.

And then he was there, flattened up against the back door of the church, which, naturally, was locked. Breathing slightly more deeply than usual, he pulled up the hem of the camouflage jacket and felt around for the key Reverend Fromberg had given to Nate. When his fingers closed around it, he spared a backward glance at the wide expanse he had just crossed. His footprints were there, a beacon for anyone who cared to look. He was counting on Jed being too drunk to notice.

Inside, the church was dimly lit and warm. The day's gray light poured through stained glass, creating crazed patterns of jewel-like colors across the floor and pews. The bell tower acted as an amplifier, funneling Jed's curses and shouts down into the nave as Micah stripped off the camouflage and his combat boots. He tucked the boot knife into his belt, next to his holster.

On silent, bare feet, he climbed the tower, stepping close to the wall to avoid causing a stair to creak.

You'll be careful?

Faith's question whispered through his mind. No woman had ever asked that of him. No woman had ever given enough of a damn to ask that of him. It made him uneasy. He shoved the whisper of her concern away, having no time to deal with it right now. Later...later he would think about all the ramifications in that one little request. About the tie that it implied.

Jed had stopped shooting, but he was still shouting some creative obscenities down at the deputies below. When Micah neared the top of the stairs, he found the trap door open. Edging up another step with caution, he found Jed with his back to the trap door. The drunk was hollering something about Nate's ancestors.

Now!

Just as his upper body emerged through the trap door, Jed swung around drunkenly. Micah froze as the business end of the pistol centered dead on him.

"Damn half-breed," Jed mumbled. "What the hell...?"

"Put it down, Jed," Micah said in a tone that had been unhesitatingly obeyed by men under extreme conditions. "Put it down before somebody gets hurt."

"Yeah," Jed said, and staggered to one side. His hand instinctively tightened on the pistol and squeezed the trigger.

Micah took the shot dead center on his vest. It jarred him a little, but some instinct made him grab the sides of the trap door before he fell down the stairs. Pain blossomed in his chest, momentarily threatening his consciousness, but he gritted his teeth and battered down the blackness by sheer force of will.

"Holy . . ." Jed gaped, the pistol slipping from his hands as Micah thrust himself up into the belfry. "Hey, man, I didn't mean to—"

"Maybe not," Micah said through gritted teeth, as he kicked the pistol away. "Maybe not. And maybe you better get facedown fast, Barlowe, before I think about the fact that you could have killed me."

The sun had come out from behind the overcast clouds around noon, and toward three it had sunk low enough in the western sky to slant golden light across the soft, white snow dunes. Fascinated, Faith watched the light change. She hadn't realized that plain white snow contained so many colors, from dusky blue shadows to sparkles of red.

Earlier she had run across Micah's clothes hamper and had been glad to busy herself washing his clothes. Now she set up the ironing board facing the kitchen windows and ironed his uniforms while she kept an eye on the stew she was simmering for dinner.

And for just a few moments, while no one was watching or judging her backbone, she admitted to herself that this was the kind of labor she loved. She enjoyed cooking and cleaning and washing and ironing; and all she had ever wanted out of life was a home of her own, a good husband to look after, and a house full of children. She had never felt any burning desire to build bridges or make money or go to the moon. What she wanted was a family. Her own family.

But that was not to be. Now she had to find strength and purpose so that she could give her baby all that it deserved. The trust fund her father had left her would maintain the ranch and pay the most essential bills, but she would have to earn anything extra herself. She wondered if Micah might want to hire her as a housekeeper.

The sight of a shiny red Blazer pulling up in the kitchen yard startled her out of her thoughts. While she wondered if she should pretend no one was home, she watched a man climb out and walk around to the passenger side. As he turned, the light caught his face, and she was able to see that he had a full golden beard.

Faith instinctively backed up from the window—she had little cause to trust men—but then stopped as she watched the man help a woman out of the car. He bent, laughing, and brushed a kiss on the woman's cheek before they both turned toward the house. That gesture reassured Faith as nothing else could have. There was no hesitation when she went through the mudroom to open the door.

The golden-haired man smiled at her from the bottom step. "You must be Faith Williams. I'm Ransom Laird, and this is my wife, Mandy."

This was the man who had rescued Micah from the VC. Faith felt her face break into a wide, welcoming smile. "Please come in. I just made coffee and was about to make some tea."

When everyone had settled around the table, and Mandy and Faith had shared a few laughing remarks about the joys and discomforts of pregnancy, Ransom turned to Faith.

"I hate to be the heavy here, but Micah asked us to come over and tell you he's going to be a little late. He's not hurt," he hastened to add as Faith drew a sharp breath. "Well, bruised a little, but not hurt."

"He was shot, wasn't he?" Faith felt everything inside her grow terribly still, and hardly felt Mandy reach over to take her hand. No, she thought. No. Not Micah!

"He's all right, Faith," Mandy said, squeezing the other woman's hand. "Honestly. I talked to him myself. They think he's got a cracked rib. Painful but not serious."

"Then why isn't he here now?"

Ransom answered her. "Because he neglected to tell anyone that when Jed Barlowe accidentally discharged his weapon, the bullet hit him. Micah thought he was okay except for some bruising, thanks to his vest, but later, when the adrenaline wore off, he realized it was a little more than that. Anyhow, they only just X-rayed him, and I guess they're wrapping his ribs right now. They're going to hold him for a couple of hours to make sure there are no internal injuries, then he'll come home. But he's fine, Faith. Really."

It was dark when Ransom and Mandy, assured repeatedly by Faith that she was quite all right by herself, took their leave. She wondered, as she stirred the stew one more time, what Micah had told the Lairds about her. They had seemed to think she would be upset and worried, which indicated they thought she had some kind of long-standing relationship with Micah. She felt as if she did, she realized. She felt as if she had always known him, and yet in many ways she had just met him.

Closing her eyes, she could imagine him coming through the door, his Stetson cocked low over his eyes, his shoulder-length black hair tousled from the wind outside. She could imagine those dark eyes settling on her in that measuring way they had, revealing nothing, yet missing nothing.

And when she held her breath, she could remember the touch of his lips on hers just last night. Her experience of men wasn't wide—her stepfather had made certain of that—but she knew the kisses she had received from Micah were special. He had made her feel that if she just entrusted herself to him, he would show her delights beyond imagining. The kind of things a young girl had fantasized before her rude awakening in marriage. The kind of things she still fantasized about in unguarded moments.

She shivered a little, realizing that she hadn't felt trapped or threatened when he wrapped his arms around her. No, she had felt good. Treasured. As if a previously unperceived yearning had been suddenly answered.

By the time Micah was released from the hospital, he was feeling like a caged lion. He had stayed only as long as he had because he wasn't stupid, and he recognized the potential danger of internal injuries. That hadn't kept him from chewing on the bit, though. He hated to be confined in any way.

The night was clear and cold, the waning crescent moon little more than a silver arc in the sky. When he parked the Blazer by the back door, he waited a couple of minutes in the dark, listening to the silence of the vast open spaces around him. There was no sound save the sigh of the wind, a lonesome, lonely sound.

It suited him to a T.

Inside, though, someone was waiting for him, and he felt a little guilty. He'd gone out of here this morning like some kind of macho fool, promising the little woman he'd be home from war in time for dinner. Dinner hour was long past, and when he'd checked with Ransom just before leaving the hospital, Mandy had taken the phone to give him an earful about how worried Faith was.

Well, hell. The woman had been in his life for a mere forty-eight hours. Surely it was too soon for her to be getting all wound up about his health? But then, he admitted reluctantly, time was no measure of feelings. He'd seen the concern in her eyes that morning, and he knew damn well that if their positions had been reversed, he would have been concerned for her. It was no big deal, just ordinary human caring.

He grunted as he climbed out of the Blazer. His ribs were just bruised, but they hurt like hell whenever he bent wrong. The tape helped, but only time would heal him.

Once again his dinner awaited him beneath plastic wrap on the counter beside the microwave. This time, however, Faith didn't make an appearance, for which he was perversely grateful. He'd had enough fussing today to last him a lifetime. After eating a huge bowl of her stew, he switched out the light and headed upstairs, thinking that the years eventually caught up with a man, whether he wanted to admit it or not. He was plumb tired tonight.

He got his shirt off with only a few muffled groans, but when he sat down to take off his boots, he knew he was in trouble. There was no way he could bend far enough to reach the laces. He tried, but pain brought a cold sweat to his forehead. Well, he could sleep with his boots on. It wouldn't be the first time he'd done it. Damn, he hated that. It was the grungiest feeling in the world to sleep with your boots on.

A soft tap on the door alerted him to the fact that Faith must have overheard some of his grunts.

"Micah? Micah, are you all right?"

"I'm fine, Moonbeam. Just fine..."

She wasn't buying his assurances without seeing for herself. The door to his room opened slowly, with almost visible uncertainty. She peeked around the edge until she found him sitting in the straight-backed chair beside his bed.

"I heard you groan," she said tentatively. "Do you need help?"

Well, hell, he thought, she was already here, and it *would* be nice to sleep with his boots off. "I can't quite reach my boot laces," he admitted.

"Oh, they've got you all taped up!" she exclaimed softly as she came into the room. All her hesitation had vanished with his request for her help. The white tape wrapped him mummylike from his small coppery nipples to below the waistline of his pants. "Can you breathe?"

"That doesn't seem to be a problem." Damn, he thought, not wanting to notice, but noticing anyway, that she looked adorable in a pink chenille robe and fuzzy pink slippers. Her hair was a wildly tossed mass of fairy curls, and one of her rosy cheeks bore a crease from her pillow. "Sorry I woke you," he said.

"Don't worry about it." Trying not to stare, she knelt before him and fumbled at his boot laces. His chest was magnificent, though, and her gaze kept straying upward as she wondered if that skin was as smooth and warm as it looked. She loved the warm tone of it. And those arms! She had never dreamed that real men had arms like that, so muscular and powerful.

Micah saw her straying gaze, caught a glimpse of her yearning, and felt the immediate response of his body. No, he told himself. No. He wanted no woman in his life, and this particular woman was not meant for casual relationships.

Besides, he had put the ladies of Conard County off-limits with good reason. It was hard enough to face old flames day after day, but even worse when the whole county gossiped about it and shared in all the juicy details. He reckoned that the aftermath of a failed love affair in Conard County must feel something like reading about yourself in the supermarket tabloids. Just look at poor Miss Emma, who probably still heard about her traveling man more than a decade later.

Faith's hands fumbled at his laces, but she finally managed to loosen them enough that he could kick the boots off. "Thanks," he said roughly.

Still kneeling before him, she tilted back her head and smiled up at him. "You promised you'd be home for dinner, Micah."

He didn't want to, but he felt himself smiling back. Just a small upward lift of the corners of his mouth, but he knew she saw it when her eyes began to sparkle. "So I did," he agreed. "Guess I should apologize."

"Apologize?" She shook her head. "I don't want an apology."

Before he was foolish enough to ask what she wanted, she started to stand, and he reached out to steady her. And suddenly she was standing right before him, between his legs, his hands on her hips, her gently swollen womb right in front of his eyes. Almost as if he couldn't help himself, he leaned forward and pressed his cheek to her. He felt a small soft kick, and a rusty chuckle escaped him.

"She's driving me crazy tonight," Faith confided impulsively. "Kicking and turning so much I feel like I'm on a roller coaster."

"She?"

"She. I'm sure it's a girl."

Micah felt another poke. And at almost precisely the same instant Faith's soft warm hand slipped into his hair and pressed him even closer.

"Micah?" Her voice was little more than a shivery whisper.

"Hmm?"

"Thank you for letting me share this with you. I've wanted so badly to share this. I never dreamed how hard it could be to be pregnant and not have anyone to share it with." Looking down at her hand against his dark head, she had the craziest feeling that he was like a wild thing, consenting to be touched only briefly, that at any moment he would rear up and disappear. The thought brought a deep pang.

The tendrils drawing them together were invisible, but he could feel them in the air around them. Reluctant to lose the warmth and closeness, yet needing to preserve his solitude, he pulled back, lifting his cheek from her womb. Her fingers trailed slowly down from his hair to his shoulder as he straightened.

Two things hit him simultaneously, shaking him: her warm fingers were touching the bare skin of his shoulder, and her breasts were now right at eye level. The belt of her bathrobe rode up over her tummy and just under her breasts, accentuating their fullness.

"Faith..." He had no idea what he was going to say, and speech became impossible when her palm settled on his shoulder. It had been too damn long.

She edged closer to him, as if she missed the warmth of his cheek against her. Tilting his head back farther, he looked up and wished he knew what she was thinking. It was a totally uncharacteristic wish in a man who cherished his solitude and wanted to share it with no one. He couldn't remember the last time he had given a damn what anybody was thinking.

Her gaze, he realized, was locked on her hand resting on his shoulder. Turning his head, he could see her milky skin against the duskier color of his own, the long strands of his dark hair trailing across her pale fingers. The contrast was an erotic jolt that zapped straight to his groin.

"Micah?" Faith's voice was now barely a whisper, a shaky whisper at that. "Micah, I feel ... funny...." Shaky. Hot. Cold. Paralyzed.

At once his powerful arms wrapped around her, and the next thing she knew, she was perched on his thigh, her side pressed to his chest.

"What's wrong?" he asked. "Do you feel sick? Does something hurt?" But even as the questions sprang to his lips, a look at her told him that she wasn't sick at all. Her hand remained on his shoulder, and now she moved it. Slowly. Testingly. Her eyes still focused on his shoulder.

"You feel...so warm," she whispered shakily. "So nice. Micah, I..."

She couldn't seem to complete the thought, but he really didn't need her to. He could feel it in the unsure, restless movement of her hand against him, could see it in the way she licked her lips and stared at him in fascination.

The same fascination was blooming in him. For two days now he had been fascinated by the warm, living satin of this woman's skin, by the tousled curls that looked as if they had been spun from moonlight. Her fragrance had been a continuing temptation, her soft woman's body a lure he had struggled to resist.

Now she was perched on his knee, so close he could hear the whisper of her soft, short breaths and feel the radiance of her body warmth like a welcoming aura. Closing his eyes against the visual temptation she presented, he struggled to find his famed self-control, a control so strong and unbreachable that some of his comrades had nicknamed him the Robot. This small, slight woman did what no threat had ever been able to: she made a joke of it.

And her small, soft hand continued to knead his shoulder. In that single touch there was a world of yearning and a wealth of uncertainty. He opened his dark eyes again and turned her face toward him. "Look at me, Faith," he said hoarsely. "Look at me."

Slowly, almost dazedly, her blue eyes lifted to his. Her pupils were dilated, her lips parted, her cheeks flushed. And damn it, she was confused. The woman didn't even know what was happening to her! How the hell was that possible?

"Micah?" A mere breath. A mere puff of sound. As if in the mindless grip of hypnotic suggestion, she leaned toward him.

His control might be disintegrating into dry dust around him, but part of his mind was still analyzing, thinking, concluding. Right now it was concluding that Faith's former husband had abused her in another way, that Frank had taken his sexual satisfaction from her without concern for hers. If she had ever experienced even the earliest twinges of arousal, it wouldn't have been long before carelessness and lack of affection would have smothered them.

Now she was sitting on his knee and experiencing for the first time feelings she couldn't name and impulses she didn't understand. If he exercised his own control right now and set her aside—surely the only wise thing to do—he would wound her again. She might never again let these feelings surface, might never again dare to touch a man. He might well put the seal on what Frank had done.

Well, hell!

Yet he hesitated, wondering if he had enough control to carry her any further without giving in completely himself. It was a question he had never needed to ask himself before, and it set him back on his heels. But he couldn't leave her like this, with her barely born feelings crushed under a ruthless dismissal—or even a kind one.

Trapped. It was a feeling he hated, even when it came about through his own scruples. He was feeling trapped right now, and it gave him the edge over his shattering control. Feeling again firmly in the driver's seat, he drew Faith closer and urged her head to his shoulder.

"Hush, Moonbeam," he said, his voice as dark as the night. "Just lean against me and close your eyes."

Ignoring the temptation of her belt, he brought his hand to her cheek, where he felt the smooth warmth that had so enticed him. She was so small, so soft, so delicate, and she woke the tenderness he kept buried in his soul. He touched her now with that tenderness, tracing the curve of her jaw until she shifted restlessly and her head unconsciously turned into his touch, seeking more.

He caught his breath, then steadied himself. Her trust, he realized uneasily, was penetrating barriers that had never before been pierced. How could she trust him so readily, so easily, after what she had been through? Was this leftover conditioning from that long-ago summer when he had watched over her?

But what did it matter? She was leaning into him, trusting him, receptive to him, and he wanted her more than he had ever wanted anyone or anything. She was a song in his blood, like his Cherokee ancestry. She was a hope he had never allowed himself and a dream he had hardly dared to have. For just these few brief minutes he was going to sacrifice caution and succumb to feeling.

Catching her beneath the chin, he turned her face up and settled his mouth over hers. There wasn't an ounce of resistance in her. She opened for him like a blooming rose, inviting his invasion and possession. Starved to learn her taste, he plunged his tongue into her.

Warm, sweet, eager. She welcomed him as if she had been waiting forever, and her tongue shyly imitated his movements. He teased her gently, taking care not to frighten or overpower her, making sure she never felt trapped. Gently he held her, and tenderly he kissed her, slipping his tongue playfully along hers, careful not to let eroticism grow beyond friendliness.

And then he forgot why he was being careful, because she turned into him and lifted her arms snugly around his broad, bare shoulders. God, how he *needed* to be held! The thought slipped past his guard and bounced around in his mind like a pinball, zinging here and there and leaving everything changed in its wake. The man who needed nothing suddenly needed her until he ached with it, until his throat tightened and his diaphragm froze on an unborn sob of longing. Gasping, he lifted his head and battled his own weakness.

Micah Parish had just faced his own loneliness.

"Oh, Micah." Faith's whisper was shaken as she pressed her face into the curve of his neck and inhaled the wonderful scent that was peculiarly his. "Oh, Micah..." she sighed again. At the worst possible time in her life, it suddenly appeared that fairy tales weren't lies. She hardly knew how to cope with the shock of this unexpected yearning. For months now she had been imagining a life that would be free of men. Completely. For months she had been building a castle in the air where she could be safe because she would be beyond reach. Now this. Now the terrifying, wonderful, awesome possibility that a man could actually make her want and need, that he could actually bring her pleasure and a sense of security. Why now, when she least needed another complication?

In her sigh he heard none of her reluctance. What he heard was her yearning, and since it exactly matched his own, he tipped her face up again and claimed her mouth. This time he kissed her with unabashed eroticism, his thrusting tongue telling her exactly what he wanted to do with her.

When her head fell back against his shoulder in complete surrender, he knew a warrior's fierce triumph at sweet victory. Sucking her lower lip between his teeth, he growled softly and felt for the tie of her robe. A tug released it, and his hand, with unerring instinct, found its way inside, searched out a path past buttons and fuzzy flannel, and then surrounded its objective, a warm, full, firm breast.

"Oh!" The sound escaped Faith on a sharply drawn breath. "Micah..."

Their eyes met, his dark and deep, glowing like black fire, hers blue, bright, slumberous with awakening passion. Her lips were swollen and wet from his kisses, parted to accommodate the rapid breathing that pressed her breast rhythmically into his grasp.

"Did he ever touch you like this?" Micah demanded suddenly, angry at himself for handling her this way, furious at Frank Williams for abusing her. "Did he ever make you feel this way? Did he ever, just once, make you feel *good*?"

Faith shook her head slowly, just once. Then she ripped the breath from him by the simple act of turning to press herself hard against his hand, by the simple, broken statement, "Never. Oh, Micah...I never...ever..."

The brutality she had lived with had never been clearer to him. In that instant he found his sagging control and battered down the wrath that could do no good. Had there been a way, he would have erased from her memory all the bad things, but there was no way. All he could do was show her that it didn't have to be bad. That a man could give her good things. She deserved to know that.

Gently, as if unwrapping the most priceless piece of porcelain, he brushed back the front of her nightgown and bared her breast to his gaze. She had the finest, palest skin, with a delicate tracery of blue veins that only heightened his awareness of her incredible fragility.

Tucking the fabric under her breast, he lifted her nipple to his mouth. He heard her gasp at the first touch of his tongue, and then she grew completely still, holding her breath in anticipation. He had heard that a pregnant woman's breasts became terribly sensitive, so he took exquisite care.

Her nipple had already begun to swell, but he lapped gently at it with his tongue, listening to her soft gasps, until the nubbin was hard. Then he took her into his mouth to suck her gently and listened with deep pleasure to her muted groan.

"Micah..." His name was little more than a moan that trailed away, but there was no mistaking her reaction when her hands found his head and held him close and tight. Her fingers tunneled into his hair and hung on tensely.

"This is how it should be, Moonbeam," he muttered roughly against her soft, satin skin. Lifting his head, he looked down at her dazed expression, at her soft breast, at the hard peak of her reddened nipple. She was beautiful. Exquisite. He wanted her naked; he wanted her garbed in nothing but her God-given beauty. He wanted to hold her swollen belly in his hands and press kisses there to let her know she wasn't at all fat or ugly, but was perfect in her pregnancy.

And then he saw the scars.

Chapter 7

He didn't like this. He didn't like this at all. Pausing after he shoved another of Faith's suitcases into the rear of the Blazer, Micah took a moment to stare out across dazzling snow at an equally dazzling blue sky.

She wasn't anywhere near as sure now that Frank knew nothing about her ranch. When he had questioned her closely this morning, she admitted that she might have mentioned the place to Frank. Maybe she had mentioned it several times. But Frank, she insisted, had never been interested in the ranch.

That was the giveaway, Micah thought now. Frank had never been interested. How could she know that if she had never discussed it with him? What it came down to was that Faith desperately needed to believe that Frank would never even think of looking for her there, so her mind had played little games with the facts and nearly convinced her that he didn't know about it.

Micah figured that if Frank really wanted to get Faith, he would remember the Montrose ranch fast enough when he discovered she had left San Antonio. Finding it wouldn't be easy, with everybody in Conard County alerted to a dangerous stranger looking for the Montrose place, but it wouldn't be impossible.

So he had tried to persuade Faith to stay with him until Frank was apprehended. That was when he discovered that although she might be small and fragile, she could be as cussedly stubborn as an army mule. Somehow, at some point, the woman's mind had diddled with reality and convinced her that she would be safe at the ranch. Micah had tried every argument his agile mind could manufacture, but Faith had refused to budge an inch. In her mind, her father's home was an unbreachable fortress, a sanctuary no evil could penetrate.

Damn it, he should have made love to her last night. Hadn't he read somewhere that lovemaking released that bonding hormone, whatever it was? He'd had the perfect chance to make her want to stay, and he'd blown it because he got mad about her scars.

Aw, hell! Turning, he stomped back into the house for another load. It would have been unscrupulous to take advantage of her that way, he told himself. He would never have been able to forgive himself. She probably never would have forgiven him. She wasn't a casual type.

The phone started ringing the instant he set foot on the porch. He stamped his feet twice to knock the snow off and then stepped inside to answer it.

"Parish."

"Micah, it's Dirk Bayard. About the white Honda you had me tow in?"

"Right. How bad is it?"

"I can have it running by noon if you want. It just needs a new radiator. I won't be able to fix the body damage until next week, though, but it can be driven until I get the new grill in."

"Go ahead. The lady needs a car."

She needed more than a car, he thought irritably. More than the pickup truck he'd been planning to lend her when she wouldn't even allow him to use the lack of car as a reason for her to stay with him. She could use a new brain, one that thought clearly.

Talk about getting a wild hair.

He hated the feeling that it was at least partly his fault she was in such an all-fired rush to get out of here. When he'd seen those fresh red scars where her husband had stabbed her, he'd gotten furious. Blind angry. And Micah Parish in a rage was a scary thing. A terrifying thing. He'd been told so often that he never let his temper get out of hand.

But it had almost gotten out of hand last night.

He could hardly blame her for wanting to get out of his house as fast as possible. He hadn't hurt her or anything, but if his temper was terrifying to other men, then it must be even more so to a woman who was accustomed to being battered by a man when he got even a little bit annoyed.

Inside Micah, the full-fledged fury of a thunderstorm existed. When he became truly angry, the air seemed to snap with energy around him, and it was almost possible to feel the lightning. There were times when he even fancied that he could feel the atmosphere warp around him as if bent by incredible force.

No, he could hardly blame Faith for wanting to get away from him. How was she to know that such force and strength could be harmless, that he would never hurt a hair on her head, no matter how furious he became? He was willing to bet that Frank Williams had promised her more than once that he would never strike her again.

Picking up the box that contained her meager supply of kitchen utensils, Micah stomped out of the kitchen and into the bright, cold day. The propane truck and the phone installer were supposed to arrive at her place at ten, and time was getting short if they were going to be there to greet them.

"Micah?" Faith's light voice called him from the porch. "Gage is on the phone."

Well, hell, what now? He shoved the box into the back of the Blazer and strode back to the kitchen. This morning Faith wore jeans and a fuzzy lavender sweater. She had a liking for soft colors and fuzzy fabrics, and Micah was discovering that he did, too. And he had never guessed that they made jeans for pregnant women.

Why the hell hadn't he just loved her silly last night?

He picked up the phone. "Morning, Gage."

"Morning. I thought you'd want to know that a buddy of mine up at the state lab says they should be faxing the results of their examination of Jeff's cattle late this afternoon, around four. He hinted that things weren't adding up."

"Thanks, Gage. I'll come in this afternoon."

"How are the ribs?"

"Okay." He'd had to wear cowboy boots so he could use the bootjack to remove them later. They weren't half as stable as his preferred combat boots, but there weren't any laces to fiddle with, and as long as he didn't have to do any running or cover rugged terrain, they would do. At least they made it possible for him to get by without help.

Bending to pick up Faith's boxes and suitcases hurt, too, but it was only a brief, sharp pain that let up as soon as he straightened. He could endure that quick jab without much trouble, and he sure as hell wasn't going to let Faith heft this stuff.

When he hung up, he turned to find her watching him with concern in her blue eyes. "I'm fine," he said gruffly.

Her brief nod was more of an acknowledgment than an agreement. It occurred to him that if he claimed he needed her help, she would stay to look after him. But that would be dishonesty, and he wasn't dishonest. Nor did he want any dishonesty in his relationship with her, wherever it led.

"Why don't you rest a moment and have some coffee?" she suggested.

It would, he realized abruptly, be all too easy to get addicted to her concern. It wasn't that he wanted to be fussed over, or that nobody would care if he dropped dead. He had friends, good friends, who would grieve at his death. But never in his life had he had someone who cared about him in the small ways—the ways that mattered.

He glanced at his watch and figured they could spare a few minutes. Maybe if he took another stab at it, he could get her to give up this craziness.

This time, though, instead of telling her all the reasons why she shouldn't go, he simply asked her to stay.

Her hands tightened around her mug of herbal tea, and she regarded him solemnly. "I have to go, Micah. I have to stand on my own two feet just once in my life."

"Before you got married—"

"Before I got married I lived at home with my mother and her husband. I've never once been truly independent."

He thought about that a moment and inevitably wondered how it had come about. These days most kids flew the nest just as soon as they had the opportunity.

"My mother was sick," Faith said after a moment. "Someone had to look after her, and I don't regret it, but I missed the experience of being on my own. I think if I'd had that experience, I never would have stayed with Frank for so long. I keep thinking that if I had known I could manage by myself, I wouldn't have been so afraid."

She made a small sound, something like a sad little laugh. "It's pathetic, isn't it? Spineless."

"I'm sure there was more to it than that." As a cop, he knew a little something about the spiral of domestic violence, and as a Green Beret he knew something about psychological warfare. "You love someone, so you forgive them. Make excuses for them. And you think you must be somehow at fault, so you feel guilty. And finally you feel so worthless, so totally like a failure, that you believe you deserve the abuse."

She looked at him wonderingly. "You really do understand."

"Hell, yes. It's Basic Brainwashing Technique 101. From childhood we're conditioned to believe that if we're bad we'll be punished and if we're good we'll be rewarded. Religions are built on the concept, and most children are raised with it. It's straightforward operant conditioning, and it doesn't even have to work at a conscious level."

He reached across the table and touched her hand. "Unfortunately, cause and effect don't have to be apparent. If the effect is bad, the cause is assumed. That's what happened to you, plain and simple. People don't find it easy to believe that bad things just happen, that there doesn't have to be any direct cause when they become the victims of violence. Invariably, the first assumption they make is that they did something to bring it on themselves."

Faith nodded, a suspicious shine in her eyes. This was more than she had hoped for, she realized suddenly. That anyone other than another abused wife would understand. That a man could actually understand what had happened. It had all been explained to her, of course, when she went for counseling. She had desperately needed to know how she had let herself come to that, and she had been told pretty much what Micah had just told her. But somehow, hearing it from him validated it in a way that her psychologist's explanation had never done.

And the most comforting realization, the one that warmed her, was that he didn't think she was weird or sick or crazy. He thought there was nothing wrong with her, that she had simply been an ordinary woman caught up in things she didn't have the means to battle.

She watched him glance at his watch yet again and then rise to carry his cup to the sink. He was a genuinely unique man, she thought. Hard in ways that would make him a truly formidable enemy, yet surprisingly compassionate.

He faced her, leaning back against the counter, resting the heels of his hands on the edge. "Are you sure you won't reconsider?"

He would make it so easy to stay, she thought. Micah Parish was a caretaker, and he would take care of her so well that she would probably never notice a lack in her own fortitude and independence. But that wouldn't be fair to either of them.

"I have to," she said again, and rose to carry her own cup to the sink.

He was big, he was a cop, and he was a man, but she felt perfectly safe approaching him. Just three days ago she would have found it impossible even to think of doing such a thing, yet here she was doing it. He had an untamed appearance that probably frightened many people, and there was a hardness to his features that could be intimidating, but she knew she could walk right up to him in perfect safety. If he lifted a hand to her it would be only to comfort or to bring her pleasure.

Reaching out, he caught the back of her neck in one of his large hands and drew her close. When she stood against him, her face pressed to his chest, he closed his arms around her and felt her wrap hers around his waist. "If you need anything at all, you just call me, Moonbeam. Don't ever hesitate to call me."

They arrived at her ranch in time to meet the woman from the telephone company. After the phone was installed and working, the propane tank was filled and all the appliances checked out, they headed into town to get Faith's car from Dirk Bayard's shop. From there, Faith went grocery shopping and Micah went over to the sheriff's office.

He still didn't like it, but he was beginning to accept the fact that he couldn't stop her. He could, however, make sure that the patrolling deputy in the area checked on her at least once during his shift. Most of them, being the westerners they were, would probably check on her even more often than that.

"Well, well, well," said Velma Jansen, the department's dispatcher as Micah came through the door. "It's the famous deputy himself. How are the ribs, big boy?"

Velma was sixty, scrawny, leathery and as tough as a marine drill instructor. She had a shamelessly big mouth, a heart that was even bigger, and she mothered the deputies until they begged for mercy.

"Prime, Velma," Micah joked back. "They're prime."

"There's a club for cops like you, you know," Velma said. "You big, tough macho types who are idiotic enough to let someone else get off the first shot. You can only join if your life is saved by your body armor. Big honor, right?"

"Ignore her, Micah," Charlie Huskins advised from the duty desk. "She's been holding body armor checks all day. Nobody gets out that door without proving they're wearing it."

Micah had no difficulty whatsoever imagining the scene this morning as the day shift tried to get out that door and were confronted by a determined Velma, all four-foot-ten of her. He wondered if she poked their ribs to check or made them take their shirts off. It was almost enough to make him grin.

He held his hands up in the universal sign of surrender. "I'm not on duty, Velma."

"Nate was hoping you'd come in," Velma said. "He had to go over to the high school, but he'll be back shortly."

"Trouble?" Micah asked.

"Oh, no," she hastened to assure him. "Nate and Marge had to talk to the guidance counselor. One of their daughters is having trouble in algebra or something."

Charlie spoke up. "He wants to ask you again about pressing charges against Jed Barlowe."

"Jed didn't mean to shoot me," Micah said flatly. "The man's a fool, but he isn't a murderer."

"Then you're a fool, too, Micah Parish," Velma snapped. "The man's a danger, whether he means to be or not."

"We can charge him with drunk and disorderly," Micah said patiently. "We can charge him with public endangerment, illegal discharge of a firearm, and a whole bunch of other stuff, but I'll be damned if I'll press an attempted murder charge."

"See, Velma?" Charlie said. "I told you Micah's as honest as the day is long."

"It'll be small comfort if Jed Barlowe gets drunk again and shoots somebody."

"I don't think Jed will be out on the streets for a long time as it is," Micah said.

An hour later he was telling the same thing to Nate, only Nate was a lot quicker to agree than Velma. "I just needed to be sure, old son," Nate told him. "The county D.A. wants to make some headlines, and I need to be able to assure him you weren't just confused yesterday. Consider it finished."

Micah started to rise, but Nate waved him back. "Gage said the state lab is going to be faxing down the results of the necropsies on those cattle of Cumberland's."

Micah nodded again. "He called me this morning. That's part of the reason I stopped in."

"Good. Now, what's happening with Faith Williams?"

"She's moving out to the Montrose ranch today."

"Damn. You couldn't stop her?"

"Short of committing a felony?" Micah shook his head. "She's stubborn."

"Then she ought to fit right in with a neighbor lady I can think of." Nate sighed and shuffled the stack of waiting paperwork. "What is it with these women, Micah? They sail along like a ship before the wind, and then all of a sudden, at some little provocation, you find they've tossed the anchor overboard and ain't going nowhere, nohow. They're all scared and frightened and then, bam! They've got a backbone made of unbending steel. And always at the wrong time.''

''Trouble with Marge?''

Nate glanced up wryly. ''Does it show? Never mind. Faith Williams is a bigger problem. I don't cotton to the idea of a pregnant woman out that far all by herself. Not in my county. Short of condemning the property, I don't guess there's much to be done except to alert the patrols to keep a close eye on her. Damn it,'' he said in annoyance, ''doesn't she understand how fast a body can get into serious trouble?''

''She's never been alone before.'' Micah stretched out his long legs. ''I asked Mandy and Ransom to keep an eye on her, too.''

''Maybe Mandy can talk some sense into her.''

Micah's face remained expressionless. ''Mandy Laird? The woman who said no mad arsonist was going to drive her from her home? The woman who was planning to conduct her own solitary pregnancy at a ranch every bit as far out as the Montrose place?''

Nate suddenly laughed. ''That's what I mean about women!'' A moment later, all vestige of humor had vanished from his face. ''I have a bad feeling about this, Micah. A bad feeling.''

Micah nodded. ''Tell you one thing, Nate. At the first sign of trouble of any kind, I'll carry that woman out of there bodily.''

''You do that, son. You do that.''

''Well, hell.'' Micah's comment pretty much said it for all of them as they pored over the necropsy report. He'd been hoping for something, anything, to add to the not-quite-right feeling he had about the mutilations. All the lab had come up with, however, was a more detailed description of what he already knew.

They were Cumberland's cattle, all right, but Micah had already judged that by the apparent age of the brand mark.

Cause of death for both was exsanguination, followed by excision of the tongue and genitals. He'd already figured that from the lack of blood around the wounds or at the scene. Detritus from around the animals' hooves was awaiting further analysis.

"Sure to be good old Wyoming clay," Nate said sourly.

"Aw, be optimistic, Nate," Gage said. "Maybe they'll find the seed of a plant that grows only in the desert or something."

Nate looked hard at him and then gave a short laugh. "Maybe you Feds are used to that kind of break, but out here in the boonies, all we get are a slap, a lick and a prayer."

Micah looked at Gage. A Fed? Past or present? But before he could pursue that intriguing line of questioning, Nate was moving on.

"The guys at the lab are good," Nate said. "I shouldn't put them down. They try. They just don't have all the facilities and experience bigger localities have." He turned to Micah. "Head out, scout. I don't expect to see you in here again before Monday, and then you'll take the desk."

"I'm fine—"

Nate silenced him with a gesture. "You know as well as I do that an instant of instinctive hesitation could cost you your life. As long as those ribs hurt at all, you get easy duty. End of discussion."

Micah had taken orders for too many years to argue now. Outside, he pulled on his Stetson and his mirrored sunglasses despite the waning afternoon light and peered down the length of the street toward the supermarket. Faith's Honda was gone, so she must have headed back to her ranch. He decided to follow and make sure she hadn't run into any trouble.

Fifteen miles later, at the turn onto County Road 118, he was berating himself for being a fool. If the woman was bound and determined to live all alone in the middle of the godforsaken reaches of Conard County, then why the hell did he care? She could have stayed in San Antonio where, despite her protests, there were surely people who cared about her. Hell, that Ranger, Garrett Hancock, probably would have hovered over her like a protective hen. There were hospitals nearby, emergency medical services within minutes, plenty of police protection....

Scotch that thought. The woman didn't want police protection. Didn't believe in it. Didn't trust it.

With reason.

And because of that, she was hiding out in the middle of nowhere, and Micah Parish, who wanted no part of such doings, couldn't put her troubles from his mind.

"Well, hell," he growled into the silence. He should have loved her senseless last night. It would have been easy enough to do, considering that she had never before enjoyed sex. He should have loved her until she was incapable of arguing with him about a thing. Then he should have made her agree not to go haring off anywhere until Frank was caught and the baby was born. At least then he could have kept a close eye on her, and Frank would never think of looking for her at Micah's place.

But he'd gotten mad. And she had looked at his furious expression and grown frightened. He couldn't blame her for that. Not at all. But when he watched her shrink back from him, he had grown even madder and simply carried her to her room, leaving her alone in the dark on her bed. Then he had gone outside and run out to the county road and back. In his bare feet. It had been just about enough to cool him off.

Not that he would ever be entirely cool when he thought of those stab wounds. If he ever managed to get his hands on Frank Williams, he vowed he would teach the man the meaning of fear. The kind of fear Frank had taught his wife. The kind of fear no human being should ever have to experience.

His hands tightened on the steering wheel, and he pressed down a little on the accelerator.

Of course, it was a damn lucky thing he *hadn't* made love to Faith last night. There was no place in his world for a woman, and Faith was the kind of woman who would expect to become part of a man's world if that man wanted to become part of her body.

She was not, he thought, like most women. He had lived among enough cultures to understand that between most men and women, a relationship was a simple social and economic transaction. In return for his protection and support, a woman gave a man access to her body and sons to look after him in old age. It was straightforward, elemental, necessary to the survival of the species.

But human beings were capable of more dimensions than those necessary to survival. If they weren't, he wouldn't feel the forces of nature like a rush of wind in his head. He wouldn't feel the passage of the seasons like a hymn in his blood. He wouldn't be able to imagine a bond between people that transcended time and space.

And he wouldn't now be feeling loneliness like a requiem in his soul.

Faith, bless her, had hit him right between the eyes with that one. In all his life—at least, all his *adult* life—he had never been lonely. Solitude and loneliness were not the same thing. Far from it. And he prized his solitude, but how could a man remain solitary if he started to feel lonely?

He didn't want to feel lonely, and he suspected if he ever broke down far enough to make love to Faith, he would spend the rest of his days feeling lonely. Of course, he could ask her to stay, but that came right back to the central problem: he didn't want a woman in his life. He didn't want anyone in his life except a couple of good friends who knew how to keep their distance. Distance was meaningless to women. They invaded a man's space and took up residence. They certainly couldn't conceive of spending weeks in silence and separation.

So he didn't want to get involved, and it was a damn good thing he hadn't loved her senseless after all.

But his body ached, his loins yearned, and his solitude felt suddenly empty. And it was possible, in that empty aching, to wonder why he had always lacked the very things that most men took as their due. Was it something in him? Was it something about his heritage, his sixth sense, his way of thinking?

It was him, of course. He needed a mate who could enter his solitude without destroying it. Such a paradox was impossible. No mere mortal could do such a thing.

Faith heard the Blazer pull up to the house and never doubted it was another deputy coming to check on her. She had arrived home at three-thirty that afternoon, and almost the instant she started unloading the car, a Conard County Sheriff's car had pulled up and Deputy Ted Waring had insisted on helping. When all the groceries were inside, he accepted her offer of a mug of coffee and advised her that she could expect a deputy to stop by a couple of times a day.

"That's an awful lot of interest in a single citizen," Faith had remarked. She wasn't sure she wanted such a close association with cops, although Micah had gone a long way toward easing her mind on that score—at least with regard to the Conard County Sheriff's Office. It had been a shock to realize, when she saw Deputy Waring, that she no longer felt fear when she saw the tan Blazer and the khaki uniform. Micah had gotten her past that in just a couple of days.

"Sheriff Tate takes a personal interest in everyone in the county, Mrs. Williams," Deputy Waring had told her. "Some folks need more looking after than others is all."

Before he left, he had given her another advisory. "Hal Wyatt owns the spread just west of you. Some of his best heifers wandered through a break in the fence sometime in the last couple of days, and he's had some cowboys out looking for them. If you happen to see some men on horseback, don't worry about it."

Now another Blazer was pulling up as night settled over the land. This time, though, it was Micah who climbed out.

There was no mistaking the bubble of joy she felt when she saw him. It had been years, absolutely years, since she had experienced the champagne of sheer happiness, yet here she was, feeling it now. Right now. Because of this man with his dangerous, hard face, his wild aura, his exotic eyes. This man who looked as if he could snap her in two with his bare hands and whose innate gentleness made her breath catch.

And without a single thought for self-preservation, without a backward glance at the years of terror and pain that had been inflicted on her, she let Micah see that joy. She flung open the door with a huge, welcoming smile, and before he quite knew what had hit him, she was in his arms.

The winter chill clung to him, and he smelled crisply of the cold and himself. His shearling jacket was stiff against her cheek, his leather-gloved hands icy against her back, but his lips were hot when they found hers in instinctive response to her welcome.

This, he thought, was what it felt like to come home.

He was a wayfarer. He had traveled beneath the suns of alien lands most of his life. As an adult he had risked his neck more times than he could count to preserve the ideals of the country that had deprived his mother's people of everything. Ideals that far exceeded the grasp of most ordinary men. Micah believed in those ideals. The American Dream to Micah was the Human Dream and the birthright of all men. That belief had carried him into dangerous situations with nothing but his wits to protect him. He had won medals, had a drawerful of such mementos, enough "fruit salad" to throw him off balance if he wore it.

But never, ever, had he been welcomed home.

Her mouth was hot, wet, eager beneath his. In this kiss she was a full-fledged participant, and equal partner in the dizzying thrust and counterthrust of tongues that spoke in ways clearer than words.

Then suddenly, as if they both simultaneously realized that they weren't ready for the implications inherent in their actions, they broke apart.

Micah listened to the sound of his ragged breathing, knowing that he'd just had another unwanted revelation. He listened to the ragged sound of her breathing and knew that she wasn't ready for any of this. So much for his famed control.

"How are you making out?" he asked roughly, to fill the silence before it grew uncomfortable. He needed to wall off that kiss into a compartment of its own, to prevent any discussion of it or apology for it.

She astonished him with something that sounded like a very genuine laugh. "I've been on my own for precisely five hours, Micah. I haven't had any time to make out well or poorly."

He glanced down at her and liked what he saw. The pinched look that had been so evident when he first found her on the road had magically been erased. Her hair, that mass of silvery blond fairy curls, was wildly tousled around her face, and her lips looked soundly kissed.

"Coffee?" The pot she had made earlier for Ted Waring was still warm on the hot plate, and she poured a healthy mugful for Micah. "Actually, I've begun to consider some of the logistics of living here. It suddenly occurred to me that I'll need my own snowplow."

"Don't worry about it. I'll plow your drive if it needs doing."

"I couldn't ask—"

"I didn't hear you ask."

Jason Montrose had died before Micah returned to Conard County, and this house had been built maybe fifteen years ago after the original ranch house burned to the ground. It was a single story building, unlike most in the area, built of brick. Micah looked around him, noting again the relatively new appliances, the gleaming no-wax floor. He would bet that Jason had done all this with his daughter in mind.

"Mind if I look around?" he asked Faith. Earlier, he had looked over the barn and surrounding terrain and learned the layout of the house, but he wanted to check out the house again. Years of training compelled him, just in case. *In case?* God, he hoped his sixth sense wasn't involved in the urge.

The house had been surprisingly dust-free, surprisingly well kept, when she had arrived. She had expected to find dust inches thick and all kinds of spider webs, even evidence of mice. Instead, she had found a dwelling that looked as if it had been vacated only months before, not years. Oh, there had been dust and some evidence of spiders, but nothing like what she had expected.

Walking through it with Micah now, pointing out things, her instinct was to be glad he hadn't caught her with the place in a mess. She took pride in her housekeeping, and even though she had barely arrived, it would have embarrassed her to have to show a filthy house.

But even as she was chatting pleasantly about what a nice house it was, unease was nibbling at the edges of her comfort. She kept getting the most unsettling feeling that the residents of the house had walked out only moments before and might return at any time. That was ridiculous, she told herself. Silly. No one had ever lived here but her father, and he had died five years ago.

Micah never entered a room without learning all the exits and entrances within seconds. It was an old habit, another one of those that was just too much trouble to break. He also liked to know whether the windows were locked and how well. Faith watched him check out every room with an intensity that finally silenced her, an intensity even greater than he had showed that morning. In the end, she just let him do his thing.

"Jason really did a fine job," he remarked when they returned to the kitchen. "Even after all this time there isn't the slightest draft around any of the windows or doors. Wish my place was half as airtight."

They settled at the table as they had done on other nights in his kitchen, him with his coffee and her with her tea.

"I hated it when Dad's old house burned down," Faith remarked. "It was years before this place felt at all like home to me." But it was only now, as she sat there with Micah, that she realized it was going to feel lonely and empty beyond belief when he left tonight. It wouldn't be the same as her apartment in San Antonio, where she could hear other people any time of the day or night. Here, there wouldn't even be a passing car to hear once Micah left.

"Where did you grow up?" she asked Micah. "Not around here."

"No. My dad was army, and I grew up all over the world. By the time I graduated from high school I'd lived in twenty-seven different places in eight different countries."

"That must have been hard on you and your mother."

"My mother left when I was two."

"That must have made it even harder on you." She could tell he wasn't keen on this subject, but she was full of questions, and as long as he didn't get angry, she wanted to ask them.

He studied her impassively, his harsh, dark features and black eyes revealing nothing. She wanted to know, and he was a little surprised to realize that he wanted to tell her some of it.

"I don't remember my mother at all. Somewhere I've got a picture of her, but it never meant much to me. She was a Cherokee medicine woman, or so my father told me once. They met when he was posted to Oklahoma, and I guess it must have happened fast, because he was only stationed there for three months. I suspect leaving must have been a real wrench for her. After a couple of years she bailed out and took my younger brother with her. Almost a year later my father said she had died."

"Do you know her family?"

Micah shook his head. "No. I don't know a thing about them, except that her father was also a medicine man. My father either never knew about them or forgot it all by the time I got big enough to ask."

"But what about your brother?"

"Gideon stayed with her relatives, I suppose. I don't really know. My father only mentioned him once or twice while I was growing up and—" He broke off and shrugged. "He's never been real to me, Faith. I never knew him. By the time I got around to being a little curious about him, my father had died."

Faith had the worst urge to reach out and touch him, but she suspected he would reject any gesture of sympathy. "So you don't really have any family, or any Cherokee roots."

One corner of his mouth lifted a hair. "Isn't this the great melting pot? I've melted, Faith. True blue American mongrel."

"Except that I imagine there've been a lot of people who didn't see it that way."

"Well, I do find it kind of ironic that my Cherokee ancestry seems a bigger cause for interest than my European ancestry. We all go back to Eve, don't we?"

Faith smiled. "So I would have said. I think it's a shame, though, that you don't know much about your mother."

"How much does anyone really know about a parent?"

"Very little, I guess." She rose and put the kettle on. "I sometimes think I ought to do something to make sure I leave some kind of legacy for my baby in case something happens to me. I've just never been able to imagine what that could be."

Micah studied her almost solemnly as she moved around the kitchen. He was still following her with those dark-as-midnight eyes when she returned to her seat across from him. "My mother left me a name," he said after a moment. "I think it's the best legacy she could possibly have given me, because I was able to carry it with me everywhere, and no one could ever take it from me. Not even her.''

"You mean the name Micah?" Faith's eyes were wide, interested, and she leaned a little toward him. "It's a beautiful name."

He shook his head. "No, I mean the name *she* gave me. My father said she gave it to me as soon as I was born and made him write it down so it wouldn't be forgotten. She called me Speaks with Voice of Thunder." He had never told that to a living soul. Never.

"Oh, that's beautiful," Faith murmured. "Oh, Micah, that's beautiful. And it's so perfect for you! I could almost believe that she was able to see you full-grown. . . ."

Micah looked away. "Maybe she did. I don't know. I never told anyone about it before."

"I won't tell a soul," Faith promised. "Not a soul."

Why the hell was he telling her all this? he wondered, and slowly brought his gaze back to her. This woman kept unlocking the private places inside him. One at a time, little by little, she opened the doors. Like a moonbeam, she slipped into the darkest corners.

A mortar round exploded deafeningly, and dirt flew everywhere.

Micah jerked awake, instinct and training both keeping him utterly still as another hollow crash resounded through the darkness.

Thunder. Lightning flashed brilliantly, blinding in its intensity. Damn, he'd heard of it, but he hadn't quite believed it. A winter thunderstorm.

He sat up and swallowed a groan as his ribs protested. Well, that sure explained the dream, he thought as another crash of thunder ripped through the night. It had been years since he had dreamed of being in a heavy firefight. Years.

The digital clock beside his bed said it was shortly after two. His body said he was through sleeping for now. He threw back the covers and swung his feet to the floor. The linoleum was icy, and he once again promised himself he was going to rip it up. The bare wood wouldn't be quite so cold. Or maybe he would put down rugs. Faith would probably prefer rugs.

The thought jarred him as much as the imagined mortar attack had. Muttering a choice word, he rose and began yanking on his clothes. Who the hell cared what Faith would like? They lived in their own homes, in their separate worlds, and he must be losing his mind.

He considered going downstairs barefoot, but once again his training intervened. A man wasn't prepared to deal with much without his boots on. Moving cautiously, he managed to get some socks on with only minor discomfort and only a couple of four-letter words.

Downstairs, he started a pot of coffee and then stepped outside. The air was cold and would probably grow much colder by morning, if the storm was any indicator. The advancing cold front would have to be strong to generate this kind of weather.

Thunder rolled hollowly again, and lightning flashed, burning an afterimage of his barn onto his retinas. Incredible. He hoped Faith was sleeping through this. He couldn't imagine that she would feel very comfortable with this kind of violence all around her the very first night she spent alone in her new home.

But he relished it. He reveled in the way the cutting wind snatched at his hair and whipped it around him, the way his ears burned from the cold, the way the air crackled with the charge of the storm. Each and every sensation was a keen affirmation of life. With his head thrown back and the wind grabbing at him, he felt so vigorously alive that he could almost sense the rush of blood in his veins.

Alone and alive, a solitary shaman without a people, without a real home—it was his way. *Brujo.*

Into the silence and solitude, into the stormy night, borne on the breath of the wind, unease came. At first he thought it was just the storm's restlessness, but before long he knew. Something was wrong.

When the feeling wouldn't abate, he turned to go back into the house, thinking that he would get a heavier jacket and check out the animals. He had scarcely taken a step into the kitchen when the phone rang shrilly. He reached for it immediately, sure it must be the office needing him for some emergency as a result of the storm.

Instead it was Faith.

"Help me," she sobbed. "Oh, God, help me! He's going to kill me!"

Lightning flared across the sky, and with a click, the line went dead.

Chapter 8

With Micah's phone dead, he couldn't call for backup. The storm's electrical activity cut up his radio transmission badly, and he wasn't at all sure that Ed Dewhurst was able to make heads or tails of what he tried to tell him.

He didn't wait for confirmation, though. He shouted into the microphone as he roared down his driveway and skidded around the turn onto the county road. The Blazer fishtailed wildly for a moment and then straightened out. There were enough dry patches on the pavement to make it possible to speed up.

His shotgun, fully loaded, was upright in the dash rack. Beside him on the seat was his holstered .45. In the glove box was a 9mm Browning with a full clip. A damned arsenal, he thought, and it wouldn't do him a bit of good if that creep used Faith as a hostage.

The Blazer seemed to be moving in molasses, though in fact he covered the four miles of county road between his place and hers in just about five minutes. Five minutes was a long time. Five minutes was long enough to stab a person thirty or forty times. Five minutes was long enough to suffocate a person. It was enough time to die a dozen times over. And he still had to get up her driveway.

Through a blast of static he heard Ed again, and this time it sounded as if Ed had gotten the most essential bits of information. He said he was on his way.

Faith's house was completely dark. Not even the porch light punctuated the stormy night. Nor was any vehicle other than hers apparent. Of course, Frank could have hidden an armored troop carrier behind the barn, or even inside it. And although the wind had been blowing, there were still too many tire tracks in the snow to be able to tell at a glance if someone besides Faith had come but not gone.

It was every cop's nightmare, entering a dark house with no idea how much danger waited inside. Micah left his shotgun locked to the dash, deciding the 9mm Browning would be of more use in close quarters where accuracy might well be essential. He tucked his knife into his belt, where he could have instant, unfettered access to it. In his left hand he carried his aluminum, eight-cell flashlight, turned off but ready, with the butt on his shoulder and the bulb pointed downward. As such, it was a good defensive weapon.

Thunder rolled again, and lightning flickered psychedelically. The storm was moving off, softening its fury.

He listened at the door but could hear nothing from within. It did nothing for his state of mind, however, to find the door unlocked. A twist of the knob opened it, and he stood on the threshold of the pitch dark kitchen, listening intently.

He smelled ozone on the cold air, and then on the warmer interior air he scented the musty odor of a long-empty house, the faint lingering fragrance of coffee, and the even fainter perfume of Faith's presence.

He eased inside and closed the door behind him, shutting out any extraneous sounds from the storm. A *plink* came from the vicinity of the sink—a dripping faucet. The refrigerator clicked to life and hummed. There was no one else in this room. His nose was certain of that.

He flicked on the flashlight and pointed it into all the dark corners, driving back the shadows. Nothing appeared to be disturbed. He moved on to the living room and again found nothing and no one.

Frank must have found Faith asleep in bed. Micah's stomach tightened at the thought. Half-prayers mixed with curses flitted around the edges of his mind as he forced himself to concentrate on what needed doing right now. She could be dead already. Or Frank could be holding her in one of the bedrooms with a hand over her mouth and a gun at her head, or a knife at her throat. He had to find her. Now. Every second might be critical.

The first two bedrooms were also empty, as was the bathroom. That left Faith's bedroom, the one she had pointed out earlier as the room that had been hers when she visited her father. A violated sanctuary, he thought, and eased the door open quietly, carefully.

Again he hesitated on the threshold, every sense straining to detect motion, sound, smell. Here Faith's fragrance was stronger, along with the sharper tang of terror. She was in here; he was certain of it. He was also equally certain that no one else was. Had Frank fled already?

"Faith?" He switched on his flashlight again and scanned the room. "Faith?" At least he couldn't smell any blood. Still, there were a lot of ways to kill without spilling blood. "Faith?"

A small rustle, barely a whisper of sound, like the brush of fabric against skin, drew him to her closed closet. Steeling himself against whatever he might find, he reached for the closet door.

"Faith, it's Micah," he said, and flung the door open.

In the brilliant light of his flashlight, he saw her. She was huddled in a small ball in the far back corner, half buried in clothes and shoes. Her blue eyes were wild with terror, and her face was as white as the driven snow.

At that same moment he heard the growl of a powerful engine approaching and knew that Ed Dewhurst had arrived. Reaching up, he keyed the microphone that was clipped to his shoulder.

"Ed?"

"None other. I'm pulling up right behind your unit. Where are you?"

"Back bedroom, west side. The house appears to be clear, but I haven't checked the basement yet. The woman appears to be unhurt but terrified. Stay where you are while I ask her a few questions."

"Will do."

Micah squatted, taking care to keep the bedroom door in full view. "Faith?" He spoke gently, as he would to a terrified child who didn't know him. "Faith, where's Frank?"

She blinked then, repeatedly. And the terror faded from her face to be replaced by confusion. "Micah?" Her voice was a small, shaky whisper. "Micah?"

"It's me, Moonbeam." He realized suddenly that he was behind the flashlight and that she couldn't see him at all. At once he pointed it away from her. "Where's Frank? Where did he go?"

"Frank?" She blinked again, and then her hand flew to her mouth. "Oh, God, I heard something. The storm . . . it was like that night . . . and then I thought . . ."

Micah leaned forward, touching her arm gently, beginning to understand. "Was Frank here, Faith? Did you see him?"

Slowly, she shook her head. "No. I didn't see him. I heard . . . the storm . . . ." Confused, she fell silent and shook her head again.

Micah keyed his microphone. "Ed? I think it was just a flashback set off by the storm, but come in and check out the basement, will you? The stairs are behind the door to the right as you come into the kitchen."

"Consider it done. Micah? You want me to call off the mob?"

"Yeah. I don't think we need anybody else."

He rose and hunted up the light switch. As soon as the overhead fixture came on, Faith relaxed visibly.

"It's all right?" she said, looking at him with so much trust that Micah felt something inside him twist. How could she look at any man with that much trust, he wondered, let alone one as hard as he was?

"It's all right, Moonbeam," he said gruffly. "You're coming with me."

Bending, he helped her from the closet and then held her close, letting relief and gratitude wash over him. Later he could ask her what had happened, but right now all that mattered was that she was safe, that Frank hadn't harmed her.

"You're sure you're okay?" he asked her. "Frank wasn't here?"

"No. No." A ripping shudder passed through her, and she pressed closer. "I was so scared. Oh, Micah, I was so scared!"

"Shh. You're coming home with me, baby. I'll keep you safe."

For once she didn't argue.

Ed Dewhurst appeared in the doorway. "All clear," he said.

"Thanks, Ed. I'll finish up here."

"I'll wait until you get outside, then. Just to be sure."

It was 2:30 in the morning, Faith was pale and shivering, and Micah could see no point in lingering. "Grab whatever you need for tonight," he told her. "We'll come back in the morning to get the rest of your things."

It was then that she showed a spark of spirit. "But..."

"Screw it," Micah said bluntly. "You can argue yourself blue in the face, woman, but this time you'll lose."

She tilted her head back and peered up at him. In the depths of her blue eyes he could see the moment she realized he wasn't going to be budged. Moments later she was stuffing a change of clothing into an overnight bag. When she wanted to dress, Micah nixed the idea.

"Just pull on your parka and boots over your nightgown," he told her. "We're going straight home, and you're going straight to bed."

He warmed up the cab of the Blazer before he would let her leave the house, and then he insisted on carrying her across the snow so the hem of her gown wouldn't get wet.

Once again he made her feel cherished and opened a deep wound she was only just beginning to acknowledge. This, she thought, was how she had once believed that men cared for women. And although other women claimed they didn't want this kind of caring, Faith admitted she had always wanted it. Independence was a nice thing to have, but there were times when nothing would do but to have someone take care of you. Not all the time, just sometimes, like now, when the small act of carrying her to an already warmed car made her feel infinitely precious.

But Micah was not like other men, she thought as they drove back to his ranch. Not at all like other men. Twenty-five years ago he had been special, and today he was even more so, as if life had honed him until only the good things remained.

Closing her eyes, she rested her head against the seat back and tried not to think about what had happened tonight. Micah had told the other deputy it was a flashback, and she guessed it must have been. A particularly loud crack of thunder had cast her suddenly back into her apartment in San Antonio. Until the moment she recognized Micah behind his flashlight, she'd been huddled in terror awaiting the next blow of the knife, hearing Frank's threats in her head.

Bitch! I'll cut that baby out of you!

Shivering even in the warmth of the Blazer's interior, Faith opened her eyes to drive the memories back into the dark places where they belonged. The storm was nearly over now, little more than an occasional distant growl and flash.

"I'm sorry I dragged you out in the middle of the night," Faith said. "I seem to remember calling you. I must have."

"You did, but I was awake." He glanced her way, his face shadowed eerily in the poor light of the dashboard instruments. "I'm glad you called me. I'd hate to think of you huddled in that closet all night."

"But it's so... stupid. Embarrassing."

"No." Without hesitation, he reached out and covered her restless hand with one of his. She immediately returned his grip, tightly. "I've had a few flashbacks. There's nothing stupid about them. And they're only embarrassing in retrospect. When you're having one, it's as real as today. More real. I'm glad you called me." He said it again, with even more emphasis. Then he remembered the unlocked door he had found. "Faith, did you lock your door before you went to bed last night?"

Several moments passed before she answered uncertainly. "I'm not sure. I don't remember. Why?"

"Not important." But it *was* important, and he would have felt a whole lot better if she could have remembered.

The night had begun to turn truly bitter. When he climbed out of the car in his own yard, the wind that nipped his ears had knife-like icy fangs. He carried Faith once again, setting her on her own feet only when they were safely in his kitchen.

"You don't weigh more than two feathers," he remarked as he helped her struggle to get out of her coat. "Are you sure you're eating enough?"

"I've never been very big."

"Do you want some cocoa?" She looked like she needed a little time to wind down. Her eyes were too bright, her cheeks were still too pale. Her hands moved restlessly, plucking at her white flannel gown nervously. Maybe she needed to do a little talking, too.

"I'd love some."

Micah nodded and turned to the stove. "Did you bring a robe?"

"I forgot." She sat at the table and propped her chin on her hands. "I'm warm enough. It's okay."

"We'll get it in the morning, along with the rest of your stuff." He mixed cocoa powder and sugar in a pot with a small amount of water and turned on the stove.

"Micah, really, I—"

He interrupted abruptly, without apology as he poured milk into the saucepan. "Stuff it, Moonbeam. Enough is enough. There's no way on God's earth I'm going to let you stay out there alone until your ex is safely back behind bars." He muttered a word that brought a flood tide of color to her cheeks, then turned around to glare at her. "I was a fool to let you get away this morning. Damn it, woman, there's a point past which independence becomes sheer stupidity and cussedness."

"Cussedness?" She blinked. "Plenty of people have thought I was stupid," Frank and her stepfather, to name two, "but nobody's ever accused me of obstinacy."

"Well, I am and you are." Suddenly he leaned forward and peered at her. "Are you laughing?"

A surprising smile curved her mouth. "Well, yes. I kind of like the idea of being obstinate. I've been such a doormat all my life."

He was trying to adjust to this unexpected side of her when just as suddenly as it had come, her humor fled. She hunched visibly in her chair and wrapped her arms around herself. "It was so scary, Micah," she said quietly. "I was so terrified. Frank wants to kill this baby."

"The *baby?* Why the hell does he want to kill the baby?" Some things were beyond the comprehension of a normal mind.

"Because it's *his*. He told me that I was his and the baby was his, and he could do anything he wanted to us. He was mad because I tried to get away from him, and because I was taking the baby." She shrugged one shoulder. "I don't know. He was mad that I got pregnant, too, even though it was his fault for not waiting until I—" she broke off and then continued. ''If I'd ever been able to figure out what it was that made him so angry, maybe I would have been able to keep from making him so mad.''

''Don't. Don't even think like that, Faith. It'll drive you crazy. Men like that don't need a reason, and they use anything for an excuse. If it wasn't one thing, he would have found another.''

She looked up at him. ''I know, but...''

''But you're human, and you keep trying to understand it. You never will, though. All the reasons and all the excuses don't add up to understanding. There's just something seriously wrong with the man.''

And standing here, thinking about it, made him furious. How could any man want to kill his own seed? How could any man want to hurt the woman who nourished it?

It was a stupid question. He'd been around the block more than a few times, and he knew what people were capable of. It might violate his every sense of rightness and offend his every feeling of decency, but somewhere there was somebody capable of doing almost anything.

Frank Williams didn't want anyone else to have his wife, including his child. He probably felt jealous of the baby that occupied her body. The child was a trespasser, an interloper. An invader.

''Well, hell.'' He was hardly aware of speaking aloud, but he *was* aware of the rage that churned inside him. His protective instincts were aroused like never before, and his innards weren't likely to quiet down until he was sure that Faith and her child were safe from that scum.

''Micah?''

Hearing her uncertainty, he focused his dark gaze on her and saw that he was frightening her. It must be there, plain on his face again, he thought. All the rage he was feeling, all the desire to smash something in order to make her safe. And it was scaring her.

''I'd never hurt you,'' he said flatly. ''Never. But damn it, Faith, I'm human, and sometimes I'm going to get mad.

Right now I'm so mad at Frank I'd like to bash his face in.
And I'm not going to apologize for the feeling, so either go
to your room or get used to it."

Scowling, he turned his back to her and stirred the cocoa. The milk was beginning to steam. Ready enough. He
turned off the gas.

"Micah."

It was a good thing she spoke before she touched him,
because he was wound tighter than a spring, and he didn't
like to be touched without warning. He always needed the
time to stifle his defensive reactions, to steel himself for the
invasion of his personal space. She gave him the time.
Barely. His muscles turned to iron beneath her fingers.

"I know you wouldn't hurt me," she said.

Slowly, battling the dregs of his earlier tension over her
safety, battling the upsurge of a different kind of tension
because of her proximity, he turned his head and looked
down at her. The absolute truth in her expression ripped a
hole in his heart.

This woman had far more courage than she knew, he realized. More than he had guessed. Not only had she struck
off into the unknown by herself, but now she stood firm in
the face of an anger that had made some of the world's
toughest men uneasy. More, she had the guts to trust him
when she had no reason to trust any man.

Turning toward her, he wrapped his powerful arms
around her and drew her close to his chest. "I'll take care of
you, Faith. I swear that man won't get near you." Holding
this woman, he realized uneasily, was getting to be as natural as breathing. "Now, how about that cocoa?"

Faith went to bed a short while later, but Micah stayed
downstairs, hoping to shake the restlessness that plagued
him. Tonight's activities had roused primitive feelings of all
kinds, from the violent to the sexual. He didn't have any
problem with his primitive side. It was part of him, like his
face or his hands, and he accepted it as a facet of his na-

ture. Sometimes it was useful. Sometimes, like tonight, it was troublesome. And when it was troublesome, he felt restless and caged and aware that with just the smallest provocation he might try to break out.

Another long, cold run would probably help, but he didn't want to leave Faith alone. He had a strong feeling that her night wasn't over, that the fallout from the flashback hadn't really hit her yet. She couldn't possibly shelve all the feelings the nightmare had reawakened without some difficulty. At this moment Frank's vicious assault on her was as fresh as if it had happened a few short hours ago, not three months.

She was probably, he thought, lying awake in her bed, staring at the ceiling with her heart pounding and her mouth dry, trying to tell herself to calm down. Exhaustion would carry her off eventually, but for now she had to deal with it all over again. Mostly she had to deal with the immediacy of the feelings. Because of the flashback, the muffling effect of time had vanished.

Thinking about that only made him more restless. He needed to do something, and there wasn't a damn thing he could do. Every instinct and urge told him to throw something, break something, bash something—preferably Frank Williams. Every cell in his body demanded that he *fix* things. And he couldn't. Lacking a target or any kind of outlet, he paced like a wild thing caged.

An hour later—longer?—he paused at the foot of the stairs for the umpteenth time and ground his teeth. This wasn't helping a thing. Not a thing. He would go up and check on her. If she was asleep, he would go out to the barn and clean stalls. If she wasn't asleep . . . if she wasn't asleep, maybe he could comfort her.

His boots rang loudly on the wood stairs. He hadn't carpeted them and probably never would. Another one of those defensive habits, not to muffle any sources of noise that could provide a warning. Right now, though, he cursed the racket and tried to tiptoe, not wanting to disturb Faith if she was sleeping.

She wasn't asleep. When he gently pushed her door open, he found her sitting upright in the middle of her bed with every light in the room blazing brightly.

"I can't sleep," she said unsteadily. "I keep remembering...."

He hesitated, unsure what to do.

"Don't leave me alone," she whispered. "Please don't leave me alone."

That much he could do. When he held out his hand to her, she scrambled from the bed and flew to him. His large hand swallowed hers whole, and the bones of her small fingers felt incredibly fragile. He wondered if he would live to regret this night, but that didn't keep him from guiding her to his room and motioning her into his bed.

She was getting into every corner of his life and soul, he thought as he used the bootjack to yank off his boots. Now, for the rest of his solitary days, he would be able to imagine her as she was right now, sitting propped against a pillow in his huge bed, with the colorful Hudson Bay blanket pulled to her chin. In the warm cascade of light from the small lamp on the table beside her, her pale hair was a wild halo, her blue eyes nearly swallowing her face as she waited. Trusting. That was what was really killing him. All that trust he wasn't sure he deserved, not when his body kept trying to remind him that she was a woman and he was a man.

Some remnant of wisdom kept him from removing any more clothing except his belt. For comfort he unbuttoned his shirt cuffs, but then, fully clothed, he stretched out beside her on top of the blanket. He hadn't lost it all—yet.

When he opened his arms, she turned into them without hesitation, finding a comfortable spot on his shoulder to rest her head. The bedside light remained on.

"Talk," he said. "It helps."

"Nobody wants to hear this stuff."

"Well, I don't want to hear it, either. But it needs telling, and I'll listen." His tone was gruff, but his hand was infinitely gentle as it found its way into her soft-as-silk-and-moonbeams hair.

"Nobody ever listened before," she said in a voice tight with choked feelings that ranged from bitterness to anger. "I tried to tell my stepfather, and he told me Frank beat me for my own good. It was a man's duty, he said."

Micah swore under his breath. "I'm listening, honey. I'm listening. It's a man's duty to protect those who are weaker, not punch them around. Your stepfather was wrong, baby. Dead wrong." God, he hated to think how that had undermined her attempts to find help. "The cops didn't help you, either, did they?"

"No. I thought they would have to, but...but..." The breath she drew was almost a sob. "They've got some kind of code about getting each other into trouble...."

He hugged her closer and dropped a kiss on her temple. "I know. That kind of thing happens when you don't know who's going to be guarding your back. It doesn't make it right. Every one of them who failed to help you deserves to be horsewhipped."

"I just...couldn't believe it when they walked away." Her voice was thick with the tears that still hadn't begun to roll down her cheeks. She needed to cry, he thought. She really needed to let it all out. "I felt so alone. So alone!"

He held her and rocked her gently and waited for the tears that never came. She fell asleep eventually, curled against him, and he continued to hold her.

He wondered what she would think if he told her how much he wanted her and decided she would probably be horrified and frightened. She had no cause to expect anything good from a man.

And then he remembered how just last night she had responded to his kiss and his touch. If he hadn't seen those scars, they would have made love right then. He was certain of it.

But no, he told himself. It would be wrong. He didn't want to get involved, and she was too emotionally fragile to handle an uninvolved relationship. Or any kind of relationship. He had to give her time and space to heal. And maybe, in giving her the time and space, he could get over this incredible urge to make her his.

He'd never felt like this before, he realized uneasily. He had never wanted anyone or anything quite this badly. And he had never gotten this degree of satisfaction from holding any other woman, from comforting any other woman. It was as if Faith were attached to his heart by an invisible string, and her every feeling was transmitted to him somehow, tugging and pulling on his own feelings.

They *both* needed time and space.

A sunbeam woke her in the morning. Blinking awake, she stared at dancing dust motes that sparkled against the incredibly clear blue backdrop of the winter sky. For an instant she felt like a child again, waking to the excitement and promise of a spanking new day. A sense of wonderful contentment remained with her even when she realized that she wasn't a child anymore, and that she was waking up in Micah's bed. Or maybe it remained *because* she was waking in his bed.

Her flashback last night had freshened all her fears, but sleep had once more muffled them with distance and time. What remained fresh in the morning light was all that Micah had done last night. He had come racing at her call, ready to protect and rescue her. He had drawn her out of her terror and comforted her. Then he had taken her home with him and held her through the night.

She didn't think her own mother would have done half as much for her as Micah had done since her car ran off the road.

And now she was lying in his amazingly comfortable bed beneath warm blankets with a sense of well-being she knew she owed directly to him. He had made her feel as if she mattered, a feeling that had been sadly lacking in her life.

Her baby stirred, giving a series of rapid little kicks and pushes right across the front of her womb. She's turning over, Faith thought, and smiled in pleasure at the life growing within her.

"Morning, sleepyhead."

Micah's deep voice drew her gaze to the door. He stood on the threshold, dressed in jeans and a red and black flannel shirt, and in his hands he held a tray.

"Breakfast in bed for the lady," he said, coming toward her.

"Oh, Micah," she murmured as he set the tray on the bedside table. "You shouldn't have gone to so much trouble."

"No trouble. You had a rough night, and you could stand a little pampering. Hell, you could stand a lot of pampering." And he had never in his life wanted to pamper anyone. He piled the pillows behind her, then drew up the chair beside the bed so he could help her.

"Face it, Moonbeam," he told her with a definite twinkle in his midnight eyes, "your lap is gone for the duration. You'll just have to borrow mine." With that, he picked up the tray and balanced it on his knees so she could reach it.

"It's a cold, beautiful day out there," he told her. He'd brought a mug of coffee for himself and sipped it while she ate. "When you get dressed, we'll go back for your stuff. I don't want any arguments about it, either."

"But it isn't right, Micah. I don't want to put you to so much trouble!"

"No trouble. Hell, woman, you're less trouble than a mouse in the house by far. And a mouse never cooked me dinner."

Her shy blue eyes lifted to his. "You like that?"

"I should have said so. Yeah, I like it. After living alone most of my life, it's really a luxury to come home and find a meal waiting for me. You're a good cook, too, so I'd consider it a fair trade, if you need to do something to keep from feeling like you're imposing.'' He'd figured that out about her. Her drive for independence needed to be assuaged, so he would assuage it.

"I also noticed," he added, "that you did my laundry and ironing. Now, I have to draw the line at that. That's too much bending and lifting, and too much time on your feet. If you try to do it again, I'll feel bound to take my clothes to the cleaners in town to keep you from doing it.''

She peered at him, gauging his seriousness. He meant it. "Okay, I won't touch your laundry. But, Micah, women all over the world work in the fields and . . .''

"I know all about the rest of the world. I also know about the infant mortality rate. No heavy work or I'll take you with me wherever I go. No scrubbing floors. No laundry and ironing. I'll concede on the vacuum cleaner, but not another thing.''

Impossibly, Faith felt the corners of her mouth lifting in an irrepressible smile. Even when he was being domineering, Micah made her feel good.

That smile was nearly Micah's undoing. He was putting on a good show of being a friendly, thoughtful guy this morning, but every cell in his body was remembering that he had held this woman's sleeping body for hours last night, and that he had suffered for it.

Oh yes, he had suffered. Throbbed. Ached. Hungered. *Hell.* He felt like the wolf in Red Riding Hood. Deceptive. Underhanded. Conniving. Reprehensible. This woman was beginning to trust him, and he was sitting here with a wolf's smile on his pretend-sheep's face while wanting to fall on her and bury his body so deeply in her that they would both forget they had ever been alone.

God! And he had the nerve to think Frank Williams was a crud! This woman had more than enough to deal with. She didn't need some oversize half-breed savage slavering after her. . . .

The thought drew him up short and opened a surprising window in his mind. *Slavering? Half-breed savage?* The words that Dawn Dedrick's rejection had branded on his soul. Was he actually applying them to himself? Was he actually assuming that Faith would apply them to him?

How many times had he heard those words in his mind and then walked away before some woman could actually say them? Why had he always assumed she would? Why had he never lingered to find out that she might not?

Because women didn't stay. Had never stayed. Not his mother, not all his father's "housekeepers" and "friends."

Good God, did he really think this way?

"Micah?"

He had turned to stare out the window as veils of self-delusion were stripped away. He suddenly felt oddly naked and raw. He had thought he knew himself. A man who spent so much time alone felt comfortable even with the dusty places in his soul. Except that there had been corners and rooms he hadn't even known existed until this very moment.

"Micah?"

He turned slowly and looked at her. Moonbeam. Fairy princess. The icon he had cherished in his shaman's heart through all the dry and empty years. But she was no icon, no fairy princess, no moonbeam. She was a woman who had suffered and was now locked in the prison of her fears, just as he was.

She was a woman whose gentleness somehow touched him in places that no one else had touched. He didn't know if that was good, or if he liked it, but like a wolf drawn by the brilliance of fire, he just kept circling closer anyway.

What he wanted right now, this very minute, was to lie down beside Faith and hold her close. What he wanted was to kiss her softly, gently, repeatedly. He wanted to learn her shape, her hills and hollows, with his huge hands, hands he would make as gentle as a man could. He wanted, touch by touch, kiss by kiss, to draw her into his world, into his passion, into his need.

She was through eating. He gripped the tray and stood. "Get ready. We need to get your stuff."

Faith watched him walk from the room and wondered what she had done to bring that desolate look to his dark eyes.

The day was extraordinarily cold and bright, and the glare of sunlight off the snow was almost painful to her eyes. Micah disappeared behind his mirrored glasses, and Faith thought she might be wise to get a pair of her own.

Once again she watched him as he drove and wondered at his self-containment. She envied his apparent self-sufficiency and wished she could emulate it. She couldn't, though. There was a part of her, she realized, that would always feel empty unless she could share it. There was a part of her that needed to love, and while she might never have the husband she dreamed of, she would now have at least a child to love. Maybe that would be enough. It had better be. Her need to love and be loved had made her vulnerable before, and she didn't want to risk that again.

Micah drove slowly along the county road, taking time to enjoy the pristine beauty of the winter day. There would be plenty of other days like this before spring thawed Conard County, but familiarity would jade the eye and deprive the view of its breathtaking quality. That was one thing twenty years with the army had taught him: to take time to appreciate beauty wherever he could find it.

"Look!" He braked gently and pointed off to the right. "A jackrabbit."

Faith looked but couldn't see it until it took flight across the rugged snow-covered ground. She was still smiling delightedly when the rabbit had disappeared and she turned back to Micah. "I'd forgotten," she said. "I'd forgotten how beautiful it is here."

As he turned into her driveway he braked suddenly, bringing them to a halt at an angle across the road. He recognized both his tire tracks and Ed's from last night. All the department's Blazers used exactly the same heavy-treaded, studded snow tires. Overlaying his tracks, however, was a fresher set from a smaller, lighter vehicle.

It might be nothing. It certainly looked as if the smaller vehicle had come back out. He hesitated another moment, then pulled the Blazer to one side of Faith's driveway.

"Micah? What's wrong?"

He glanced at her, but his mirrored glasses completely hid his thoughts from her. "Not a thing," he said. "I just want to check something out."

Probably a neighbor, he told himself, but couldn't remember any of the local people owning small vehicles. People who lived on the ranches hereabouts needed full-size trucks and four-wheel drive. Some of them owned Lincolns or Cadillacs, but none of them would have made tire tracks this size. This looked like the imprint from a Japanese car or truck. It could have been somebody from town, but . . .

He climbed out of the Blazer anyway and squatted by the tracks ignoring the fierce ache of his ribs. From his pocket he pulled a notebook and made a swift sketch of the tread marks. They were recent. One set considerably more recent than the other, hardly melted yet in the morning sun. Walking a little farther up, he looked for some flaw that would make this set of tires stand out from any other, but he didn't see one. There were a whole lot better substances for taking an impression than snow, unfortunately.

And it probably didn't matter, he told himself as he returned to the Blazer. No reason it should.

"Is something wrong?" Faith asked again when he slid into the vehicle beside her.

"Not a thing. I was just curious about those tire tracks. They're fresh this morning, and I don't recognize the tread. That's all."

"Do you always devote so much attention to things like that?"

He turned his head and looked straight at her. Tan Stetson, long black hair, mirrored lenses. Just the look of him was enough to jam her heart into high gear. So male. So virile. And for the first time in a long while, that recognition didn't strike her as a threat.

He spoke, his voice a deep, smooth sound. "For twenty-one years I couldn't afford to ignore things like that. Not ever. It's become a habit."

Her car was still parked where she had left it yesterday, apparently untouched and undisturbed. Faith reached for the door handle as soon as Micah brought the Blazer to a halt, but he reached out and restrained her.

"You wait here," he said. "I want to check things out first."

"Why?" She was beginning to get irritated by his caution and felt she at least deserved to know why he was acting this way.

"Why?" He gave her a faint smile. "Because I'm a cop, lady. It's what I do."

He unnerved her even more by removing the shotgun from the clamp on the dashboard. "You ever fired one of these things?"

"When I was a kid," she admitted reluctantly. "Dad taught me."

"Good. I'm sure you won't need it, but do me a favor and hang on to it anyway. It's loaded and ready. I'll leave the engine running, but I want you to lock the door after me. Got it?"

She nodded slowly, understanding that something had disturbed him. Micah Parish wasn't a man who tiptoed through life, and if he was taking this many precautions, he had a reason. Without another question or any objections, she handed him her house key.

"Lock it," he said as he climbed out, and he waited to make sure she did. When she pressed down the button on his side, she heard all the other locks click with a solid thunk.

He gave her a thumbs-up and then turned toward the house. She noticed that he pulled his jacket back away from his gun, and that he unsnapped the holster. And to think she hadn't even noticed he was carrying his weapon when they left his house!

He would have checked the yard for footprints, but so many servicemen had come and gone that the ground was thoroughly trampled. At the door, Micah tested the knob and found it locked, but loose. Ed had locked up last night, right? Chances were a neighbor or even a salesman had stopped and left upon finding no one at home. But Micah didn't take chances. When he opened the door, he was standing to one side so he wouldn't be silhouetted against the brilliant day, an easy target for anyone inside.

Then, moving swiftly, he removed his sunglasses, stepped inside and closed the door. The glasses had kept him from adapting to the brilliant outside light, so he was able to see quite clearly. The kitchen was just as he remembered it from last night, and the refrigerator hummed exactly the same note. The hot water heater gurgled quietly and then fell silent.

There was a new odor in the house. A sour smell. An unwashed body smell. Someone *had* gotten inside.

Micah pulled his gun and cursed his cowboy boots as he tried to move quietly across the kitchen. The odor was absent when he opened the basement door and peered down the stairs, so the intruder had not gone down there. Instead, he followed the odor into the living room. There a framed photograph lay facedown on the coffee table in a spray of shattered glass. Nothing else, not even the TV, had been touched.

Touching nothing, he moved on, certain now that someone had deliberately come to terrorize Faith.

Neither of the spare bedrooms had been touched, but in the doorway of Faith's bedroom he froze and stared in total disbelief. He'd seen a lot of terrible things in his life, but nothing had ever quite affected him as much as the destruction of Faith's room did. It wasn't the mess. It wasn't the holes punched in the wall, or even the word scrawled in red lipstick over the headboard.

It was the way her clothes had been slashed. Each and every single item had been pulled from the closet and methodically shredded.

Chapter 9

The sun had gone down more than an hour ago. Faith stood at the kitchen window of the Laird house and peered out into the night, wishing with all her might that Micah would come for her and take her home with him.

He was looking for Frank. So was every available lawman in Conard County. From time to time Ransom Laird called the sheriff's office and asked for the latest developments, and each time Nate Tate told him they were still chasing leads. Frank had been seen at Maude's diner, Nate had said. Just yesterday. Maude hadn't thought much of it because he hadn't asked any questions. He'd been a stranger, though, so she'd remembered him well enough to recognize a mug shot.

Micah had left Faith in the care of Ransom and Mandy, telling her that Ransom would give her the best protection available, but that since Frank would never look for her there, it was just an added precaution.

Faith understood his motive and was grateful for his care and the care of the Lairds, but the day had been an incredible strain. Trying to be polite and pleasant for hours when worry was stretching her nerves to breaking was almost more than she could stand. Mandy clearly didn't expect her to make the effort, but Faith had been raised to believe that no situation excused discourtesy.

Closing her eyes, she vividly remembered the look on Micah's face when he had come out of her house that morning. He had been furious, so angry that his face had turned as hard and cold as stone. Micah didn't get angry the way most people did, Faith realized. He didn't shout or yell or throw things. He grew quiet. Cold as glacial waters. Silent and still. It was scary. The air around him seemed to crackle with power, and she got the feeling that if he let go, nothing on earth would stop him. Faith had seen him that way twice now, and both times she had had the wild fancy that he might reach out and grab handfuls of energy from the very air like a sorcerer.

Despite that, she couldn't wait to see him again. Couldn't wait for him to show up and take her away with him. If she had half a brain, surely she would feel safer here with Mandy and Ransom. But even though the Lairds made her feel welcome and safe, they didn't make her feel as safe as Micah did.

"Faith?" Mandy spoke from behind her. "Shouldn't you put your feet up or something?"

Faith turned, managing a smile. "Probably. I'm too tense to sit, though."

"I can imagine. At least join me at the table for a cup of tea. I hate herbal tea, you know. And I'm still not convinced caffeine is bad for the baby."

Faith nodded. "But you don't want to take a chance."

Mandy wrinkled her nose. "Exactly. I've never been much of a risk taker." She put the kettle on the stove.

Just then Faith heard the roar of an approaching engine. "That's Micah." She turned and all but pressed her nose to the glass in her eagerness.

Ransom was suddenly beside her, his hair and beard looking like polished brass. "Let me make sure first, Faith." He was holding a shotgun, and he urged her gently back from the window.

It was Micah. He came onto the porch and into the kitchen looking weary and a little frustrated. Without a word, he held out one arm to Faith. When she came to him, he hugged her to his side. Even through her sweater she could feel the outdoor cold that clung to him. "You okay?" he asked roughly.

"I'm fine, Micah. I'm fine. Frank?"

"Not yet. But if a termite sneezes in the county tonight we'll hear about it. The man can't make a move, Faith. Not a move. We'll get him."

"Coffee, Micah?" Mandy asked.

"No thanks, Mandy. I just want to sack out so I can get on this first thing." He looked down at Faith. "You want to come with me?"

"Of course!" She was astonished that he needed to ask. "I'll get my jacket."

He watched as she hurried to the living room, and he managed to ignore the significant looks exchanged by Ransom and Mandy. Let 'em speculate, he thought. He was taking care of Faith because somebody had to, and he didn't see any army of volunteers lined up. That was all. And this damn sexual attraction he was feeling would just have to burn out with time. It was that simple, and he would be damned if he was going to complicate his perfectly simple life by letting things go any further than they already had.

He was still telling himself that when they were closed up in the cab of the Blazer and driving down the county road, Faith's tempting feminine scent wafting all around him, carried on the blast from the heater. He had never in his life known a woman who smelled so damn good. Afterward, he thought of that drive as twelve miles of sheer hell.

"Sheriff Tate said Frank was seen at Maude's diner," Faith said. "Is that in town?"

"Yeah. Right across from Good Shepherd Church and two blocks from Main Street. Not too many tourists find it."

Faith turned a little on the seat. "You think he knows the area?"

"Maybe. Maybe not. Hard to say." Hard to think when his body had decided that his self-imposed celibacy ought to end *right now*. Even his brain was trying to join the mutiny by throwing up erotic images faster than he could erase them. "He's been seen a few other places in the last day or so, too. Scranton's Service Station. The drugstore. He's not staying at any motel or rooming house, though." It really bothered him to think that if the storm hadn't scared Faith last night she would have been at that house when Frank arrived. That he probably would have shredded her with the knife, just as he had shredded her clothes out of thwarted rage. "Nate has a couple of deputies watching your house tonight, in case he goes back."

"God, Micah, doesn't it ever end?" What had she ever done to Frank except try to love him? Why couldn't he just leave her alone? It was over. *Over.*

Micah reached across the seat, found one of her hands and squeezed it gently. "We'll get him. If he stays in Conard County, we'll get him."

"And if he doesn't stay?"

How the hell could he answer that? "Faith, I'll make you a promise right now, on my honor as a man. I'll keep you safe, regardless of what it takes. I promise you that."

It was a rash promise, but he was fully prepared to keep it. He had been trained to hunt men across continents, and after twenty-five years of risking his neck for faceless principles, he wouldn't hesitate to risk it and everything else for someone he cared about.

But Faith astonished him. Before the sound of his words had even begun to fade, she turned toward him. "No, Micah. Don't make promises like that. I'd never be able to live with myself if anything bad happened to you."

Well, hell, he thought. He had every intention of keeping his promise, whether she wanted him to or not, but it moved him that she was concerned for him.

He felt a gentle touch on the back of the hand that clasped hers and glanced down to see her other hand caressing him, stroking him gently, softly, in the way no one else had ever touched him. As if he were precious.

God, how the hell was he going to withstand all this temptation? Not only did she manage to make him hornier than he had felt in years, but she was driving him crazy with the need for her gentleness, of all things!

That touch pierced him in other ways, too. It said so much that she wanted to touch him that way, that she felt safe to do so, free to do so. It made him want to touch her back, made him want to encourage her to touch him in other ways, other places.

Micah looked so tired, Faith thought as he helped her down from the Blazer and into the house. He looked as if he had missed too much sleep last night, as if he had been hurting all day—and he probably had been, from his bruised ribs. And after saying he just wanted to sack out, the first thing he did once they were inside, even before he took off his jacket, was to start a fresh pot of coffee.

As soon as the pot was bubbling, he turned toward the table, shucking his jacket with movements that seemed a little stiff.

"You're sore," Faith remarked.

His dark eyes snapped to her face and then drifted away. "A little. The second day is always the worst."

"Do you want me to take care of the animals for you?"

He hung his jacket over the back of a chair and looked at her, wondering which one of them was losing their marbles. She couldn't seriously be proposing to perform that kind of heavy work in her condition? He opened his mouth to argue with her, question her, scold her and then snapped it shut. It didn't matter, and he only wanted to fight with her to get his mind off the impossible ache in his loins.

He answered her question curtly. "I took care of the chores before I came over to get you." Because he had needed to work off a huge quantity of steam. Because he hadn't wanted her to be alone for even the short time it took him to look after his livestock.

She edged closer. "Won't that coffee keep you awake?"

"Moonbeam, *nothing* can keep me awake when I decide to sleep. I learned a long time ago to sleep anywhere, any time, under any conditions."

She watched him settle in a chair and lean forward, resting his elbows on the table while he massaged the back of his neck with his fingers. He must have refused Mandy's offer of coffee because he didn't feel like socializing, she thought, because he clearly didn't want to get to bed all that fast. It was, in fact, still early. *She* certainly didn't feel like going to bed.

Instead, she had the worst urge to reach out and touch him. She would have liked to rub his neck for him, to feel again the wonderful warmth of his smooth skin. She would have liked to sit on his lap as she had the other night and feel safe as only Micah had ever made her feel. His embrace had been engraved in her memory during childhood, she thought. Closing her eyes, she could still remember how warm and secure she had always felt when Micah snatched her out of harm's way.

That feeling had lingered into adulthood, and after the past few days, she didn't think it was misplaced. With Micah she was safe, and that understanding unleashed a whole flood of yearnings.

But he was tired and sore, and she was still a little afraid of how such feelings could enslave her, so she redirected her attention.

"Are you hungry, Micah? I could fix you something."

He looked up slowly, and just as slowly shook his head. "Honey, what I'm hungry for, you aren't serving."

"Oh." And then understanding struck. "Oh!" She could feel her cheeks burn.

He'd said it because he expected the truth to send her scurrying off to her bedroom. The blunt admission of his desire was a far cry from what happened when he kissed her and held her, and in the absence of seductive heat, he really thought she would run, which would be best for both of them.

But she didn't. Instead, she stood there staring at him with wide, startled blue eyes that were framed by a profusely blushing face and riotous pale curls. She looked, he thought inanely, like an alarmed Dresden doll, all pink and white porcelain. Fragile. Sexy. Damn!

"I...see," she said uncertainly. Breathlessly. Her hands curled into tight little fists at her sides.

"I doubt you do," he said drily. If she did, she would certainly be running. And sparing him this draining exercise of willpower that was rapidly disappearing.

"No, I...do see," she insisted in that same breathless voice. "Don't you...have a lady friend?"

He was stunned by that question and what it revealed. She was talking of physical needs that could be assuaged by any body, and while there were times when a man could and would settle for precisely that, it wasn't the kind of thing a gently reared woman should consider to be the norm. Unless someone had... "Did your husband keep a lady friend?" he asked harshly.

Her color heightened even more painfully, and she clasped her hands over her swollen womb, twisting her fingers tightly. She looked down. "Of course. I couldn't...I wasn't...he said..."

For a long moment Micah didn't move. He didn't even breathe. The coffeemaker burbled and popped and then finished brewing in a hiss of steam. He hardly noticed, though five minutes ago he would have said he'd kill for a cup of coffee. Right now he *could* kill, but not for anything so measly as a cup of coffee.

He couldn't leave her like this, he realized. The understanding sounded in him like the clear note of a crystal bell, whole and irresistible. He couldn't leave her with such a low opinion of her attractions.

The air became thick with portent. He could feel it, registering it in the depths of his shaman's soul. A cusp had been reached, a critical point of decision. There would be no going back from this moment. Whatever he did now, he would have to live with it forever.

Faith stood there before him, eyes down, hands knotted, and he could feel her painful vulnerability. She had, he understood, revealed something to him that she had never revealed before. She had exposed what she believed to be her deepest flaw. She had laid her soul naked before him, and that certainly must mean she trusted him not to wound her further. It must mean, too, that she was reaching out in hope of a healing touch.

And why did the gods give power to a shaman if not to heal the hurts of others?

The chair scraped on the tile as he stood up. He waited, and after a bit Faith found the courage to look at him again. She was so small, he thought, so tiny. How could anyone find it in him to mistreat her?

"I've got," he said slowly, "a burning in my soul, a crying need for a woman's gentle touch. *Your* touch. And I can tell you right now, Moonbeam, that nobody else will do."

She caught her breath and bit her lower lip. Her eyes remained fixed on his face, her expression mirroring a mixture of hope and terror. "I'm . . . I'll disappoint you!"

The words burst from her in a rush, and they were all he needed to hear. They conveyed her consent as well as her deepest fear, and her consent swept away the last barrier, the last defense, the last objection.

"Aw, Moonbeam," he said huskily, "you couldn't begin to disappoint me."

Ignoring her protests that he would hurt himself, ignoring the ache of his bruised ribs, he lifted her into his arms and carried her up to his room. When he reached his bed he lowered her feet to the floor and drew her comfortingly against his chest.

"I want you," he said in a rough whisper. "God, woman, you've been driving me out of my mind. The way you smell, the way you look, the way you touch me sometimes..." He unleashed a ragged breath. "I promise I won't hurt you. I promise I won't do anything you don't want me to. I know I'm big and scary, I know I look mean, but honest to God, Moonbeam, I'd never hurt you."

"I know." Her whisper was broken, a tattered breath. "Oh, Micah, I know." Slowly she tilted her head up and looked at him. "I trust you." She did. Oh, God, she did! Her heart hammered wildly, and she knew he must see that she was trembling, but as terrified as she was, she trusted him. It would be enough, she thought, to give him what he needed from her, such a little thing compared to all he had done for her. It would be enough, and if along the way she rediscovered the warmth and tingles that he had given her before, she would feel blessed, because she had never felt such things before. She would believe, just a little, that perhaps someday she could be a normal woman.

He bent and pressed a soft kiss on her forehead. "I'll be careful of the baby, too."

He stepped back and reached for the hem of her sweater, lifting it slowly. She battled an urge to stop him, not because she feared what he was about to do, but because she was suddenly conscious of all her flaws. Her pregnant belly was certainly no sensual inducement, and the red scars from the stab wounds were ugly in the extreme. But Micah knew they were there, knew she was pregnant. Hiding herself would be futile, because he already knew.

"I wish..." The words escaped her on a sigh.

"What do you wish, Moonbeam?" he prompted quietly when he had cast the sweater aside. She stood before him in a lacy white bra and her maternity jeans, an incredibly arousing sight. His body began to throb in earnest.

"I wish I were beautiful for you," she said truthfully. "Not all fat and—"

He silenced her with a finger across her soft lips. "I told you before, a woman is beautiful in all her seasons. Carrying a child enhances your loveliness, Faith."

"But it's not even your child!" And with a sudden, sharp pang, she wished it were.

He hooked his thumbs in the elastic waistband of her jeans and gently pulled them down, until the entire smooth swell of her abdomen was visible. He pressed both warm palms against her, as if cradling her womb, and smiled when he felt the faint stirrings of the child within her.

He looked straight into her eyes, a look meant to give weight to his words. "When I spill my seed in you, this child becomes mine, Faith. I mean it."

Before she could absorb his words or even react to his enigmatic statement, he released the clasp of her bra and her breasts fell free. The lacy scrap flew across the room to join her sweater, and then, while she was still drawing a quick breath, he lowered her to the bed and was tugging her boots off, then her jeans.

"Tonight," he said, "I expect nothing from you except your permission to touch you. I don't want you to do anything unless the urge takes you. I don't want you to feel that you have to do anything at all except close your eyes and experience what I want to give you."

"But you—"

"Shh. I want you to pretend that this is the first time ever, that you know nothing at all about any of this. Forget what you think you know, Faith. This is *our* first time."

Totally naked now, she lay on his bed and looked up at him. He had turned on the bedside lamp, but even in its warm glow he looked dark, huge, mysterious. Forbidding. And lying there nude, when she should have felt utterly self-conscious, she was conscious only of him, of his power, of his innate majesty. Of his virility. Suddenly, more than anything in the world, she wanted to see him as naked as she was. Unclothed, in his natural state, he would be magnificent.

Inside her, cold places began to heat, and deep in her center a strange unfolding began to happen. She was unfurling for him, softening, opening.

His dark gaze raked her from head to toe, but instead of embarrassing her, it heated her more. "Truly beautiful," he said quietly, and meant it. From the crown of her head to her impossibly dainty feet, she was exquisitely formed, and her pregnancy merely added to her womanly ripeness. She was a woman meant for a man's hand, a man's *gentle* hand. She was meant to be a vessel of love and life. She was meant to be the hearth around which a man could center his entire existence. She needed to be cherished and protected, and in return she would give him meaning, purpose and her loving, gentle care.

His chest squeezed with yearnings he had long buried and refused to face. Ignoring them even now, he turned his attention to her and to her needs. She was meant to be cherished, but she had been abused. Kneeling beside the bed, he bent over her and pressed a soft, warm kiss to each of the scars Frank had dealt her. There were nearly a dozen, some clearly superficial, others clearly worse. As his lips found each one, he heard her draw a quick breath and felt her heart leap.

"How can you trust me?" he asked, resting his cheek against her womb. His voice was rusty with feelings he tried to hold in check.

"How can I not?" she asked softly. He had cared for her tenderly since the instant he'd found her. Reaching out, she touched his head with her hands, caressing his smooth cheek, slipping her fingers into his long, soft hair. She gave him the gentleness he craved in the deepest places of his soul, and she did it without even knowing he needed it. She did it because it was hers to give, and it was what she gave best.

He felt that gentleness and squeezed his eyes shut, swallowing hard against the sudden locking of his throat. It had been a long day, he told himself. He was tired and worn. His ribs had ached like hell every single minute, and no matter how fiercely he'd concentrated on the job, Faith had been at the back of his mind. All day long he had worried about her, worried that she was worrying, worried that she was frightened. Hoping to God nobody told her what that man had done to her clothes.

Now she was here, trusting him when she had no reason to trust, lying naked and warm in his bed, waiting for him to do what men did to women, expecting it to be whatever she had experienced with Frank. Expecting the worst but ready to give it to him because it was what he needed.

Damn it, he didn't want it unless she wanted it, too!

And it was up to him to make sure she did.

Straightening, he pulled the blanket over her and then rose to his feet. "Do you want the light on or off?" he asked, waiting.

She swallowed but met his dark gaze bravely. "I want to see you." Her words were a tight whisper, barely audible, but he heard them and smiled. It was a warm, genuine smile, unlike him, yet somehow very like him. It was a part of him he seldom shared, and Faith hugged the knowledge to her heart.

He moved around the room casually, as if he were preparing for bed on any normal night. She had half feared he would stand over the bed and disrobe, making her absorb it all at once, but he didn't. First he shrugged out of his shirt, balled it up and threw it in the hamper beside his dresser. Standing there, with his back to Faith, he removed his watch and emptied his pockets, taking his time about it.

It gave her time, too. Time to soak in the glistening breadth of his shoulders, the rippling muscles in his upper back. Time to notice the old, puckered scar in his right shoulder. A bullet wound?

Then he strode to the bootjack, giving her a chance to admire his chest once again, above his taped ribs. To think that she had never seen a man so beautiful, or dreamed that one could be.

He was tall, muscled, broad-shouldered, narrow flanked, copper-skinned. He reached for his belt buckle, neither facing her nor turning away. She held her breath as he popped the buttons and yanked the zipper. The sounds were loud in a silence that seemed to have grown thick, as if the air were turning into molasses. He dropped his jeans and gave a grunt as he bent to free his ankles.

"Damn ribs," he muttered, and kicked the jeans aside. His legs were smooth, free of coarse hair. Smooth, sleek, powerfully muscled, the same gleaming, dusky tone as the rest of him.

He faced her then, a pair of plain white briefs the last barrier between them. Faith's hands knotted into the sheets, and she licked her dry lips, waiting, wondering, hoping, dreading. Nothing, she reminded herself, ever lives up to its billing. Reality never measures up to hopes and dreams.

But that didn't keep her from hoping and dreaming.

When she didn't shrink, cower or protest, Micah knew she meant to stay. With one quick movement, he skimmed his briefs off and slipped under the blanket beside her.

"Come here, Moonbeam," he said gruffly, and tugged her into his arms, tucking her snugly against his powerful body. So small, he thought again. So fragile. A careless touch could shatter her.

How good it felt to hold her! Without the barriers of clothing, her skin was like warm silk against him. She made his heart feel full, made his arms feel full, filled holes he hadn't even known were there.

She reached up and touched his cheek, and when he looked down into her blue eyes, he knew this embrace pleased her as much as it pleased him.

"You don't have a beard," she murmured, stroking his cheek.

"Nope. A convenient gift from my mother's people."

"I like the way you feel. So smooth and warm."

"I like the way you feel, too. Like satin. Like silk." Like all the forbidden things, all the things he'd denied himself and had been denied. Her womanly perfume filled his nose, her softness pressed him and made promises to him, and her lips beckoned him. Bending his head, he kissed her. At any moment, he thought, tenderness was going to incinerate in the inferno of passion.

But he wanted to hang on to the tenderness for a while longer. He'd known so little of it in his life, and this woman so easily gave it and evoked it in him. Letting it swell in him now, he kissed her gently, exploring the heated depths of her mouth with a coaxing tongue until she softened even more against him and answered in kind.

And then his hands began to roam, palms warm and rough against her as he quested over her hills and hollows. He sought to awaken in her the same hungers he was feeling, longed to bring her to the fulfillment he expected to find.

One of his huge hands swallowed her breast, stroking it gently, kneading it until it became an aching mound. When he felt her hands in his hair, tugging his mouth toward her, he knew fierce triumph. It was there, the need, the hunger, the human yearning for love and its release. It hadn't been thoroughly battered from her. Sliding down on the bed, he took her nipple into his mouth and sucked. Each pull of his mouth drew an echoing throb from his loins.

"Oh, Micah . . . Micah . . ."

Her broken sigh filled him with deepening heat and satisfaction. In a moment of honesty so stark it shook him, he faced his need and acknowledged the barrenness of his shaman's soul. For a young man, a good cause was enough, but he was no longer young. He needed more, so much more.

Shivering with feelings she had never felt before, Faith pressed his head closer and gave herself up to the inner storm. Something primitive and earthy was rising in her, something wild and free and never before unfettered. She wanted ... she wanted ... oh God, how she wanted! She wanted the fulfillment of dreams that life had never granted; she wanted the touches and caresses that she had once dreamed would bring pleasure but had only brought a cold ache and sense of self-disgust. She wanted the rightness that had always been denied her.

She reached out in need and found warm, smooth skin, the resilience of flesh and blood. When she touched him, when her hands began to stroke his shoulders and back, to knead his hard muscles and tug him yet closer, he shuddered, and a deep groan escaped him.

"I'm sorry," she said swiftly, instinctively, as fear swamped her burgeoning hunger. "I'm sorry." Frank had called her a whore when she had touched him, and then, when she had done nothing, he had called her frigid. She was no good at this. No good at all. Everything she did was wrong.

She tried to twist away, but Micah caught her and tucked her face into his shoulder. "Shh," he said. "Hush, Moonbeam. It's okay. I'm sorry I scared you. It just felt so good when you touched me."

Shock turned her instantly rigid. It had felt good? He had liked it? "Good?" she repeated numbly, lifting her head so she could see him.

"Good," he repeated softly, holding her gaze steadily. This night, he thought, was going to demand a frankness and honesty from him that he had never before given anyone. The women he had shared this with in the past had all been experienced enough to interpret a shudder, a groan or a caught breath. He had never before needed to talk about what was happening, how he was feeling.

His arms were around her, holding her close. Now, while her eyes were still locked on his, he brought his hand around and began to fondle her breast. Her blue eyes darkened at once, and her lids drooped. She caught her breath.

"Do you like this?" he asked, his voice a deep, quiet rumble.

"Y-yes." The word emerged on a hiss of breath.

Her nipple swiftly beaded, and he plucked gently at it. "And that?"

"Yes . . ."

"You liked it when I sucked on you."

She wanted to close her eyes in embarrassment, but somehow she couldn't. Somehow, as if he possessed a sorcerer's power to bend her to his will, her eyes remained opened and locked on his. She could sink into the dark depths of his eyes, she thought hazily, dimly aware that her hips had begun a gentle, helpless rocking. She wanted to sink into him. "I liked it," she admitted huskily.

"I'm no different than you," he said quietly. "I like to be touched. And when I groan, it means I like it a whole hell of a lot. You go ahead and touch me however you want, whenever you want, and don't worry about it. You couldn't hurt me if you tried."

But before she could test his assertion, his mouth had fastened to her nipple, and his hand had swept down to touch her between her legs. She was instantly caught on the arc of a welder's torch that seemed to burn from breast to belly. Her every nerve turned into a ribbon of silken fire, and her mind gave up any attempt to think. No one had ever made her feel like this before. No one.

He felt her surrender to the heat, felt her melt as his fingers stroked her dewy core. There was a time to take things slow, but he knew with deep certainty that this was not it. She was riding a crest of feelings she didn't understand, and at any moment they might well frighten her into awareness and reluctance. At any moment he might do something that jarred her with remembrances. He needed to move swiftly and bring her through to the other side before some self-protective instinct pulled her back from the precipice.

Her legs parted readily for him, and he settled between them on his haunches. Gently, he reached out and touched her soft, velvety folds with his fingers, watching her every nuance of expression, listening closely to the tempo of her breathing.

"Micah. Oh, Micah." His name passed her lips as a breathless whimper, and her hips rolled upward toward him. Her eyes were scrunched closed, but that was fine with him. Somehow he felt that right now was not the best time for her to see him hovering over her, a large, cruel-looking man with a fully aroused body. Right now she needed to find what was inside her.

He slid forward a little and lifted her hips onto his knees, her heels onto his shoulders. Her eyelids fluttered, but when he stroked her slick folds a little harder, she groaned and lifted toward him. Leaning forward, he pressed himself into her.

She caught her breath, then shivered, as she felt him enter her. A deep, clenching thrill seized her, and she wondered vaguely why she had never before realized how good it could feel to be stretched and filled by a man's desire. Deeper he pressed into her, pushing her legs up toward her head, but not too much. Dimly she realized that he had put them in a position where he could not possibly place his weight on her, where she could at any time thrust him back with a shove of her legs. He was making sure he did not hurt her.

Her eyes flew open then and looked into the fierce face of a half-breed warrior, a man who, despite his own needs, was placing her comfort and safety above all else. His face was a grimace of passion, and his restraint was testing him sorely as he eased slowly into her hot depths.

And then the wildness in her broke free.

Passion thrummed in her blood, and instinct took precedence over thought. She needed him. She needed his deepest possession. She needed him to fill her, take her, claim her, empty his seed into her. Separating her legs, she dropped her heels to the mattress and opened herself fully to his hunger.

"Deeper," she said hoarsely. "I need to feel all of you."

His eyes widened a little before narrowing again with desire. She locked her legs around his waist and pulled him closer. He leaned over her, on his hands and knees now, and sank slowly into her with a groan that rose from the soles of his feet. Hot. Wet. Slick. Her silken depths surrounded him.

"Micah!" She sounded frightened, but he understood. She needed more. She needed pressure he wasn't providing. She was afraid she would hang in this exquisite limbo between heaven and hell forever. He wanted to promise her he wouldn't leave her there like that, but his voice was gone, his larynx incapable of anything but the deepest groans of pleasure.

Slowly, cautiously, he stretched out over her, pushing his knees back little by little until his manhood was buried in her to the hilt. Still, he kept his weight from her womb, though he wanted like mad to feel her beneath him from shoulder to knee.

He moved. Gently but firmly, he pulled back a little and then thrust into her all the way. In. Out. In. The pressure building in her center was intense, causing her to arch against him in irresistible need. All of him. She needed all of him. Again and again and again.

"Micah!" A gasp made of yearning and fear.

"Easy, honey. Easy." He forced the words out and shifted onto his left elbow, keeping his weight off her as he slipped his right hand between them. His ribs objected, but he damned them and kept on. His touch affected her like an electric shock. Her eyes grew huge, and she bucked once, wildly.

"Micah?" Now she sounded desperate.

"Let go, baby. Let . . . go."

Her legs tightened around him, drawing him deeper than he would have believed possible, making him feel surrounded by her slick heat. Her heels dug into his buttocks, and within her he felt a wild, uncertain fluttering of muscles.

And then she rose one last time against him and the rippling contraction gripped them both, hurling them over the cliff edge to completion.

She didn't seem to want to let him go, so he eased away and then pulled her half onto him. Someday, he thought, he would feel her completely under him, breast to breast and belly to belly. Someday, when there wasn't a baby to consider, he would show her just where passion could lead. Someday.

She stirred, her curls tickling his smooth chest. "I never dreamed it could be like that," she murmured.

He smoothed her hair with a gentle hand. "Not bad, huh?"

"Not bad?" She repeated the words uncertainly, fearfully, and then lifted her head. When she saw the glint in his dark eyes, she smiled. "Micah Parish, you're teasing me!"

"Could be." He ran his thumb along her lower lip, realizing with something like amazement that he wanted her again. Right now. This woman had an incredible effect on him. First she broke down a few barriers that hadn't been breached in years, if ever, and then she turned him into the hormonal equivalent of a sixteen-year-old. Dangerous stuff. Dangerous lady. "I'm starving," he announced. "I just remembered I haven't eaten since breakfast."

"I'll make you—"

"No. You'll stay right here. I'll bring you something to eat. And tea. Or would you rather have milk?"

Downstairs in the kitchen, he pulled out sandwich fixings, intending to create a masterpiece that might tempt Faith's appetite. No way did that woman eat enough.

He froze suddenly, mayonnaise jar in one hand, mustard in the other. Well, he'd sure as hell done it now. He'd taken the woman into his bed, and since she was going to be his next-door neighbor, he'd as good as taken her into his life. Of course, she'd already been there, but not this way.

Well, hell. Didn't he know better? Hadn't he learned long ago that women were scheming connivers who—

Abruptly, he silenced himself midthought. What he'd learned about women in the past didn't apply to Faith, and he damn well knew it. It was because she was so different that she had slipped past all his defenses to end up where she was at this moment.

Still, this was not one of his brighter moves. Nope. The last thing he was interested in was a long-term relationship, and Faith wasn't made for any other kind. Stupid. Sheer, utter, incredible stupidity on his part.

And yet... Yet he was going to go back up there, feed her, and then love her with every bit of patience, caring and passion he could find in himself. He was going to love her until she never again was able to hang her head in humiliation because she believed she wasn't what a man wanted or needed. Until she never again thought herself lacking.

It sounded pretty, too, this noble desire to make her feel better about herself. The truth was, he wanted her like hell on fire. Again. And again. And yet again.

He wanted to do with her all the things he'd set aside because he had first needed to sweep her over the fortress wall of her fear. He wanted to spend hours learning every inch of her. He wanted to prop himself over her in the lamplight, touch her softly from chin to toe and discover every little place that could cause her breath to catch. He wanted to learn every one of her textures and temperatures and tastes.

And then he wanted her to learn him the same way. He paused in the act of spreading mayonnaise and closed his eyes against the swift shaft of need that stabbed him. He hadn't wanted a woman to touch him like that in so long that he couldn't remember ever having wanted it. That kind of touching was a drawbridge flung over an emotional moat. Dangerous. More than sexually seductive, it would be emotionally seductive.

It required no great leap of his imagination to know how it would feel to have her gentle fingers running all over him like that. He wanted it so badly that his mouth turned dry and his hands shook.

They hadn't yet begun, he realized. A blistering word escaped him as he faced what was happening. The two of them hadn't even begun.

And it was already too late to stop.

Chapter 10

Before going downstairs Micah had given Faith one of his flannel shirts to wear. He knew she would still feel miserably self-conscious with him for a little while, and he wanted to spare her as much discomfort as he possibly could.

He found her wearing the blue shirt, buttoned right up to her chin, although it didn't achieve quite the closed up effect she wanted, since her neck was a great deal slenderer than his sixteen-and-a-half inches. The collar sagged, revealing an enticing amount of creamy skin.

Funny, he thought as he set the tray on the bedside table, he'd never thought about skin color before, but he was thinking about hers, and he had to admit the sight of his darker skin against the paler canvas of hers was arousing to him. But then, everything about the two of them together was proving to be arousing.

Wearing only his jeans, he sat on the edge of the bed beside her and pretended he didn't notice her trepidation. Second thoughts. Hell, there were always second thoughts. He was having them, and so was she. Naturally. But just as naturally, he didn't want either one of them to do too much thinking before morning. That would be time enough to retrieve his solitude and distance and give her back hers. For now they had this one night, and they would be fools not to seize it.

Leaning forward, he damned his usual reserve and kissed her warmly on the lips. For this little while he could step out from behind his walls and give her the cherishing she needed. He could open up enough to let her know she was special to him.

His kiss was like the answer to a prayer. "Oh, Micah," she whispered brokenly against the astonishingly soft heat of his lips. She had watched him come into the room moments ago and felt again the impact of his raw masculinity, the burst of fright at his size and strength, at the harshness of his face. Her heart had started hammering, and her insides had quailed, unsure what to expect now that he had gotten what he wanted from her.

And he gave her this, this incredible, surprising tenderness, the amazing softness of a mouth that looked unyielding, the awesome gentleness of hands that surely could crumble stone.

"Oh, Micah," she breathed again, shakily, and lifted her hands until she could tunnel her fingers into the wild silk of his hair and feel the strength of the bone beneath. And after years of silence about her own feelings, she couldn't hold back the words another minute.

"You're so beautiful," she said brokenly, holding him closer, afraid he would vanish in a wisp of smoke like the magical creature he surely was. "So beautiful. Like the hawks in the sky, or the wolves on the tundra."

She heard him swallow and felt his hands knot on the pillow beside her head. He lifted his head enough so that their eyes could meet, midsummer blue and midnight black. Once again she felt that behind those dark pupils was hidden a light too bright for mortal eyes.

"Moonbeam," he said roughly. "All gossamer and silk. Too fine, too precious. You're going to blow away in the next blizzard if you don't eat something."

He shattered the moment as effectively as he might have shattered a brick with the blade of his hand. Her eyes darkened with hurt, and she looked away. In that instant he would have snatched back the words if he could have, but it was too late. She had opened something painful in him, and he had reacted instinctively. Now it was too late.

But deep inside, despite the hurt, Faith understood. She needed to draw some deep breaths and blink fiercely until she found her control, but she understood, and understanding kept the wound from becoming too deep.

Outside the wind kicked up, rattling window glass, causing the old house to groan. Inside, they ate their sandwiches by warm lamplight and gradually the instinctive distance he had thrust between them evaporated.

Micah spoke casually to her of his years in the army, confining himself to tales that would make her smile, and coaxed her into speaking of her summers in Conard County with her father. Clearly, whatever good Faith knew of men had come primarily from Jason Montrose. She spoke of him with evident love.

"I miss him," she admitted to Micah. "It's been more than five years, and I still miss him."

When he was convinced she wouldn't eat another mouthful, he carried the tray back downstairs. Faith took the opportunity to go to the bathroom and wash up a little. She considered getting her nightgown from her own room but decided that Micah's shirt felt better somehow. Comforting. And then she began to wonder nervously if Micah expected her to sleep in her own bed or stay with him.

Uncertainty swamped her and she hesitated, finally leaving the bathroom to hover doubtfully in the door of his bedroom. He was already there, standing at the window, the curtain pulled back in one hand as he stared out into the night.

So beautiful, she thought again, wondering why that word had disturbed him. Her palms itched to touch him, to feel again his hot, smooth skin, his bunching muscles like resilient steel as he hovered over her. Other more intimate places were already yearning to know his possession yet again. She would never, she thought fearfully, get enough of what he had given her tonight, not if he gave it to her all day, every day, for the rest of her life.

And she didn't even know if he'd had his fill of her and wished her gone.

He turned suddenly, a sleek, supple movement, and saw her in the doorway. His shirt practically swallowed her whole, the tails reaching to her knees. He smiled.

The smile brought her farther into the room, though she moved hesitantly. He smiled so rarely, she thought, and even more rarely did he smile with his eyes. His dark eyes were smiling now. At her.

"That shirt never looked that sexy on me," he said, his voice as deep and dark as the night outside.

Sexy? The word caused her heart to leap. He thought her sexy? She thought of herself as pale and colorless, as exciting as white rice.

"You're going to get a chill, standing barefoot on this cold floor," he said, as he walked over and picked her up in a swift easy movement, then tucked her into his bed.

That answered one question, she thought with a relief so strong that she trembled from it. He hadn't had his fill of her. Not yet.

He plumped the pillows behind her so that she could lean back comfortably, and then he sat beside her on the edge of the bed, facing her.

"How do you feel?" he asked. "Seriously."

She searched his dark eyes and saw that he wasn't kidding. He was genuinely concerned. "I feel fine," she told him. "Wonderful, actually."

"Nothing hurts? Nothing aches? Nothing is cramping?"

She shook her head, understanding the direction of his concern, and was so touched by it that her throat tightened. "It's perfectly safe for pregnant women to have sex, you know. Unless there's some kind of problem, and I don't have any problems."

Have sex? Had she actually used that term? That troubled him in ways he didn't want to analyze. Not right now. Not when his distance was vanishing in the smoke of re-igniting passions. Instead he leaned over her, propping himself on his elbows and catching her head between his huge hands.

"Sex," he said gruffly, as he gently ran his thumbs along her cheekbones, "has always been something I've had whenever I needed it, like taking a shower or eating a meal." He watched the color heighten in her face, watched her lips part as she caught her breath in growing awareness. "Making love," he continued just as roughly, "is something I may have done a half dozen times in my whole life. What I'm doing with you, Moonbeam, is making love."

He kissed her then, gently, intent on taking each step slowly, savoring each touch until they both went half mad from need. His lips molded hers, sucking, tugging, sensitizing, and then his tongue slipped into her mouth, playing a surprisingly erotic game of tag with hers.

All the while his mouth seduced her, his hands worked the buttons of the shirt she wore, and the next thing she knew she was bared from shoulder to thigh, and he was looking down at her, drinking in every detail with his dark eyes. Before she could react, he bent and kissed the mound of her belly. Then, taking care to miss nothing, his hands began to travel everywhere his eyes had already been.

"Shh," he said softly when she opened her mouth and stirred as if she might stop him. "Shh... You remind me of a rosebud, all soft and satiny, with so many dark, fragrant secrets hidden in your folds." His fingertip slipped into some of those folds, and he watched himself touch her with unabashed pleasure. "So perfect. So hot. So sweet. And right here is this secret little button...."

She gasped and arched, and she saw him smile in the instant before he bent and took her breast into his mouth. His hands went everywhere, traveling gently but missing nothing, until she felt as if she were lying in the center of a silken whirlwind. He was showing her all the secrets of her body, secrets she had never imagined existed. How could she have suspected that the back of her knee could be so sensitive, or that strong hands kneading the arches of her small feet could feel so exquisite?

How could she have dreamed that she could need to touch him back, that discovering him could become an irresistible drive?

When she plucked at the button of his jeans, Micah didn't hesitate. He rose and stood right beside her, letting her see what he had earlier barely let her glimpse. This time he yanked the zipper and dropped his jeans and there were no briefs beneath to maintain his modesty. Not that he was feeling any. The touch of her gaze on his loins affected him almost as strongly as a physical caress.

Kicking his jeans away, he faced her and waited, letting her look as she would. He knew how much he liked to look at her, how much he enjoyed the sight of her feminine attributes. He wouldn't deprive her of the same enjoyment, if she felt it.

She did. He was absolutely perfect, and the sight of him heightened her excitement. When she held out her arms he lay beside her on the bed, and when she pushed him gently onto his back he complied, watching her from heavily lidded dark eyes.

She reached out and then hesitated, glancing up at him.

"Whatever you like," he said huskily. "I'm hungry for your touch, Faith."

The words unlocked something inside her, and she reached out eagerly. It was like stroking a great big mountain cat, she thought, all smooth, sleek and wild. His muscles bunched beneath her caresses, almost as if they were reaching out for more, and little by little she grew bolder, especially when he growled and purred just like a sunning lion.

"Here," he said on a husky breath, and drew her hand toward his nipple. "Just like I do to you."

Understanding streaked through her like wildfire, and she took full advantage of realizing that he liked what she liked. He jerked sharply when her tongue touched him, and groaned deeply when she nibbled at him.

When her hand began wandering lower, he encouraged her with husky, hoarse mutters of "Yes, yes..." and he tightened like a tightly strung bow when at last her hand found him.

"Oh, Moonbeam..." he groaned, and she knew how much she had pleased him. And pleasing him, she realized, was at least as erotic as anything he did to her, and far more satisfying.

Suddenly he caught her beneath her arms and lifted her so that she straddled him. Startled, she looked down into his sleepy, sexy, dark eyes and saw the upward lift of the corners of his mouth.

"Like this," he said. "You're in charge."

The possibilities were already occurring to her, but she felt so exposed like this. Smiling even more broadly, he reached out and cupped her breasts, swallowing them in his huge hands. Pleasure zig-zagged through her like an electric current, from his touch to her center.

"Like this," Micah said again, his voice deep. "I want to see you. I want to watch you. I don't want to have to worry about you. I'm so big, Moonbeam...."

His hand left her breast, found her moist heat and touched her persuasively. She lifted herself and allowed him to guide her with his amazingly gentle hands. Moments later she was drawing a long, shattered breath and throwing her head back as he filled her. So deep. So hard. So big. So satisfying.

He was right. This way she didn't have to worry, either, and she could control every sensation. He held her hips, moving her gently until she seized the rhythm and began to rock against him in a way that made him moan and made the tightening coil in her grow tighter.

"Like that," Micah mumbled. "Yeah, like that . . . come on, baby . . . reach for it . . . ."

More. Harder. Deeper. Closer. Oh! Oh . . . She shattered in a shower of sparks and collapsed.

His breathing was as ragged as hers, his chest as slick with sweat, when she returned to herself. She lay on his chest, their bodies still joined. He had his arms around her and was holding her close. She couldn't remember anyone ever having held her like this, as if he simply didn't want to let go.

"Beautiful Moonbeam," he whispered, and buried his fingers in her hair to cup the back of her head and keep her close. For now he was past worrying about anything. It was enough to hold her, to keep her close, to know that later, when the urge rose again, he would be able to reach for her and know the miracle of her loving again.

He ran his hand down her back, savoring the feel of her skin, the fragility of her structure. So perfect, so tiny, and she had come to *his* bed, had trusted him enough to be vulnerable, had wanted him enough to reach for him. There was a miracle in that, never mind the explosive satisfaction she had given him.

Tomorrow, he told himself, would be soon enough to face the emptiness she would leave behind her in his life. For now, he didn't want to waste a minute of heaven.

"I'm crushing you," she mumbled.

"Faith, you're no heavier than the damn blanket."

Her head popped up, and to his amazement she was grinning. "Since when does a blanket weigh a hundred and fifteen pounds?"

"You weigh that much? I don't believe it."

"I weigh that much now."

He ran his hand down over her smooth flank. "I'm relieved to hear it. I was sure you didn't weigh anywhere near enough. You look like you'd blow away in a strong wind."

Giving up what was apparently going to be an unequal battle, she dropped her head to his shoulder. Her knees were supporting her so that she didn't squash her stomach, and for the moment she really wasn't any more eager to give up this intimacy than Micah evidently was. She liked the way he was stroking her back and bottom, as if the feel of her pleased him. He made her feel as if Faith Montrose Williams were enough for him all by herself, as if she didn't lack a thing he wanted or needed. The feeling was priceless.

Later he pulled the blanket over them, turned out the light and tucked them together like spoons. His arm cradled her, and beneath it he felt the stirrings of the life she carried. In the dark he smiled and spread his hand over her, to better feel the baby.

"Sleep," he said quietly to both of them. "Sleep."

Faith slept, knowing that she and her child were safe in the magic circle of strong arms.

During the night Micah woke. As always, he was instantly alert, instantly clearheaded. He was lying on his back now, and Faith was tucked against his side, her head on his shoulder. The whisper of her warm breath on his skin was a caress. Reaching out with his senses, he felt the air, searched the house, checking internally and externally for the cause of his waking.

A gust of wind rattled the window, and the house seemed to shake, but that was natural. Minutes ticked by in silence as he listened and waited, but finally he relaxed. Everything was as it should be, at least here within his walls. Faith must have moved or made a sound. He was not accustomed to sharing his bed with a woman. In fact, not once in his entire life had he actually spent the night with any woman other than Faith, or slept with her and held her while she slept.

He liked it. Or rather, he amended honestly, he liked having Faith here like this. He quite frankly couldn't imagine doing this with anyone else.

Closing his eyes, he gave himself up to the rare pleasure, keeping one corner of his mind attentive to anything unusual, but allowing the rest of himself to wallow in the warmth and closeness he felt right now.

He lay there feeling the darkness as if it were tangible. For years the night had been as much his fortress as his solitude was. Much of what he had done in Special Operations had been accomplished under the sheltering cloak of night. It had given him his greatest freedom of action, his greatest safety.

Now, with Faith lying beside him, the night was taking on an entirely different character, bringing back the magical sense of wonder and awe that he had felt as a youth when he stood beneath the stars and felt as if he could fall upward into the vastness of the Milky Way.

He remembered that boy with sudden vividness, almost as if he had been cast back to that moment in time. Micah Parish had once been eighteen and had stood beneath the diamond-studded black velvet of the Wyoming night sky, aching for things never known and lost, aching with homesickness for a home that had never been his. He had wondered and yearned and felt the ineffable sorrow of grieving for something he couldn't remember.

His throat tightened in remembrance, then tightened even more when he realized that Faith's hands were moving with gentle purpose. He opened his mouth to speak her name, to verify that she was awake, but he swallowed the sound. Determining whether she was sleeping or not didn't matter as much as not frightening her. Let her touch him as she would.

He was emotionally raw right now, emotionally vulnerable. He wasn't sure why, but for once he didn't fight it. For once he felt it was all right to let the floodtide of feeling wash over him, to give himself up, to trust.

Her hand stroked him as if she wanted to learn his every plane and angle, as if she wanted to memorize a tactile map of his contours. And she touched him gently, so gently, as if she found him precious. His throat tightened up again, and when he swallowed, the sound was loud in the quiet room.

"Micah?"

She *was* awake. Her hands moved boldly lower. He liked that boldness, liked that she felt comfortable enough with him to be bold. "Hmm?"

"Do you mind?" Her voice was a shy whisper.

"Hell no, Moonbeam," he said gruffly. "Seems like I've been aching my whole life for a woman to touch me like you do."

Her hand stopped, and he could feel her shift until she was looking up at him. Once again the night protected him from exposure. She couldn't read a thing, and he knew it.

"How do I touch you, Micah?"

"Like you care." The words were out before he'd made a conscious decision to speak them. Stark, truthful, they seemed to hang in the air. They could become a weapon, or they could become a foundation. Life had taught him that women used that kind of confession as a weapon, which was why he never shared his innermost self with anyone. He didn't know why he'd felt compelled to do so now, but he would have to live with the results, whatever they were. Unconsciously, he tensed.

"Oh, Micah..." The words escaped her in a shattered whisper. "Oh, Micah...I *do* care."

She turned into him, throwing her arms around him in an attempt to offer him the same sense of security and warmth his embrace gave her.

Her hand began to wander again, lovingly, no longer shy or hesitant, but simply gentle and tender. He liked it, and now she knew it. He remained wary—she could feel it, almost as if he were resisting the very silken bonds he craved—

but he remained still beneath her hands, though from time to time a rumble of pleasure rose in him.

This, Faith thought, must be what it was like to pet a grizzly bear. Even as she took pleasure in touching him, pleasure in his pleasure, she couldn't quite forget that he was a man, that he was big, and that he was dangerous. A grizzly could break a horse's neck with one snap of its powerful jaws. Micah Parish could probably break a man in two with his hands. She couldn't quite forget that, even as she held her grizzly enthralled with the gentle stroking of her hand, even as she reminded herself that he had always treated her with the utmost gentleness.

Her soft touches were reaching him in ways he had never been reached before. Sunlight seemed to be flooding into dark, dusty places as she made him feel treasured and precious. No one had ever made him feel treasured before. No one.

But gradually the tenor of her touches changed. He felt her growing need as acutely as he felt his own. Pressing her gently back, he sent his mouth foraging where before he had sent his hands. He felt the ripples of shock shake her as he claimed her with his tongue, but he felt, too, the ripples of profound pleasure. She cried out, and he felt fiercely triumphant when he heard the sound. She was so quiet, so inhibited, so repressed. He wanted her open, free, confident, able to shout out her pleasure or her pain.

The lash of his tongue drove her higher and higher. The sounds that escaped her became almost frantic mewls as she clutched at the bedsheets and writhed in the grip of his hands and mouth. "Beautiful..." she thought she heard him say once, and then fulfillment lifted her on its crest and flung her high, so high, beyond thought to pure feeling.

The ringing of the bedside telephone awoke Micah to the clear light of a winter day. Grabbing the receiver from the cradle, he dragged it to his ear.

"Parish," he said.

"Well, old son," said the gravelly voice of Nate Tate, "we caught the sumbitch just fifteen minutes ago."

Micah sat bolt upright. "You did? Where? What happened?"

"He walked bold as you please into Maude's this morning and ordered breakfast. Maude obliged him and then slipped out back to call us. He's being booked right now. I called the Texas Department of Public Safety, and I guess they're going to ask for extradition, so maybe we can get the bastard out of the county by the end of the week.

"Regardless, you tell Faith Williams that he stays behind bars until his extradition, so she doesn't have to worry about him anymore."

After he hung up, Micah turned and found Faith watching him with wide, hopeful eyes. She had pushed herself up a little against the pillows, but the blanket was drawn snugly to her chin, concealing her nudity. For some reason that almost made him smile.

"Frank's in the slammer, Faith."

She drew a deep breath and squeezed her eyes shut. "Oh, thank God," she whispered.

"Nate said to tell you he'll stay behind bars until he's extradited to Texas, so you don't have to be afraid of him anymore."

She opened her eyes, and two big tears appeared on her lower lashes. "Oh, Micah." Suddenly she forgot modesty and flung her arms around his neck, squealing with delight and relief. "Oh, Micah! I'm so relieved!"

He held her, listening to her mixed laughter and tears, and wondered why he couldn't shake the chill grip of premonition. Somehow, he thought uneasily, he knew this wasn't over, they weren't finished with the mess yet.

"I want to celebrate," Faith said suddenly, leaning back to beam up at him from a tear-streaked face. "Oh, please, I haven't celebrated anything in years...."

"Sure," he said swiftly. "What kind of celebration do you want? A party? I bet I could get a crowd together for—"

She reached up, silencing him with her fingers. It said a lot that she dared to do that. "I don't want a crowd," she said huskily. "I just want to celebrate with you."

Micah had celebrated many times in his life, almost invariably with a group of his comrades-in-arms. They had celebrated successful missions, their marriages, even the births of their children. Never, though, had anyone wanted to celebrate with just him. As if only he could add to the joy by sharing it. As if he were truly special. As if he were the only one who mattered.

"Sure," he said, putting a tight rein on strangely active emotions. "That sounds great to me. What do you have in mind?"

Suddenly she bit her lower lip and flushed a little. "I guess I sound awful."

"Awful? Why?"

"It's terrible to feel so jubilant because somebody's been sent to jail."

His face softened a little, and he reached out to touch her halo of pale hair. "Faith, after what that man did to you, I wouldn't think you were awful if you wanted to go to the jailhouse and poke sticks through the bars at him."

She glanced up at him from the corner of her eye. "You wouldn't? Really?"

"I wouldn't. Really. I definitely think a celebration's in order. Champagne is out of the question, but maybe we can drive over to Laramie for the day and find something to do."

"Wonderful! But I need to go home and get something decent to wear. I only brought one change of clothes."

Well, hell, Micah thought. He hated to do this, but he didn't see any way around it. Why did he have to be the one to inflict Frank's final blow?

He settled back against the pillows, tugging her down with him so that he could hug her and see her at the same time. Her expression was expectant, smiling, still flushed with the joy of her fresh liberation from terror. Hell!

"Faith, I'm afraid you don't have any clothes at home anymore. Frank ruined them."

The joy faded, to be replaced by the all-too-familiar pinched look of fear. "Ruined them?" she repeated hesitantly. "All my maternity clothes? Not that there were very many. It seemed silly to spend a lot of money on clothes I'd only wear for a few...*all* my clothes?" She bit her lip and blinked hard. "What did he do? Burn them? He did that once before and made me wear the same clothes for a... Did he burn them?"

He looked away and wished she hadn't asked that. He really wished she hadn't asked that. He'd been planning to get over there and clean up the mess before she saw it. Why couldn't she be satisfied with knowing the clothes were ruined? Why did she have to know exactly how? Why couldn't he simply lie about it? Because he had never in his life consciously lied about anything. Because she didn't deserve to be treated like a child, however much he might want to protect her.

He tightened his arm around her and felt her child stir against his hip. The incredible, wonderful miracle of life. Why did folks always have to muck it up somehow? "He cut your clothes up pretty bad," Micah said finally, avoiding the word *slashed*, even though it had been the first to spring to mind when he saw the destruction. "Anyhow," he added, trying to move past the matter quickly, "I'll wash out your things this morning, and maybe we can find a place at the mall in Laramie to get you some new clothes."

Slowly he turned his head again to look down at her and found she was lying stiff and still, worrying her lower lip with her teeth, her eyes tightly closed.

"Aw, babe," he said huskily, suddenly feeling totally helpless. A moment ago she had been so jubilant, and now she was lost and afraid all over again. He wanted so badly to make it all go away, but he couldn't.

"M-Micah?" Her eyes popped open suddenly, wide, luminous with tears she kept blinking back.

"Yes, Moonbeam?" He shoveled his hand into her hair and tried to soothe her by gently stroking his fingers against her scalp.

"I don't think it's e-ever going to g-go away completely. Not ever."

"It will. Believe me, it will. You should be feeling a whole lot better already, with the man in prison."

"I thought I was safe last time he was in jail!"

There wasn't any way he could argue with that. "I know," he said finally. "I know."

Her hands tightened on his shoulders, and he responded by tightening his arms around her. "At least," he said after a moment, "at least right now we know where he is. At least, right now, you don't have to be afraid."

She pressed her face hard into the hollow of his broad shoulder, and he felt her tears scald his skin. Too much, he thought. She had been through just too damn much. Even her moment of joy was shadowed. How could one slender, fragile woman withstand so much? How could she just keep taking blow after blow?

"I'm sorry," she said brokenly. "I'm sorry. I never cry...."

"Damn it, woman, don't you dare apologize to me for crying!" Great, now he was losing his patience. Torn by her pain, he was blowing his cool. Wonderful. Next thing he knew, Faith would be cowering from *him*. But somehow he just couldn't shut up. "You've been through more than anybody should have to endure. You've survived, and you've come through strong, whether you know it or not. If you need to cry a little—well, hell, woman, people have murdered for less! What's a couple of tears?"

Instead of shrinking from him, she burrowed even closer, and he held her for a long, long time. It would be all right, he told himself grimly. Somehow, by God, he would make it all right.

Chapter 11

Washing Faith's clothes had been quite an experience, Micah thought in bemusement hours later as he sat in the concourse of the mall and watched her hunt through the clothing racks in the store facing him. He'd insisted on doing the washing himself while she sat at his table wrapped in the Hudson Bay blanket and drinking tea. He hadn't bargained on the tininess of the articles. He was accustomed to doing his own laundry, which was full of large, sturdy items. He hadn't been prepared for the fragile wisps of her lace panties and bra, or how small even her maternity sweater was. Awe and sensual pleasure were not two feelings he expected to experience at the washing machine.

Watching her now, he suspected she was on a tight budget. He would have liked to help her out, would have loved to buy her every pretty thing she saw. And he could afford to, because he'd always been thrifty with his earnings and had invested wisely over the years. He could buy her those things without blinking, but he wasn't sure how she would take it.

Damn her independence, he thought with something between affectionate amusement and frustration. She reminded him of a feisty kitten, all sharp little claws and determination. He admired her for it, but she kept frustrating his protective instincts. And around her, his protective instincts rose sky high. Frank might have battered her, Micah thought now, but he sure as hell hadn't killed her spirit. She would be all right. He didn't know if his nerves would survive her recovery, though.

She was hesitating over a cardigan sweater, he saw, a gentle lavender color that would suit her perfectly. Probably too expensive, he thought, watching her return it to the rack. The reluctance in her movement brought him to his feet and into the store.

"I liked that sweater," he told her as he came up beside her. He saw the look on the saleswoman's face, and it would have taken a moron not to know what she was thinking of the big bad Indian hovering over the tiny Dresden doll. He recognized the look but ignored it, as he'd been ignoring such things all his life.

"It's nice, but really, Micah, it's too expensive, and I don't need it," Faith said. "I'm buying that blue one."

"Lavender's your color, though."

She looked up at him and smiled, a glow in her eyes that plucked utterly new feelings out of his soul. "You think so?"

"I know so. Let me get it for you. Call it an early Christmas present."

"But..."

He shook his head slowly and smiled at her. "If you don't let me get it for you now, I'll just have to come back on my next day off to buy it. What a waste of a trip."

The saleswoman waited on him as if he were a contagious disease. He hardly noticed. Some things mattered and some things didn't, and this saleswoman was definitely in the latter category.

Later, though, as he helped Faith carry her purchases out to the Blazer, she remarked, "I wonder what got into that salesclerk. She was so friendly at first."

Micah opened the back of the Blazer and dumped his bundles inside. Then he turned and took Faith's from her, tossing them in after.

"I guess," he said slowly as he locked the tailgate with his key, "she doesn't like Indians."

Faith drew a sharp breath. For a moment he hesitated, not wanting to see whatever was written on her face, uncertain of what he might find. At last, though, he turned his head. Slowly. And looked down into a pair of very blue, very indignant, very pained eyes.

"You get this all the time, don't you?" she asked.

He tilted his head a little, not quite a nod, not quite a shrug or a dismissal. Just an acknowledgment.

"Doesn't it make you mad, Micah?"

"Not since I was a kid."

"But..." She trailed off, uncertain how to express herself.

"Moonbeam, getting angry doesn't do a damn bit of good. It doesn't fix a thing, it doesn't change a single mind. All it does is eat a hole in my stomach. Now, if you don't mind being stared at because you're hanging around with a big, ugly Indian, let's go find a place to eat."

He guessed she didn't mind, because when they entered a restaurant fifteen minutes later, her arm was tucked securely through his, and her head was held high in an unmistakable challenge. Micah smiled inwardly and ached a little as he realized that this small, frightened woman was teaching him what it meant to be cherished.

He'd been in this particular restaurant on several occasions with Nate Tate when they'd come into Laramie on business, and he already knew he wouldn't encounter any trouble from the staff. He'd chosen it specifically for that reason, because he wanted Faith to eat a good meal, not spend all her time being indignant about the way somebody spoke to him.

The menu was a good one, full of the plain, hearty foods he preferred. The waitress was a friendly redhead who remembered him from other visits, and gradually he saw Faith begin to relax again.

"Don't be defensive for me, Faith," he told her. "It really doesn't bother me, and you're beating your brains out against a brick wall if you try to argue with bigotry."

"It has to bother you, Micah," she argued. "It *has* to."

"It did, once upon a time. Not any more. Moonbeam, listen. I've lived all over the world, thanks to Uncle Sam, and I can tell you one thing for sure—damn near *everybody* is bigoted about *somebody.*

"In the army I got quite an education in psychological warfare, and some of it was like having a light come on in my head. One of our instructors explained bigotry as a leftover genetic component of the race from the days of tribalism, when there were just two groups of people, us and them. Fear of outsiders still operates at an instinctive level."

He smiled up at the waitress as she placed their plates in front of them and then resumed his discourse. "In my case, it's even worse because chances are the people who see me today were hearing from granny, or great-granny, how she lived in terror of losing her scalp. After I got to thinking about it like that, it stopped bothering me." And he was running on like motor mouth again. He'd been doing that a lot since Faith arrived. Falling silent, he watched her slice into her steak. "*Your* scalp," he heard himself say suddenly, "sure would have been a prize."

She looked up, startled, and then laughed. God, how he loved to hear her laugh. And it struck him suddenly that right now, at this moment, she was no longer afraid of him, that she was willing, like a tigress, to take on the world to protect *him.*

Well, hell. He didn't like the feeling. It made his throat tighten, for one thing, and it made other things inside him feel ... different. Damn, he thought longingly, what had happened to his distance? What had happened to that carefully maintained space between him and the rest of the world?

He had the worst urge to get out of there, to go back to his ranch and run barefoot in the icy snow, to run naked in the cold until the soft, warm feelings were frozen out of him.

Coward. He was a damn coward. He could handle this. Hell, he'd handled far worse than a crazy desire to let a woman curl up in all the empty corners of his life. It was just a temporary aberration, he told himself. She had her life, and he had his, and now that Frank Williams was caught, they would both go their separate ways again. After all, no Dresden doll, no vision of moonbeams and gossamer, would settle for a hardened, used-up half-breed. Just as soon as she realized she was safe, just as soon as she understood that she no longer needed protection, she would gladly give him back his distance.

He had planned on suggesting a movie, but Faith was looking tired by the time they finished dinner. Neither of them had slept much last night, and Faith was pregnant besides. As soon as he paid the bill, he bundled her into the car and turned them back toward Conard County.

When Faith yawned for the second time, he coaxed her into stretching out on the seat and resting her head on his thigh. She fell asleep in moments, and he was alone again in the dark, with nothing ahead of him but a long gray ribbon of empty road.

Faith awoke in a state of total terror. Strong hands gripped her and were lifting her in the darkness, like the night that ... the night that ...

She screamed.

"It's okay, Moonbeam. It's okay. Shush, honey. Easy..."

Micah. Oh, God, it was Micah. Drawing deep gulps of blessed air, she turned into him, let him lift her from the car and carry her toward the house. "I'm sorry," she whispered raggedly. "I'm sorry."

"Forget it. You've been through hell, woman. It takes time to get over it. That's all. Just time and patience."

He would know, Faith thought suddenly as he climbed the steps. He knew what it was like, didn't he? He'd been nearly buried alive, tormented while he was helpless, tormented for days by men who must have seemed demented.

He knew.

Releasing the last of her terror with a shuddering sigh, she turned her face into the fragrant warmth of his neck. They passed through the darkened kitchen and started climbing the stairs.

"You know what I wish?" she whispered. "I wish I could have been there for you the way you've been here for me."

He didn't answer immediately, just continued climbing steadily while she soaked up his heat and listened to the thud of his steadily beating heart. Even that heartbeat was a strong, contained sound, she thought dreamily. It was with gladness that she realized he had carried her into his room, not hers.

Micah lowered her onto his bed and pulled her boots off. They fell with a thud to the floor, and then he reached out to turn on the lamp, to drive the night away.

"I'll go down and get your clothes," he said. "Want anything else?"

She shook her head, studying him from strangely solemn eyes.

He gave her a brief nod and headed out of the room. At the door, though, he hesitated, then said over his shoulder, "You were there for me, Moonbeam. You were there."

Leaving her feeling utterly confused behind him, he stomped down the stairs and decided that finally, after years of suspecting it, he was at last utterly losing his mind. Why had he ever admitted such a thing? It was crazy. Totally crazy!

But as he stomped down those stairs through his dark house and out into the cold winter night, he remembered being twenty years old. He remembered being in excruciating pain and in a state of terror so total it defied description. He remembered standing in that hole in the darkness, expecting to die at any moment, knowing that at any time the trap door above his head might open to unleash another hail of dirt and offal onto his head. He remembered thinking that if he accomplished nothing else, he wanted to die unbroken.

Pressing his palms against the tailgate of the Blazer, he locked his elbows and leaned against the vehicle, head down. She'd been there. Her little girl's voice had called him out of that hole and tugged him back to Conard County. Memories of that summer, memories of teaching Faith to ride and swim, to throw a lasso and catch a fish, had kept him sane. He had, quite simply, closed his eyes to what was really happening and relived the best summer of his life.

It had been the best summer of his life because of Faith. Without her, he would have been just another inexperienced, underpaid cowpoke on the Montrose ranch. Instead, she had drawn him to her father's attention, had drawn him into an almost-family. Jason Montrose had treated him like a son, and Faith Montrose had treated him like an adored older brother, and for ten short weeks Micah Parish had known what it meant to belong.

He hadn't been able to keep his emotional distance from that little girl, so what in hell had made him think he could keep his distance from the woman she'd become? She had grown up, she had changed, she was in no way like the child he remembered, but she still had the power to fascinate him, although the fascination was of an utterly different character now.

An utterly different character, he thought again, and straightened. It was cold out here, a cold that was making him feel lonely, and if he had an ounce of the sense he had always believed he owned, he would be inside thawing his soul against Faith's warmth. Whatever distance he'd had was shot, whatever solitude he'd once preserved had vanished, and he might as well just take pleasure in whatever good came his way. There would always be time later to deal with the inevitable pain.

The shower was running when Micah returned upstairs. He would like to shower with her, he thought as he set the bags containing her clothes to one side. He would like to get under that hot spray, soap her all over, then have her soap him. He didn't have the slightest difficulty imagining just how she would feel, all shivery and slick against him.

Whoa!

No way. That kind of thing would be dangerous as hell when she was so pregnant.

He smiled slowly, realizing that it had been years since he had felt as playful as he did at this moment. And if he felt playful, why not play?

Faith turned beneath the shower spray and squeaked when she saw Micah watching her. He'd pulled the curtain back a little at the other end of the tub, and just his head and one gleaming shoulder were visible as he leaned in and watched her with the strangest smile on his face.

"Sorry," he said. "I didn't mean to startle you."

She gave an unsteady little laugh. "I just didn't expect to see anyone...."

"Why not? Did you think I could resist a chance to see all this beauty?" His smile broadened.

"I'm not beautiful."

"Maybe not to someone else, but to me, you are most definitely beautiful. Exquisite. A fairy tale princess."

Another protest died on her lips as he stuck his arm into the enclosure with her and reached out to touch one of her nipples ever so lightly with the tip of his index finger. At once both her nipples rose and swelled in response.

Impossibly, his voice seemed to have dropped another octave when he spoke, sounding now as deep as a distant rumble of thunder. "Perfect," he said. "Absolutely perfect." His finger trailed down to trace a circle on her belly. "A fertility goddess." Slowly, he raised his gaze to her face. "Do you suppose you might be about ready to get out of there?"

She supposed she was about ready to collapse. She had known terror could make her knees weak, but she had never guessed desire could do it, too. Micah steadied her as she stepped over the edge of the tub onto the mat, then toweled her dry with exquisite care.

He was wearing only his jeans now, and Faith leaned over him, gripping the smooth strength of his broad shoulders for support. This, she thought as he lifted her foot and dried it with breath-stealing gentleness, was the way it should be between a man and a woman. She felt safe, cared for, eager. She felt free to bend over and kiss the top of his dark head, felt free to smile when she heard his breath catch at the gesture.

He dropped the towel and closed his brawny arms around her waist, shutting his eyes and pressing his cheek to her for a long moment in a sweet, sweet hug.

And then, lifting his head, he blew a raspberry on her belly.

Faith shrieked.

Micah laughed out loud for the first time in more years than he could remember, then scooped Faith up to carry her laughing and squirming into the bedroom. He laid her on cool sheets and then lay down beside her, intent on keeping her laughing.

But Faith had other ideas, and when she tugged the snap of his jeans open, his breath left him in a rush, and he forgot all about teasing her and tickling her gently, about blowing raspberries on her tummy and all the other ideas he had for making her giggle.

Propped on his side on one elbow, he froze in agonizing anticipation and watched as she pulled his zipper down and then reached inside to touch him. Other women had done that over the years. Other women had touched him with practiced hands and knowing fingers, but no one, no one at all, had touched him as Faith did.

Her hands trembled, fine little tremors he could feel, and that electrified him. What electrified him even more was knowing she found this difficult but wanted to do it anyway, for him. And for herself.

"Tell me," she murmured, her breath catching. "Tell me if I do something wrong."

"You don't do anything wrong. Not ever."

She turned her head and looked straight at him, and the vulnerability he saw in her eyes ripped a Wyoming-sized crater in his heart.

"I like the way you touch me," he told her, things inside him aching, crashing, shifting, in the emotional earthquake she had set off. "I like it, Moonbeam. God help me, I *love* it. Don't stop."

Was that really him saying those things? He'd never... But now he was, and he meant them, and to hell with what it might cost. He needed whatever touches she wanted to give him, and he didn't want her to stop because she didn't realize how much he wanted it.

"Help me," she whispered breathlessly, tugging at the denim of his jeans.

He lifted his hips and pushed his jeans down, helping her to wrestle them off his legs. When she began running her hands ever so slowly up his legs in teasing sweeps that came closer and closer to his sex, he decided he must have died and gone to heaven.

Along about the time she reached his upper thighs, she looked up at him, and something in her expression reached out to touch his soul. Then, before he could do more than register the impact, her mouth found him. *Hot, sweet, wild.*

A deep, wrenching groan escaped him, and along with it went the civilized veneer he wore. The touch of her lips and tongue turned him into man elemental, unleashed the raging fires he kept carefully banked, and set Micah Parish free of a lifetime of carefully accumulated control.

He wanted. He needed. Nothing else mattered but his needs and this woman. He forgot all his hard-learned emotional lessons. He forgot all the walls and barriers he had built. He forgot the myth he had tried to live up to. He forgot everything except that never, not once, in his entire life had he received what he needed from a woman.

With another groan, he drew Faith up over him and covered her hungry mouth with his. His woman. *His woman.* Possessiveness rose in him savagely, stronger than thought, a deep-running instinct. He needed to love her so well that she would give herself totally. Completely. Forsaking all others.

He needed a woman who was his, just his. He needed his mate, the mate he'd never had. The mate he had foolishly thought himself quite happy without—until Faith. She was reaching him at a level so elemental, so basic, that he could almost feel the connection of his soul to hers. If she left him—oh God, if she left him . . .

He couldn't even bear to think of it.

He swept her beneath him, taking care not to burden her with his weight. Possessiveness made him protective. She was his to care for, to shelter, to cherish, to love. He would place himself between her and every danger or fear. He would ensure that with him she was always safe. He would give her nothing but joy and comfort.

"Micah . . . oh, Micah . . . oh!"

He plundered her gently with his mouth, transforming his need to keep her into sensual, silken bonds that would make her want him more. He would make her his by giving her what no one else ever had. It was that simple. A man didn't hold a woman by making her his slave, his toy, or his victim. He didn't hold her through terror, or fear, or superior strength. A man kept his mate by making her want to stay. A man kept his mate by pleasing her.

He brought her close to the edge by gently sucking her breasts. It took nothing else to bring her to writhing impatience, but he gave her more anyway. By the time he joined himself to her with a slow, deep, gentle thrust, she was gasping his name on every breath and begging him to please, *please,* love her now.

And somewhere, in the grip of his powerful need, he made the mistake of declaring his possession.

"You're mine," he said raggedly as he pumped into her, his body nearly convulsing with each lunge. "You're mine, Moonbeam." He wanted her to know he wanted her that much, forever, if she would just have him.

She heard something else entirely.

When Micah's alarm went off at six, he was alone in bed. He could smell coffee, though, and guessed that Faith, bless her, had awakened early and decided to make him breakfast before he went to work.

Smiling, he rose to the new day with more eagerness than he had felt in years. Today, he thought as he gave himself a sponge bath, he was going to ask Dr. MacArdle to take him out of this damn tape. Surely they had something removable he could wear so he could shower. He suspected the doctor had taped him up only to keep him from taking the stuff off. That would be like MacArdle, all right.

Still smiling, he dressed in a fresh uniform, strapped on his holster and gun, grabbed his Stetson, and headed downstairs to give his woman the good morning kiss she deserved.

On the threshold of the kitchen, he froze. Faith was sitting at the table, fully clothed, rigidly upright, her hands tightly folded. Beside her sat her suitcase and the bags of clothing.

"Moonbeam?" His voice cracked almost imperceptibly on the pet name he had given her. He really didn't need an answer. He knew a woman who was leaving when he saw one.

"I-I'd really appreciate it if you'd take me home this morning, Micah," Faith said, her voice wobbly.

He didn't move a muscle. In an instant he became cold granite, head to foot. "Why?" he said.

"Well, F-Frank's in jail, so I'm safe now, and ... and I r-really need to be independent. I-I told you, Micah. I have to stand on my own two feet!"

She was afraid of him. He could see it. Damn it, she was afraid of him! Why? *Why?*

Still he didn't move, didn't even blink. He stared at her, facing a loneliness he knew was going to damn him for the rest of his days. She had shattered everything that held that loneliness at bay, had disintegrated his distance and torn away his solitude, and now she was going to abandon him. And it was his own fault, because he knew better than to trust a woman.

"Tell me the truth, Faith," he said flatly. "Just tell me the truth."

Slowly she lifted her head, until she was looking straight at him. He saw the fear in her blue eyes, saw the tears she was fighting, saw the courage that sustained her despite everything.

"I don't belong to you," she said tensely. "My baby doesn't belong to you." She closed her eyes suddenly, hearing Frank in her head, seeing once again the evil gleam of the knife in his hand. *You're mine, Faith. That kid's mine. I'll do anything I want with either one of you.* And just as clearly, she heard Micah telling her that when he spilled his seed in her, the baby became his. Telling her last night that she was his. *Mine.* God, how she hated and feared the sound of that word! Her eyes flew open. "I'm not yours," she said again, almost desperately. "I'm not anyone's!"

Every single feeling inside Micah shut down. Of course she wasn't his, he thought distantly. Why the hell had he ever thought she might want to be a half-breed's woman? Ignoring her as if she had ceased to exist, he poured himself a cup of coffee and a bowl of cold cereal. He ate standing at the counter, his back to her, unwilling to see her fear, her tears, her anguish. Unwilling to feel anything ever again. Damn, he'd known better.

When he finished, he rinsed his bowl in the sink and then turned, lifting the suitcase and bags without glancing at her. "Let's go," he said harshly. At the door he paused a moment to grab his uniform parka and throw it over his shoulder, but he didn't put it on. He needed the cold. He needed the kind of cold that would numb him all the way to his soul, but for now he would have to settle for Wyoming's November ice.

He didn't speak to her again until they reached her house. He felt her looking at him repeatedly, but he ignored her. He wasn't going to give her an opportunity to try to smooth over her rejection of him, nor was he going to listen to her plead for his understanding, the way women often did after they shafted a man. She had said all that needed saying, he figured, and he wasn't going to give her a chance to drive the knife any deeper.

When he parked at her door, he told her to stay put. "I'm going to clean up the mess Frank left before you go in there," he said roughly.

"Micah, I can—"

He rounded sharply on her. "No."

She shrank back against the door, but he was damned if he cared anymore. Leaving her outside in the locked vehicle, he made his way to her room and began gathering up all the shreds of slashed clothing. He was not a vindictive or vengeful man, and his only thought was that no one, absolutely no one, should ever be faced with evidence of such hate being directed toward them.

He found a large trash bag in the kitchen and filled it with the scraps of cloth. Then he found a rag and some pine cleaner and went to scrub away the threats and filthy words that had been scrawled in lipstick across the wall above her bed. Nobody should have to see that kind of thing. Nobody.

"Okay," he said to her twenty minutes later. He helped her down from the Blazer, escorted her into the house, then carried in her bags. Without looking at her, he checked the phone to be sure it was working, then picked up the bag of scraps. He would burn them at home; he sure wasn't going to chance Faith looking in there and seeing what Frank had done.

At the door, he stopped and spoke over his shoulder. "You can still call me if you need anything," he said gruffly. "That's what neighbors are for."

Outside he tossed the bag into the back of his vehicle and paused a moment to draw a couple of deep breaths of cold air. Nothing had changed, he told himself. He had only thought it might, but it hadn't, so everything was just the way it had always been.

Except that now he knew what it felt like to have his heart torn out by the roots.

Chapter 12

"Jeez, Micah," Charlie Huskins said to him as he entered the office, "you look awful. Are you okay?"

Before he could dismiss Charlie's concern with a remark about a sick animal keeping him up all night, Nate butted in.

"Get your backside over to Doc MacArdle and have him look at those ribs."

Micah turned right around and marched back out the door without argument. He'd been planning to see the doctor anyway, and it saved making excuses to conceal the truth. And what had happened to his poker face, anyway? He was usually unreadable, but this morning he must be an open book.

The doctor's office was in his home on Front Street, a prosperous avenue of elderly, elegant homes that housed Conard City's higher social classes. Dr. MacArdle wasn't back from morning rounds yet, but the nurse, Joanne, took one look at Micah and put him right in the examining room, assuring him it wouldn't be long.

Yep, he must look like hell. Curious, he walked over to the small mirror that hung over a sink and peered at himself. He didn't think he looked any different.

Shrugging inwardly, he wandered over to the window and stared out at the cold, gray day. There wasn't a speck of color left in the world, he thought. Not a one. The trees were barren, the snow dingy, the sky overcast.

"Howdy, Micah." Ben MacArdle stepped briskly into the room, carrying a clipboard and wearing the knee-length white coat that was his habit. The coat was beginning to get a little snug around his middle since he'd married last spring.

"Morning, Ben. I was hoping you could get this tape off me."

"I figured you'd be about ready to rip it off yourself by now." Ben glanced up with a smile. "Come on, take off your shirt. Nate's worried about you."

"He is? What'd he do, call you at the hospital?"

"He called Joanne. Said you looked like a vampire who'd missed his last meal."

"Well, hell."

"You look a little drawn, all right."

"I'm just tired, that's all." He *was* tired, he thought as he hung his crisply pressed shirt—Faith's doing—on the hook and turned back to the doctor. Tired in a bone-deep, soul-deep way he had seldom felt before.

Removing the tape wasn't a difficult task, requiring only that Ben clip away at it with scissors, since a layer of cotton batting lay between the tape and his skin.

"Will you look at that?" Ben said with a whistle as he pulled the tape away. "All the colors of the rainbow and a few I don't think I ever saw before."

Micah looked down at the bruise that covered his entire left side from nipple to waist. Experimentally, he poked at it with a finger. "Not tender."

"Bet this is, though," Ben said, and pressed on a bruised rib. Micah drew a sharp breath. "Thought so. Take a deep, slow breath."

Micah emerged twenty minutes later with an elastic bandage around his middle that he could remove when he wished, and a clean bill of health. Ben had offered the opinion that it wouldn't hurt Micah to take a few more days off, Micah had made a few noncommittal sounds, and Ben had thrown up his hands.

Nate was waiting when Micah returned to the office. "Ben said you could use some more time off."

Micah stared stonily back. "Not today," was all he said.

Nate studied him a moment. "Okay. Not today."

"Frank Williams is in the tank?"

Nate nodded. "His extradition hearing is Wednesday. Garrett Hancock is flying up tomorrow, and he has every intention of taking Williams back to Texas with him."

"Won't be soon enough for me."

"How's Faith doing?"

"She moved back to her own place this morning." Micah turned toward the stairway that led upstairs to the jail. "I think I'll go take a look at the guy. If I ever run into him, I want to know who he is."

Conard County didn't have much need for a jail and boasted only six cells in an armored room on the second floor of the building. A deputy sat guard around the clock, but the necessary security was provided by locks and bars. Usually the tank held petty thieves, joyriders, drunks and brawlers. Today it held only Frank Williams. Jed Barlowe, the drunk who had shot Micah, had been sent off to Casper to a detox program.

Frank Williams, like many of the world's worst people, looked perfectly ordinary. He looked like ten thousand other cops: young, healthy, a little pudgy around the middle from spending too many hours in a patrol car. He was nothing special, nothing frightening.

Except, Micah thought, for a strange wildness to his eyes. They were the eyes of a Charles Manson. Looking into those eyes, he found it possible to believe everything he had heard about Williams, and possible to suspect there was plenty more as yet untold.

"You're sure a unique-looking deputy," Williams remarked, half smiling as he watched Micah approach.

It was a friendly smile, Micah noted with detachment. From anyone else, under other circumstances, he would have accepted it as a friendly overture. From this man, friendliness was bound to be manipulative. "I'm a unique man," Micah answered levelly. He stopped two paces away from the cell and simply stared at the other man.

Finally Williams began to get unnerved. "What are you doing?"

"Memorizing you."

"Memorizing me?" Frank came to his feet. "What for?"

"So I'll know you the next time I see you, whenever I see you, wherever I see you."

Frank shifted uneasily. "Why? What difference does it make?"

"Well," Micah said slowly, "I spent twenty years in the Special Operations branch of the army. It's a habit to know my target."

"Target?" Williams backed up a step. "What do you mean by that? I'm not your target."

"Not at the moment." Micah took a step toward the cell. "I'll tell you something, Williams. If you so much as lay one finger on Faith ever again, if I ever so much as catch wind of your stinking scent within fifty miles of that woman, I'm going to track you down and teach you the meaning of fear. I don't care how far you go, I'll follow you. I'll track you to the ends of the earth and I'll get you. I swear it." Turning, he started to walk away.

"You threatened me!" Williams shouted after him. "I'll sue you for that!"

"Prove it," Micah said flatly without looking back, then disappeared through the door.

Nate insisted that Micah take desk duty, so the day dragged. He finished all his own paperwork and half of

Nate's, while listening to Charlie Huskins tell old jokes and talk about his wife and baby daughter. Charlie liked to talk. All in all, it was a quiet day in Conard County.

Just before five, Gage Dalton showed up. Wearing his usual black from head to foot, Gage entered the office like doom on an already gloomy day. Charlie gave Gage the kind of uncertain look people always gave him, even when they saw him frequently. Gage nodded to him and looked at Micah.

"Got a minute?"

Micah nodded and followed Gage into Nate's office. Gage closed the door behind them.

"What now?" asked Nate when the two came in, his tone the resigned voice of a man who had found life a little too exciting lately.

"I spoke with a guy I know up at the state lab to see if they've learned any more about Cumberland's cattle. He told me they're having a big fight about it up there, and the lab director is demanding the necropsies be reperformed by someone else."

"Why?" Nate was sitting up straight now. Micah still leaned against the wall, but he felt the tension inside.

"The pathologist is insisting those cattle were cut with surgical instruments."

"Hah!" The sound escaped Micah. He'd known it.

Gage acknowledged the fact with a nod. "There's evidently some more stuff, but my contact doesn't know what it is. I want to go up there and see if I can rattle their cages a little. I don't like the idea that they're sitting on evidence."

"They probably aren't convinced yet that it's accurate evidence," Nate said. "But yeah, Gage, you go ahead, and turn in a travel voucher when you get back. If you have any trouble, give me a holler."

Gage left moments later, and Nate and Micah exchanged looks.

"You were right, old son," Nate said. "But then, you always are. What the hell is going on in my county?"

Micah shook his head. "Wish I knew."

"It used to be so peaceful around here," Nate said. "I could count on handling little stuff, the kind of crap you take care of so your neighbors are happy, the kind of thing you do to keep friends out of trouble. Hell, son, we haven't had a murder in this county since John Grant took it in the chest from that escaped convict four years ago. How many places can say that?"

"Not many."

"Damn straight." Nate scowled at him. "Then we had Mandy Grant kidnapped a couple of months ago by that she-devil who wanted to get back at Ransom. Now we got that Williams character, and cattle being surgically mutilated." He shook his head. "Damn."

"Maybe you ought to kick out all of the outsiders. We seem to bring the trouble. Me, Ransom, Faith, Frank Williams. Gage isn't from these parts either, is he?"

"Nope."

"Where's he from?"

Nate looked up at him. "Hell, Micah. He's been in hell. Anything else, you need to ask him."

A typical Nathan Tate response, Micah thought as he headed back to his desk. Absolutely no information at all. Nate probably said the same damn thing when anyone asked him about Micah.

By quitting time, Micah felt like himself again. One weekend's lovemaking with a woman wasn't enough to throw him off kilter for long. He'd just somehow blown it all out of proportion last night and this morning. Hell, it hadn't even been a whole week since he had rescued the woman from the road. Too short a time to become genuinely attached to her. After forty-three years, he'd suffered from a few hours of craziness, that was all.

Some of the stew Faith had made was left in the refrigerator, so he shoved it into the microwave and headed out

for the barn to tend his animals. The work made his ribs
ache, but he welcomed the pain. Maybe later he would go
for a run.

Pain was a great touchstone, he thought. It reminded him
of what was real. It focused and centered him in himself. It
was a goad that drove him.

He could feel himself recovering his distance, he thought,
as he returned to the house sweaty and aching from his la-
bors. He could feel his barriers rising as if brick after brick
were slipping into place, filling in all the chinks. She was
only a woman, after all. Just a woman. He'd gotten along
just fine before she showed up in his life, and he would get
along just as well now.

He was just fine the way he was.

That being true, why did he feel as if he were standing at
the bottom of a very narrow, dank, dark hole waiting to be
buried alive?

When Faith watched Micah drive away, her initial reaction had been one of relief. She had escaped without harm.
Standing alone in the solitude of her father's familiar house,
she allowed herself to feel safe. Frank was in jail, and she
was never again going to be any man's possession. Never.

Closing her eyes, she pressed her hands to her womb and
felt her baby's vigorous movements against her palms. It
was just the two of them now. Just her and the baby, and it
was going to be all right. In this house, where she had
known joy, she was going to make a real home for her child.
A home full of love and light and warmth, a home without
any shadows of fear.

The smell of pine cleaner was strong, and it grew stronger
as she walked back to her bedroom. She was able to see a
faintly pink smear where Micah had sponged away the
words she had heard mentioned but had never seen. The
holes in the wall were still there, but Micah couldn't have
done much about those.

Suddenly, without any kind of warning, her legs gave way and she sank onto the bed. Wrapping her arms tightly around herself, she rocked back and forth, and cried and cried and cried.

Frank had followed her here. He had followed her. If she hadn't had that flashback that made Micah take her home with him, she would be dead now, she and her baby both. So what if they came and took Frank back to Texas and put him in prison? So what? How long would it be before he got out again? What if he escaped again? Oh, Lord, Lord, was she ever going to be safe?

At some point she curled up into a tight ball on the bed and fell into exhausted sleep. She hadn't slept last night, but had lain awake staring into the dark, hearing Micah's voice claim her as Frank's once had, trying to deal with the fear she couldn't seem to escape.

At last she left it behind, for a little while, in sleep.

It was dark when at last she awoke. A day had slipped by, lost in the velvet reaches of slumber. She freshened up a little in the bathroom and then answered another imperative call of nature, heading for the kitchen and the refrigerator. She was starved, and the bag of melon balls she had stashed in the freezer on Friday suddenly sounded irresistible.

It wasn't until she was sitting at the table, a half-eaten bowl of melon balls in front of her, that the sleepy sense of well-being slipped away, leaving her horribly conscious of the emptiness around her.

Horribly conscious of missing Micah.

She turned and looked at the phone, wondering if she should call him and explain what had sent her into flight this morning. Surely he would understand? He seemed to have understood all her other craziness. This time she had been running from an idea of men that Frank had pounded into her with fists and words, an idea that had little relationship to Micah. Micah would understand that.

Or would he? Recalling the way he had seemed to harden into granite this morning when she told him she was leaving, recalling how distant and cold he had become and remained, she wondered. For the first time since last night, she was able to look past her fear and consider that she might have wounded Micah, that she might have insulted him by the way she had fled.

And if that were the case, he would never want to speak to her again. Or see her. Or hold her.

Trying to ignore the aching sense of loss that thought engendered, she scooped up her bowl and put it into the refrigerator. Time to get her mind off morbid things, she told herself. Time to read a book. Time to enjoy the total solitude she had been trying to find for ages.

Wasn't this what she'd wanted, to be utterly alone? Wasn't this what she had been telling herself would solve all her problems? That once she was alone she would be safe?

But her solitude mocked her with emptiness, and her heart treacherously remembered how full it had begun to feel.

Uneasiness began to ride Micah like a goad. He couldn't settle down with his book, couldn't sink into the music he put on the stereo. He found himself pacing restlessly through the house, upstairs and down, too often catching a whiff of Faith's elusive fragrance. That would wear off with time, and so would this damn restlessness and sense of loss. Or so he told himself.

Stepping outside, he stood staring up at the starry night sky. He hadn't bothered with a jacket, so the cold seeped through his shirt and made his skin prickle and sting. He needed a good long run, he thought, and turned to run down his driveway, but the uneasiness stopped him.

Somehow, for some reason, he didn't want to be too far from the phone. Shrugging, he gave in to intuition and stayed where he was, studying the stars as if they held some answer to the pain he kept buried in his soul.

Around him he felt the night, the miles and miles of space and distance, the emptiness of Wyoming's wide open spaces. He felt the abiding power of the land beneath his feet, the strength of the rock that had endured for millennia, and tried to imagine himself part of that rock and clay, as strong and as enduring as they were. He drew strength from the earth, he reminded himself, and solace from the wind.

And, like the eagle, he was free.

Gage Dalton found Micah there twenty minutes later. Micah had turned when he heard the approach of a vehicle and waited patiently while Gage's Suburban crunched slowly to a halt a dozen feet away. Gage climbed out and approached slowly, as if he sensed the magnitude of his intrusion into Micah's privacy. For a moment the two men regarded one another silently across a span of about six feet.

"Coffee?" Micah said finally.

"Thanks."

Inside, Gage sat at the table, slouched in the chair, legs loosely crossed. Dark from head to toe. Micah leaned back against the counter, crossing his booted feet at the ankles, and waited.

Presently, Gage looked at him. "I was out wandering the roads, feeling restless. You know the feeling."

"I know."

"I figured you might. Anyhow, I was driving around thinking about the mutilations, about what you found, what the guy at the lab told me, and trying to put it all together in some way that makes sense. When I got near here, I thought maybe we could kick some ideas around."

Micah stared at him. Until this moment, he had thought of Gage Dalton as a near-stranger, someone he would probably respect if he knew him, but someone he would never really know. There were people like that, people who never opened up. Micah was one of them himself.

In that moment, though, he understood that Gage had stopped here not to discuss mutilations, but because he had heard that Faith had gone back to her own place. Gage had come as a friend.

"Yeah," Micah said after a moment, his voice a little rusty. "Yeah, we can kick some ideas around." Coming over to the table, he pulled out a chair and sat.

Every light in the house blazed brightly. Faith yawned, wondering how she could possibly feel so sleepy after having slept away the entire day—and when every dark corner seemed to harbor a threat.

In the past couple of hours she had discovered that she didn't feel secure here alone, even with Frank safely locked up. Solitude no longer offered protection.

Only Micah offered protection, she thought with a sudden, painful squeezing of her heart. Only Micah had ever made her feel safe. Cared for. The emptiness of this house would never give her that.

It would never give her the strength of his arms around her, or the heat of his gentle loving, or the wonder that filled her whenever he pressed his hand to her womb and felt her child move.

It would never give her any of the things she needed, the things she *really* needed. Things she had begun to believe didn't exist until Micah showed her that they did.

She reached for the phone, refusing to let fear conquer her again. She would apologize. Tell him she was sorry for the hurtful way she had acted. She would...

The phone was dead. Blankly, she stared at it, and then every light in the house went out.

Micah broke off in midsentence and cocked his head to one side. Something was wrong. Closing his eyes, he reached out in some indefinable way, trying to locate the source of the uneasiness that had suddenly pricked his mind. After a moment, though, the feeling faded. He looked at Gage.

"What was it?" Gage asked.

"Just a feeling."

Gage nodded, as if he had those feelings, too. Hunches. Intuitions. Something just below the level of conscious thought that you learned to pay attention to if you lived on the edge for any length of time. Gage's acceptance told Micah something about the younger man's shrouded past. It also raised a lot of interesting questions Micah didn't ask because it was none of his business.

Gage wasn't quite as taciturn as Micah, but he wasn't a whole lot more talkative. Somehow they drifted away from the subject of the mutilations, and talk became desultory, the pauses longer, the quiet somehow comfortable.

At some point Micah realized they were both waiting for something. That earlier nibble of unease had left its mark, and apparently his own sense of something about to happen had communicated itself to Gage.

And then he felt it again, only this time it was stronger. Much stronger. Something was very definitely wrong. Disturbed, he didn't hesitate any longer. He went to the phone and dialed Faith's number.

With each unanswered ring, his trepidation grew. Visions filled his head, none of them reassuring. She could have slipped in the tub, or fallen down her basement stairs, or...

He slammed the phone into the cradle. "I'm going over to the Montrose place," he told Gage.

"I'll come with you. If something's wrong, you might need help."

Micah was in no mood to dally, but some things needed doing, like it or not. He got his vest, his gun belt, his jacket, checked his .45, made sure his speedloaders were ready. There was no reason to suppose that Faith was in danger from a person, but he supposed it anyway. Instinct. Gut feeling.

Gage must have felt the same way, Micah realized as he stepped outside. The other man was at his Suburban, pulling on his own body armor. Better safe than sorry.

They took Micah's official vehicle, and as they raced toward the Montrose ranch, Micah tried to think of other things to keep himself from dwelling on what he might find.

And that was a dead giveaway, he realized. A dead giveaway. He'd been through hell many times in his life, and he'd never before found it necessary to play mental hide-and-seek with reality. If this were a routine call, he would be *trying* to imagine every possibility before he got there, so that he would be as prepared as possible. He wouldn't be trying to think about the fact that Gage had body armor and had just asked if Micah wanted him to call for backup, two clear betrayals of the fact that Gage had a long background in active law enforcement. No, he would be focused on the task at hand, not wallowing in a sense of dread.

With a sharp, inward mental yank, he forced himself to do this right, to think clearly about every potential threat. He owed that to Faith.

This was the second time in less than a week that he'd made this drive in the middle of the night in a near panic about Faith. The second time.

"When I get my hands on that woman," he heard himself say aloud, "I'm going to shake some sense into her."

"Might be a good idea," Gage agreed easily. "Seems like a damn fool thing, living alone all the way out here when she's pregnant."

Micah thought so, too. And this crap about independence... Faith wasn't meant to be independent and alone. She was meant to be loved and cherished, not to stand by herself in the cold winds of the world. He would willingly have bet that if she was asked, she would confess to wanting more than one child, and damn it, she would make a wonderful mother.

If he had to shake her until her teeth rattled, he would make her see that she had no business burying herself like this. She needed a life, a full life.

But he wouldn't shake her. He wouldn't lay a finger on her, because he knew that if he did, she'd run away like a scared rabbit—and probably for good. And he also knew that if he touched her again, he probably wouldn't be able to let her go.

She was a song in his blood, the sunlight in his soul.

When the lights went out, Faith froze into instant immobility. With the phone already dead, she didn't for an instant think this was a simple power outage. Were the doors and windows locked? Oh, God, she couldn't be sure, because she hadn't checked them yet. Frank might have unlocked them, or the deputies might have, after Frank broke in here. The only door she knew for certain was locked was the kitchen door, because she had locked it when Micah left.

Bending slowly, she lowered the receiver until she could let go of it without leaving it to swing and bang against the walls. Then, carefully, she stepped out of her pumps, knowing her stocking feet would be quieter.

The circuit breakers. Where was the breaker box? To throw off all the lights at once, the main had to be thrown or the power line had to be knocked down, and she seriously doubted anyone would attempt the latter. The basement? Could Frank be in the basement?

Her mouth felt as dry as Death Valley, and her heart was hammering so hard it seemed loud in the silence. The baby stirred, kicking gently and turning over. Please, God. Please, please, please!

If she could get her car keys, maybe she could get to her car and get out of here before...

The thought drained away as she looked at the door to the basement. It was dark, but her eyes were just beginning to adjust, just enough to see the pale gleam of the doorknob. If she stuck a chair under there...

She grabbed one of the kitchen chairs and carried it swiftly to the basement door, keeping quiet until the very last moment, when she needed to wedge it into place beneath the doorknob. The sound was excruciatingly loud in the utter silence of the house. With the power out, not even the refrigerator hummed, and the hot water heater had stopped groaning.

Her car keys were in her purse on her dresser, all the way back in the bedroom. She refused to allow herself to consider that he might already have disabled her car. She had to try.

How had he gotten out of jail this time? she wondered desperately as she held her hands out and tried to feel her way through the impossibly dark house. How had he managed to get away again?

In her mind, Frank Williams was taking on the character of a supernatural force. He just kept coming and coming and coming, and not even prison bars seemed to be able to hold him. And this time there would be no Garrett Hancock to break the door down and come to her rescue. This time she couldn't call Micah.

This time she was utterly alone.

As she eased along the counter, her hand came up against the storage block that held the butcher knives. Instinctively, she pulled out the ten-inch chef's knife and carried it with her. If he came at her again with a knife, she vowed, she wasn't going to be the only one wounded.

In the midst of her terror, as she tried to ease down the hallway without making a sound, she was suddenly drowned in a burning wave of shame over her flight from Micah that morning. It had been a reflexive reaction to his claim that she was his, but only to a point, and that was what shamed her now. Frightened or not, she was guilty of putting Micah Parish in the same class with Frank Williams, and there was just no comparison between the two. Even as scared as she felt of being a man's possession, she surely should have been able to see that Micah wasn't anything like the man she believed was pursuing her now.

She hoped she would have a chance to tell him that, to apologize, but as she took another gulp of air and slid another step down the hall, she wasn't sure she would ever again have the opportunity to do anything.

Finally—finally—she reached the door of her bedroom and slipped inside, closing the door behind her. Now for her purse, and then she would climb out the window.

Maybe it wasn't Frank, she thought as she moved cautiously across the room toward the dresser. She hadn't heard anything, after all. Maybe it was just coincidental that the lights had gone out. Maybe she was acting like a frightened idiot, and she'd better be damn careful she didn't fall on this butcher knife. Wouldn't that be ironic, to die of a self-inflicted stab wound in an empty house because the lights had gone out?

Suddenly there was a banging from the other end of the house, and the unmistakable sound of something being forced across the kitchen floor.

Oh, my God! Oh, my God! He was coming for her!

Forgetting all about car keys and the window, she scurried for the huge, old oak armoire that had been one of her favorite hiding places as a child. It had survived the fire that gutted the original house, and her dad had kept it, even though the new house had adequate closets. In it now were sheets, blankets and pillows, and she crawled quickly into it. In moments she had closed the door behind her and listened to the latch catch. Then she burrowed into the blankets and quilts until she was sure she was covered from head to toe. In the dark, perhaps all the blankets would fool him. Perhaps.

Her heart raced, and her oxygen-starved lungs drew great gulping breaths as she strained with every fiber of her being to hear.

An eternity passed while she huddled and waited, the knife in her hand, her ears straining for any sound other than the hammering of her heart. Disconnected prayers and pleas raced through her mind, and she felt herself trying to reach across the desolate distance to Micah. If only some pinprick of uneasiness could reach him...if only some prayer or wish could summon him.

"I know you're here, bitch!"

Frank's voice shattered the terrifying silence with the incontrovertible evidence of his presence. Clapping her hand over her mouth to smother an instinctive cry, Faith bit her knuckle hard.

"I'll find you. You know I'll find you!"

Faith curled up even tighter, trying to wrap her womb in the protection of her body.

"You stupid whore! Did you really think I'd let you go? Did you really think I'd let anybody else have you? Nobody's going to have you, Faith. Nobody. You're mine."

Faith swallowed another whimper and fought to keep from shaking so hard that she lost her grip on the knife. Oh, God, God, God, *please* . . .

"After I take care of you, bitch, I'm going after that redskin who's so fond of you. When I'm done with you, I'm going to cut him into little pieces and laugh all the time I'm doing it."

Profound terror gripped Faith, fueled by her vivid memory of the last time Frank had come after her. She could still feel each blow, each stabbing thrust of the knife.

This time, she thought in the instant before her mind went totally blank, this time she was going to die.

Chapter 13

The sight of a pickup truck pulled off to the side of Faith's driveway was all the additional evidence Micah needed that she was in serious trouble. A visitor would have pulled up to the house, not left his vehicle a good quarter mile away.

He jammed on the brakes and looked at Gage. "Call in and let 'em know we've got trouble. This looks planned. I'm going ahead on foot."

"I'll be right behind you."

Micah ran, keeping to the side of the driveway so the snow would muffle the sound of his steps. It was an easy run for a man with his training, a man who often ran a couple of miles just to clear his head a little. His breathing hardly deepened, but with each step he sank more profoundly into the inner stillness that brought him to the peak of preparedness.

It was the night of the new moon, and there was only starlight to guide him, but the snow reflected that little bit of light, magnifying it, making it just possible for him to see enough.

The basement window near the front of the house had been knocked in. A piece of glass had fallen outside onto the snow, and the glint of the dim light on the perfectly smooth surface drew Micah's eye instantly. He must have used a cloth to muffle the sound and made a silent entrance.

Faith was alone in the dark house with an intruder.

Rage struck him like a thunderclap in his head, leaving a deadly clarity in its wake. Time was of the essence, but he had to get into that house without alerting the intruder, who might hurt Faith if he became alarmed.

Although in truth, Micah thought grimly as he fell to the ground and began shimmying backwards through the small window, there was no doubt in his mind who had broken into the house. No one else in all of Conard County would come after Faith like this. Oh, it might be some drifter, but Micah would have bet his life savings that Frank Williams had managed a jailbreak. With only one deputy on duty as a jailer, it would have been easy enough to accomplish, and until the shift change took place at midnight, nobody would even know Williams had escaped.

What a great time, Micah thought acidly, to realize that jail security needed a good beefing up.

Once his feet hit the floor, he pulled a penlight out of his jacket pocket and scanned the basement quickly. In the shadows he saw that the door of the breaker box was open. If the guy had thrown the breaker, then there had been lights on when he got here—otherwise he wouldn't have bothered. That meant Faith had been awake. Had known someone was in the house. Was probably even now in his clutches. Micah bit back a curse and headed for the stairs, flashlight in his left hand, .45 in his right.

At the top, the door was wide open. A chair lay overturned nearby. Micah doused his light and paused, listening, and heard a sound from farther back in the house. Taking two steps, he reached the kitchen door and unlocked it, opening it wide in invitation to Gage. Then he turned and headed toward Faith's bedroom.

"I'm going to cut that baby out of you, bitch!"

Micah froze, but no sound answered Frank's vile threat. That meant Faith was either hiding or already unconscious. Micah prayed it was the former and began creeping down the hall.

"You're mine, you filthy tramp! Did you really think I'd let you walk away from me?"

Suddenly Faith screamed, and Micah quit worrying about silence. In an instant he reached the bedroom. As dark as it was, he could still make out their shadows, and he saw that Frank had Faith on the floor in front of him as he towered over her and held her by her hair. In his hand, a knife gleamed coldly.

Micah took aim. "Let her go."

Frank jerked Faith closer. He laughed. "It's all over for me anyway, but I'll be damned if I let some redskin have her!"

He lifted the knife and jerked Faith back yet again. Micah hesitated an instant, just an instant. It was dark, and though he'd never in his life hesitated to pull a trigger, he hesitated now, just a fraction, because Faith was one of those shadows. Then he fired.

Frank jerked and dropped the knife. He let go of Faith and pulled a gun from the waistband of his pants.

"Drop it, Williams," Micah ordered. "Next time, I won't just graze you."

"Go to hell." He pointed his gun directly at Micah.

A report sounded, and Frank Williams staggered wildly and then fell to the floor. Micah hadn't pulled the trigger. Slowly, he turned and found Gage right beside him.

Gage shrugged, a barely perceptible movement in the dark. "Figured you wouldn't want to be the guy who killed the father of her child." He slipped into the room past Micah, gun ready, and approached Williams. Micah covered him.

Gage knelt and felt for Frank's pulse. "He's gone and good riddance," he said with patent disgust. "Deader than a doornail, Ms. Williams. This bastard will never trouble you again."

Faith didn't answer. Freed from the necessity to be a cop, Micah closed the distance between them in a flash and knelt beside her on the floor, reaching for her, trying to hold her close, but finding she was curled up into a tight ball and wouldn't unfold.

"Faith, baby, it's over. It's over. You're safe now."

Shudders rippled through her, shaking her from head to toe. "Micah?"

"I'm here, Moonbeam. I'm right here." His voice was little more than a husky whisper as his throat closed. "Did he cut you?"

"No..." The word was a groan of anguish. "Micah, I'm losing the baby!"

The distance between Faith's house and County Hospital was 33.6 miles. Micah covered them in under twenty-five minutes with the Blazer's lights flashing and the siren howling across the desolate countryside.

"Maybe it's for the best." Faith's whisper pierced his heart.

"No," he said. "No."

"No man wants another man's child," she argued, her voice rising as another cramp seized her. "No man. And can't you just imagine the stories this baby would hear about her father? Oh, God, Micah!"

"Shh...shh..." Reaching out, he found her hunched shoulder and squeezed. "It's going to be all right, Moonbeam. You want this baby, and we're going to save her. We're going to save her."

Hell, he found himself thinking as he made promises he couldn't keep, he wanted this baby, too. He'd become attached to the little pokes and flutters and the whole damn idea of the kid. And newborns—well, hell. Newborns were the whole point of living and loving. The best part of humanity. There was a space in his heart already waiting for this child to take up residence, and it had been there from the moment he had felt the child move.

Once again he wanted to stake his claim on this woman and child, to tell Faith that the only father this kid was going to know about was going to be him. He kept the words locked up tight, though, because this wasn't the time, and because he remembered all too well how she had fled from him just this morning. She didn't belong to anybody, she had said. He wondered how long he would let her go on believing that.

When he lifted her out of the Blazer and placed her on the waiting gurney, she was still doubled over, but he was relieved to see no evidence of blood or water. It wasn't too late. Not yet.

Bending, he kissed her on the forehead. "You need me, just holler my name. I'll be here."

Then they took her away, out of his hands, and left him with nothing to do but wait. With a cup of terrible vending machine coffee, he settled down in the waiting room.

At some point he realized he was no longer alone. Looking up, he saw Ransom seated across from him.

"Mandy wanted to come, too, but I wouldn't hear of it," Ransom said.

"Good. She needs her rest."

Reaching into a nylon bag on the floor beside him, Ransom pulled out a large insulated bottle. "I know about hospital coffee," he said, and proceeded to fill two disposable cups. "I sure drank enough of it."

"Thanks." Micah accepted one of the cups and tasted it with pleasure. "Mandy makes the world's best coffee."

"How bad is it?"

Micah met his friend's concerned blue eyes. "Don't know. She was cramping, but... I don't know. They haven't told me anything."

"When Nate called me, he said he didn't think Williams had hurt her."

"No. He didn't have time." Thank God for that. Now, if they could have just one more small miracle, just one tiny little miracle... He closed his eyes a moment against a surging tide of feeling. "I wonder how that bastard got out."

"Would you believe," said Nate's familiar voice from the door of the waiting room, "that Williams conned Lou into going into the cell? Lou's in here with a dented skull, by the way. He's going to be okay."

"How'd he get Lou to do that?" Micah asked. He wouldn't have thought Lou was the gullible type.

"We may never know. He's concussed and can't remember anything past the point where Frank called him over." Nate smiled faintly. "Hell, son, this is Conard County. We're not prepared for serious criminals and jail breaks. Guess we'll be a little better prepared after this, though." He settled onto the sofa by the door. "Gage said to tell you he'll clear up the paperwork before he heads out to the state lab this morning.

"You know," he continued, "now that we've got Frank Williams taken care of, all we need to do is put a stop to the cattle mutilations."

Micah nodded. "Maybe Gage will bring back something we can go on."

"Maybe," Nate agreed. "How's Faith?"

Micah shrugged. The hours just kept ticking by, and nobody had told him anything. Years of training kept him patient, sure only that sooner or later Faith would ask for him. Until then, he didn't want to force himself on her, not even that little bit. Not after what he'd heard tonight.

Nate popped back up from the couch. "I'll go ask questions."

If anybody could get answers, Micah thought, it would be Nate. When he returned ten minutes later, though, he simply shrugged. "All they say is they're doing what they can."

The same thing they'd told him earlier, Micah thought grimly. It wasn't enough.

But with nothing else to do, he sat with the two people closest to him in the world and tried to absorb the cracks and crevices that the earthquake of today's events had made in his deepest places. Faith had been scared of him this morning. Maybe, after what had happened tonight, she would never be able to be with a man again. Maybe she would lose more than her ability to trust. Maybe she would never be able to stand being with a man again.

Maybe, he thought, he would have to start all over again with her. Maybe he would have to begin at the very beginning and show her little by little, day by day, that she need never fear him. And maybe she would never believe that.

And maybe he would just keep on trying, for the rest of his days if necessary. This morning, he admitted, he had reacted to his own old fears the same way she had been reacting to hers. His own defenses, the carapace of ancient scars he wore like a shield, had stood between them as surely as her fears had. If he hadn't been reacting to his own scars, he would never have let her go. He would have stood there and insisted they talk it out, work it out, love it out. He would have put his arms around her and held her gently until she understood that she had no need to fear his possession.

Well, that was what he would do from here on out. For the next forty years if he had to, because, by God, life was worthless without her.

It was nearly dawn when a weary Ben MacArdle appeared. "Micah? She'd like to see you."

Micah sprang to his feet. "Is she . . . ?"

"She's just fine," MacArdle said as they walked down the hall together. "As miscarriages go, this one never even got started. The baby's fine, no distress, and Faith's comfortable now. We'll keep her until tomorrow as a precaution, but physically, she's just great." He paused at the door of her room and looked up at Micah. "The rest of it is going to take time."

"I've got time. Plenty of it."

"Then give her some. She's not ready to handle anything more right now."

Thus warned, Micah entered the room cautiously. She lay on the bed, looking so small and fragile that he ached. Her pale curls made a silky halo on the pillow, and her small hand looked as pale as the sheet on which it lay. So fine, so delicate, so fragile.

He reached her bedside without making a sound and watched her sleep. God, he wanted to gather her up and hold her close and make sure no harm ever came to her again. He wanted to stash her safely away and guard her like a dragon protecting his treasure. Such a thing was impossible, of course, but that didn't keep him from feeling protective enough that he wanted to do it.

"Micah." She spoke his name without opening her eyes.

"I'm here, Moonbeam." When he saw her hand stir on the sheet, he took it in his and held it. "How do you feel?"

"Better. The baby's okay."

"I know. I'm glad. I'm so glad."

Slowly, she opened her eyes and looked at him. "Micah?"

"Hmm?"

"I'm sorry."

"There's nothing to be sorry for."

"Yes, there is. I ran from you. I hurt you. I know you're not anything like Frank. I know it, but I ran, and I'm sorry. . . ."

"Shh...shh." He gathered her into his arms and held her to his chest. "Don't worry about a thing, Faith. Not a thing. As soon as you get out of here, we'll talk, okay? But right now, don't you worry about a thing. Not a thing."

A ragged little sigh escaped her, and she softened against him, leaning into him. "I missed you," she murmured, then fell asleep once more.

He held her until they made him leave.

The following morning at ten, Nate appeared in the doorway of Micah's office. "Micah? Get over to the hospital. MacArdle's about to let the little lady out, and she'll need you to take her home. And don't come back here until you get her straightened out, hear? I don't want any solitary pregnant females out in the back of beyond in my county, and you can tell her I said so."

Micah almost smiled, but he was too busy grabbing his hat and jacket to realize it.

She was standing with her back to the door when he arrived, packing the small overnight bag he'd brought her yesterday. A shaft of sunlight fell through the window, catching her hair and making it gleam like pale gold.

"Need a ride, little lady?"

She swung around, frowning, then laughed when she saw the teasing sparkle in his dark eyes. "You know I hate that, Micah."

"I know." He crossed the room and grabbed her overnight bag. "I took care of the paperwork before I came up. You're free to leave." He didn't tell her that he'd paid the bill. She would find that out soon enough. For now he didn't want her angry, and he didn't want to ruffle her independent feathers.

The day was beautiful, without a cloud to mar the perfection of the blue sky. Snow gleamed and sparkled so brightly that it hurt the eyes to look at it. Micah helped her into the Blazer, then joined her.

He put on his mirrored glasses again, and Faith leaned her cheek against the headrest and simply watched him. She didn't think she would get enough of the sight of him if she had a million years to simply sit and stare. He was so masculine, so exotic, with his long dark hair and harshly featured face. He was a man, he was a cop, and he was big, and the thrill that realization gave her was no longer one of fear. Not at all. Not even remotely.

She expected him to take her to her house. After the stink she had made about leaving, after the way she had run and insisted she needed to be independent, she didn't expect him to turn down his own driveway. But he did, and he didn't say a word. She considered questioning him, but his mouth was set in a grim line, so she kept quiet.

He lifted her down from the Blazer, then reached for her overnight bag, saying more clearly than words that she was staying. Her heart took a leap, and her mouth turned dry.

"I moved your stuff back over here last night," he announced as he ushered her into his kitchen.

"Micah—"

"Hush." Gently, he urged her onto a chair. When she was seated, he tugged her boots off, then reached for the buttons of her jacket. "Get as mad as you want, Moonbeam, but I'll be double-damned if I'm going to let you live alone. Sure as hell not while you're pregnant." He glanced up at her from dark eyes as he struggled with a button. She didn't look mad, he realized. Not mad at all. He wasn't quite sure what her expression was, but it wasn't mad. "Nate said to tell you he doesn't want any pregnant women living all alone in the middle of nowhere in his county."

"He did, did he?" She pursed her lips. "And that's why you dragged me here without asking? Because Nate said I can't live alone?"

There was something in the tone of her voice that disturbed him, but he was no coward, and he wasn't going to back down this time, no matter how angry she got. "No, that's not why. It's because I'll be old before my time if I have to make one more mad midnight dash up that road to your place wondering if you're hurt or...or..." He couldn't finish. After a moment, he cleared his throat. "You're turning my hair gray, Moonbeam."

She lifted a trembling hand and touched the dark silk that reached his shoulders. "I'd hate to do that to such beautiful hair," she murmured.

Her touch was like a blessing to his aching soul. Of her own free will, she had reached out to him. He wanted to catch her to him and sweep her upstairs, but he restrained himself. His heart needed some signs from her, and this was but a first tentative move. Turning his head, he brushed a kiss on her palm.

She cupped his cheek then, touching him with the gentleness he so deeply craved. "*You're* beautiful, Micah," she murmured. "I tried to tell you that once before, and you didn't like it, but it's true. You're beautiful."

He closed his eyes for a moment against the welling tide of feeling, then returned to the task of removing her coat. She let him pull it from her shoulders, and she offered no protest when he leaned forward and rested his cheek against her womb. Instead, her gentle hands held him there, stroking his cheek, his hair. This was a touch he had been seeking for his entire life, he realized.

"I had a lot of time to think last night," Faith continued softly, stroking his hair, calming him. Soothing him. Soothing herself. "For the first time in years I was completely free of my fear of Frank, and I realized that all my other fears were just reflections of my fear of him."

The baby stirred and kicked Micah's cheek, a soft little poke. "I must be squashing her," he said roughly and started to raise his head.

Faith's hands stopped him. "No," she said. "No. She likes you there. *I* like you there. It makes us feel safe and warm and cared for."

Micah caught his breath, and this time he did raise his head to look her squarely in the eyes. "You were afraid of me."

"I was afraid of a word, Micah. A word that Frank abused." Her blue eyes were steady, unafraid, as they returned his searching gaze.

"'Mine,'" he said. "That word. That's what scared you. I heard him say it just before I got to you the other night."

She nodded. "He was always saying that, saying he could do whatever he wanted, because I was his. He claimed he could kill this baby because it was his."

"And I claimed you both, just as he did."

"That's what scared me," she admitted. "It was stupid, I know, but—"

"Not stupid," he interrupted her. "Not stupid at all."

"But I'm not afraid of you, Micah," she said. "I'm not one bit afraid of you. That's why it was so dumb that I managed to get you mixed up in my mind with him...." Her voice trailed off, and she looked away for a few seconds. When she looked back, her eyes were sad. "And I can't promise never to mix things up again. I don't always seem to be able to control the way my mind and feelings work."

He drew a deep breath and took her hands in his. "Moonbeam, I can handle the mix-ups if you just promise not to run again. We can always work it out."

"W-we can?" Her voice broke, then rose on a note of hope.

He heard that hope, and a vise that had been gripping his heart for two days now suddenly let go. He gave her one of his very rare smiles. "We can. All you have to do is try to talk to me. I'll get angry sometimes, and sometimes I'll probably remind you of him, but, Moonbeam, I'd burn alive at the stake before I'd ever lay a hurtful finger on you or our child."

She drew a sharp breath, and her grip on his hands tightened. "*Our...* child?"

He tugged one hand from hers and laid his palm against her stomach. "This child. Our child. I told you that when I spilled my seed in you this child became mine. I wasn't kidding."

"But..." She searched his face almost desperately. "How can you...? Is this some kind of Indian thing?"

He shook his head. "I don't think so. It's just my thing. I've always felt that loving a woman included loving the fruit she bears. It doesn't matter who plants the tree, Faith. The apple still tastes just as good."

"Oh my," she said softly. Her lower lip quivered, and one huge, silvery tear appeared on her lower lash. "Oh my."

Leaning forward, she threw her arms around his neck and clung tightly.

This woman's absence for the last couple of days had been like a hole in his heart, and now that hole was being filled in by her sweet warmth, her gentle touch, her personal fragrance. He released a long sigh and gave up the battle to remain patient. He needed her, and he needed her now, hot, warm and willing beneath him. There was a lot that they would have to settle, but it was just going to have to wait, because emotions were locking up his throat, and there was only one way he could show her all his feelings. Words had never been his way.

He lifted her easily and started up the stairs. Faith buried her face in his neck, her breath a hot caress on his skin. "Don't you have to go back to work?" she asked him, hoping against hope that he didn't.

"Nope. Not until I get you straightened out, anyway."

Once, such a statement would have thrown her into a tempest of fear, but Micah made her feel so safe that she could discern the teasing note in his voice. "Straighten me out how?"

"Flat on your back," he said huskily. "Under me. Making appropriate sounds of pleasure."

"What if I want *you* flat on your back under *me?*"

The question, sounding so coquettish even as her voice quavered at her unaccustomed boldness, caused Micah to laugh. "Moonbeam, you can have me any way you want, any time you want."

Knowing he would have to be cautious because of the baby, he lowered her gently to his bed and just as gently began to undress her. And while he removed her clothing and tempted her with the light caress of his hands, he talked as he had never talked before.

"I've been lonely my whole life long, Moonbeam. I just never admitted it to myself. I told myself that my solitude was a fortress, that as long as I stood alone no one could hurt me."

"Oh, I know," she breathed. "I know. I told myself the same thing. Oh, Micah, it's not true!"

"I finally realized that." His dark eyes, like blazing black fire, devoured her. "When I held you, I realized I had some big holes that needed filling, big holes that were aching with emptiness. You filled my arms, Moonbeam, and I knew for the first time that they'd been empty."

She lifted her hand as if to touch him, but he rose and pulled her pants from her, leaving her completely naked on his bed. Then, standing over her, he began to strip his own clothes away. She watched every one of his movements in a way that told him she hadn't been kidding when she said he was beautiful. That understanding made him ache, too.

At last, at long, long last, he was beside her and they were pressed together from head to toe, bare skin on bare skin, warm sunlight illuminating every moment of their joining. She smiled as he claimed every inch of her with his hands, and that smile grew when he groaned at the gentle touch of hers.

When he finally sank into her liquid heat, he knew he had come home. The last barrier fell, and as he moved he told her, "I love you, Moonbeam. I love you body and soul."

"I love you, too, Micah," she answered. "Oh, I love you!"·

"Stay... with... me," he gasped.

"Yes... yes..."

"You're mine." The words slipped past one of his lowered barriers, and as soon as he heard them in the air, a fist squeezed his heart. He stopped moving and opened his eyes, almost afraid to look into Faith's face. What if he saw panic, or fear, or...?

"I'm yours," she told him, her eyes wide open and steady, without a shadow of fear in their depths. "I'm yours for as long as you want me."

Cautiously lowering himself to his elbows, he kissed her on the mouth. "I'm *yours*," he said huskily. "I've never belonged to anybody before, but I want to belong to you."

"Oh, Micah," she breathed, lifting her hands to cradle his face. "Oh, I do like the sound of that. You're *mine?*"

"All yours. One hundred percent. Forever."

Her breath caught, and then suddenly she was laughing and crying and hugging his neck so tightly that he was afraid he would fall on her, and damn it, he still needed her....

She still needed him, too, and with a gentle, beckoning roll of her hips, she let him know it. "Love me, Micah," she whispered in his ear. "Love me."

"To my dying breath," he vowed, and lifted her with him to the most intense expression of his love that he could give her.

"You are the song in my blood," he told her. "The light in my soul. My Moonbeam."

* * * * *

OFFICIAL RULES • MILLION DOLLAR MATCH 3 SWEEPSTAKES
NO PURCHASE OR OBLIGATION NECESSARY TO ENTER

To enter, follow the directions published. **ALTERNATE MEANS OF ENTRY:** Hand print your name and address on a 3" ×5" card and mail to either: Silhouette "Match 3," 3010 Walden Ave., P.O. Box 1867, Buffalo, NY 14269-1867, or Silhouette "Match 3," P.O. Box 609, Fort Erie, Ontario L2A 5X3, and we will assign your Sweepstakes numbers. (Limit: one entry per envelope.) For eligibility, entries must be received no later than March 31, 1994. No responsibility is assumed for lost, late or misdirected entries.

Upon receipt of entry, Sweepstakes numbers will be assigned. To determine winners, Sweepstakes numbers will be compared against a list of randomly preselected prizewinning numbers. In the event all prizes are not claimed via the return of prizewinning numbers, random drawings will be held from among all other entries received to award unclaimed prizes.

Prizewinners will be determined no later than May 30, 1994. Selection of winning numbers and random drawings are under the supervision of D.L. Blair, Inc., an independent judging organization, whose decisions are final. One prize to a family or organization. No substitution will be made for any prize, except as offered. Taxes and duties on all prizes are the sole responsibility of winners. Winners will be notified by mail. Chances of winning are determined by the number of entries distributed and received.

Sweepstakes open to persons 18 years of age or older, except employees and immediate family members of Torstar Corporation, D.L. Blair, Inc., their affiliates, subsidiaries and all other agencies, entities and persons connected with the use, marketing or conduct of this Sweepstakes. All applicable laws and regulations apply. Sweepstakes offer void wherever prohibited by law. Any litigation within the province of Quebec respecting the conduct and awarding of a prize in this Sweepstakes must be submitted to the Régies des Loteries et Courses du Quebec. In order to win a prize, residents of Canada will be required to correctly answer a time-limited arithmetical skill-testing question. Values of all prizes are in U.S. currency.

Winners of major prizes will be obligated to sign and return an affidavit of eligibility and release of liability within 30 days of notification. In the event of non-compliance within this time period, prize may be awarded to an alternate winner. Any prize or prize notification returned as undeliverable will result in the awarding of that prize to an alternate winner. By acceptance of their prize, winners consent to use of their names, photographs or other likenesses for purposes of advertising, trade and promotion on behalf of Torstar Corporation without further compensation, unless prohibited by law.

This Sweepstakes is presented by Torstar Corporation, its subsidiaries and affiliates in conjunction with book, merchandise and/or product offerings. Prizes are as follows: Grand Prize—$1,000,000 (payable at $33,333.33 a year for 30 years). First through Sixth Prizes may be presented in different creative executions, each with the following approximate values: First Prize—$35,000; Second Prize—$10,000; 2 Third Prizes—$5,000 each; 5 Fourth Prizes—$1,000 each; 10 Fifth Prizes—$250 each; 1,000 Sixth Prizes—$100 each. Prizewinners will have the opportunity of selecting any prize offered for that level. A travel-prize option, if offered and selected by winner, must be completed within 12 months of selection and is subject to hotel and flight accommodations availability. Torstar Corporation may present this Sweepstakes utilizing names other than Million Dollar Sweepstakes. For a current list of all prize options offered within prize levels and all names the Sweepstakes may utilize, send a self-addressed, stamped envelope (WA residents need not affix return postage) to: Million Dollar Sweepstakes Prize Options/Names, P.O. Box 4710, Blair,[fj NE 68009.

The Extra Bonus Prize will be awarded in a random drawing to be conducted no later than May 30, 1994 from among all entries received. To qualify, entries must be received by March 31, 1994 and comply with published directions. No purchase necessary. For complete rules, send a self-addressed, stamped envelope (WA residents need not affix return postage) to: Extra Bonus Prize Rules, P.O. Box 4600, Blair, NE 68009.

For a list of prizewinners (available after July 31, 1994) send a separate, stamped, self-addressed envelope to: Million Dollar Sweepstakes Winners, P.O. Box 4728, Blair, NE 68009.   SWP-1292

COME BACK TO

There's something about the American West, something about the men who live there. Accompany author Rachel Lee as she returns to Conard County, Wyoming, for CHEROKEE THUNDER (IM #463), the next title in her compelling series. American Hero Micah Parrish is the kind of man every woman dreams about—and that includes heroine Faith Williams. She doesn't only love Micah, she *needs* him, needs him to save her life—and that of her unborn child. Look for their story, coming in December, only from Silhouette Intimate Moments.

INTIMATE MOMENTS®
Silhouette®

Silhouette CHRISTMAS Stories 1992

Experience the beauty of Yuletide romance with Silhouette Christmas Stories 1992—a collection of heartwarming stories by favorite Silhouette authors.

JONI'S MAGIC by Mary Lynn Baxter
HEARTS OF HOPE by Sondra Stanford
THE NIGHT SANTA CLAUS RETURNED by Marie Ferrarrella
BASKET OF LOVE by Jeanne Stephens

Also available this year are three popular early editions of Silhouette Christmas Stories—1986, 1987 and 1988. Look for these and you'll be well on your way to a complete collection of the best in holiday romance.

Plus, as an added bonus, you can receive a FREE keepsake Christmas ornament. Just collect four proofs of purchase from any November or December 1992 Harlequin or Silhouette series novels, or from any Harlequin or Silhouette Christmas collection, and receive a beautiful dated brass Christmas candle ornament.

Mail this certificate along with four (4) proof-of-purchase coupons, plus $1.50 postage and handling (check or money order—do not send cash), payable to Silhouette Books, to: **In the U.S.:** P.O. Box 9057, Buffalo, NY 14269-9057; **In Canada:** P.O. Box 622, Fort Erie, Ontario, L2A 5X3.

ONE PROOF OF PURCHASE

SX92POP

Name: _____
_____
Address: _____
_____
City: _____
State/Province: _____
Zip/Postal Code: _____

093 KAG